…espite the strang… …s …nposed by the i… …f …uscany try to carry…

…n the Royal Palace o… …e …afes at the bonds … …eremony. Meanwhi… …uille's father scents success in his search for the secret of …nmortality. Then a gypsy blade flashes at the ice fair. An …nperial emissary lies bleeding by the frozen river, and …e uneasy peace is shattered. The Eschalan overlords will …ot rest until they have revenge.

…erin saw it happen, saw the blow fall. Now she can …ever go home.

…olin Greenland's *The Hour of the Thin Ox* was praised by …he Guardian as being "both lush and compressed, like a …appy-ending *Heart of Darkness*". *Other Voices* takes us out …f the jungle up into the mountains, and the no-man's …nd between the living and the dead.

OTHER VOICES

OTHER VOICES

COLIN GREENLAND

UNWIN
PAPERBACKS

LONDON SYDNEY WELLINGTON

First published in Great Britain by Unwin Hyman, an imprint of
Unwin Hyman Limited, in 1988

First published in Great Britain by Unwin® Paperbacks, an imprint of
Unwin Hyman Limited, in 1989

UNWIN HYMAN LIMITED
15–17 Broadwick Street
London W1V 1FP

Allen & Unwin Australia Pty Ltd
8 Napier Street, North Sydney, NSW 2060, Australia

Allen & Unwin New Zealand Pty Ltd with the Port Nicholson Press
Compusales Building, 75 Ghuznee Street, Wellington, New Zealand

British Library Cataloguing in Publication Data

Greenland, Colin, *1954–*
Other voices.
I. Title
813'.914 [F]

ISBN 0-04-440309-7

Set in Palatino by Computape (Pickering) Ltd
and printed in Great Britain by
Cox & Wyman Ltd, Reading

Aux enfants terribles

This must be the jumping-off place.
Wolfgang Press

Things from the forest die here
But I don't.
Elizabeth Fraser

Contents

—1—

A Sign of Unresolved Ambition

Arethusa Guille, whom everyone called Serin, was the daughter of Dr Tarven Guille, the taxidermist. Her first home was a small dark room on Montesin Alley. Serin's mother, Amber Marchan, had formerly been a great beauty, a montano, desperately shy in the pursuit, but on more intimate acquaintance fierce and demanding. Dr Tarven Guille was not a doctor, but had been a medical student when they met, doing his military service in the borderlands. It had been as a consequence of their affair that Tarven had left college without a licence, driven into apprentice-ship to support his new wife.

Their firstborn, Tomasina, had never opened her eyes. A second, Sybilla Kay, 'was long in the coming and quick in the going', as Amber would say. The bowel cough had her before she was two. Serin knew about her sisters, but that she was not allowed to play with them.

She had got her name Serin while she was quite a little baby. Her mother, having dozed as she often did in the afternoon, came to and thought there was a bird in the room. It was Arethusa, sitting up in her cradle. She had spontaneously discovered how to whistle. She turned to her mother and gurgled, then lifted her arms and whistled more, frowning with the effort.

Amber snatched her up crowing. Lost for any other way to express her pleasure, she flung open the window. It had just stopped raining. The alley was full of cold, damp air. Snails were about. A blackbird settled briefly on the wall. The baby whistled; the bird flew off.

'You're too little to be a blackbird!' Amber told her daughter. She thought of the tiny yellow singing bird she had seen; on the peregrinage, far south, never here. 'Are you a serin? Is that it?'

Her one child was the whole joy of Amber Guille's disappointed life. She was never happy in Calcionne, even once the old man died and the Guilles came to live above the shop, among all its unsold treasures. Fox snarled by beaver; pied cat gazed impassively past bent-necked goose. They were Serin's first companions, after her mother. She would clamber on to the little shelf above the stairs and crouch in an enclave of stiff feathers, tarnished scales and dusty fur. She stared into the baffled eyes and felt their minds, dim, feral, accusatory.

'Have I not told you to come down from there?' her mother would want to know.

The child never took any notice. On the shelf she sat so still she was in no danger of falling; so her mother would leave her there, for hours on end.

Favoured customers would be invited upstairs for a cup of beer. They would exclaim at Serin and her 'pets'.

'Do they all have names?' they would ask her.

'Yes, of course,' she would say.

Then the more persistent ones would ask, 'What are they?'

'I'm not going to tell you,' said Serin.

Indeed she herself did not know what the animals' names were. She knew they had them, but they were secret. She also knew that this was not something grown-ups would understand.

For a while Amber Guille went around polishing everything. Imagine, she, whose parents had been hill people, having her own house in the city! But its gloom conspired with her fatigue. As the years went by, with no sign of an end to the war, she would grow listless and sit by the hearth, staring rapt at nothing visible. Then she would rouse herself, shriek at the fire and send Serin out for coal.

It was always one basketful, never more. The girl could carry that, to save the charge for delivery. Serin hated doing it, hated the weight of it, but she liked to be out of the house alone. She had no one to play with. At school, where she went infrequently, the boys made up stories about her dealings with dead animals. The girls passed comments in an undertone, and sucked knowingly at the ends of their hair. Serin wanted to shout at them but was tongue-tied. She would gaze at the book, pretending not to hear.

Serin had not inherited her mother's arch good looks. At nine she was sallow and skinny, her hair an unparticular shade of brown. Her best dress was yellow, with a bodice, but today she was wearing one of the plain ones, which was green and faded and did not suit her. Her boots were brown. Her breath steamed in the darkening air.

She had to wait at the coal-yard while the dame served an old man who trailed a small, hairy dog at the end of a rope.

'I'm not complaining,' he kept saying. 'Why should I complain?'

The dog stared at Serin. Then it nosed at something smeared on the cobbles. Serin pictured the dog as it would be dead, and stuffed. She liked the idea, and wondered how she might steal it, and kill it. Not that she would have attempted such a theft, not at nine, but she enjoyed thinking about it. The things she had stolen so far had been small ones, things easily overlooked, a hand-lens, a lace scarf from the back of a cupboard.

The old man left at last, with the dog after, and Serin stepped forward. The dame looked up from under her broad hat.

'Good evening, Serin. How's your mother?'

'She's quite well,' said Serin. She put the basket on the trestle.

'What's she doing today?'

'She's sitting looking in the hearth.'

The coal-dame grunted and picked up a shovel. 'And you say she's well.'

'She is. She smiles sometimes.'

Coal-dust had drifted to the corners of the yard, like black snow.

'Did she give you money?'

Serin handed over the coins and dragged the basket to her.

'And for the last time?'

Serin stared, saying nothing.

The dame sighed, and folded her arms. She looked over Serin's head. 'Next week will do,' she said, bitterly.

Bracing herself against the weight of the basket, Serin walked stiffly out of the yard and down the hill. The mountains were tinted pink and lilac in the last of the watery light. They looked insubstantial, as though some fanciful hand had painted them on the sky to make up for the bleak streets and grey-faced houses.

At the far end of the alley behind the Bunch of Chives she saw Marta, Pig Rosse and Otto Meringer. They were looking furtively round the corner, hiding from someone. Serin approached cautiously, uncertain of the reception she might get; but Marta saw her and beckoned.

Serin set down the basket and joined them.

'Who is it?'

'It's an orange man,' said Marta.

None of them had ever seen an orange man before. He was walking along the deserted Brinkway as bold as you please, in a most peculiar coat that seemed to be all folds, and leather leggings. His hair stood up at the front in a bush, and when he came under a lamp Serin could see that it went on growing all the way down his neck, like the mane of a pony. He had large rings of black metal stuck through his ears and pieces of it clipped here and there all over him. Wound over his head and under his chin he wore a white scarf, like a bandage for the toothache.

His skin was, for want of a better word, orange.

'Is it a man?' asked Serin.

'It's an Eschalan,' said Otto Meringer. 'Don't you know nothing?'

Serin believed him. It was Eschalans the soldiers were fighting. They had been fighting since before she was born. Otto Meringer's big sister had been a soldier, now she was dead.

'Is that an Eschalan? What's he doing here?'

Otto picked up a stone. Pig Rosse copied eagerly, though Marta tugged his hand.

'He'll be wishing he wasn't in a minute,' said Otto, and threw the stone.

It went wide, startling the Eschalan. He gazed about.

'People of Luscany,' he cried in a strange, squeaky voice. 'Lay down your arms! Welcome your new lords!' He did not seem to have any weapons himself. He waved a short stick, with a piece of cloth tied to it.

Pig Rosse threw his stone. It went no distance, but the noise attracted the man's attention. He came towards them.

'Run!' gasped Marta, pulling Pig with her. But Otto stepped out into the street and flung another stone. It hit the man on the forehead. He clutched his head.

Otto and Serin went nearer.

Between his fingers the Eschalan's blood was ordinary red.

'People of Luscany!' he shouted at them. 'Lay down your arms!'

'He can't even talk proper,' said Otto. 'Hark at him.'

They pelted the Eschalan with refuse from the gutter. They chased him down the alley and into the backyard of the Bunch of Chives.

'Welcome your new lords!' he besought them, waggling his stick. Otto and Serin had him at bay. Marta and Pig Rosse were still hanging around, watching from a safe distance. For a moment it seemed there were no grown-ups anywhere in the whole world; then the back door of the inn crashed open and Mad Polly the potwoman came out with a tub of slops.

Mad Polly too had been a soldier once. One of her arms was missing below the elbow, and there was a great scar where someone had cut her face in two and the two pieces had never fitted back together properly. Perhaps it had also sundered her wits. They were all afraid of her, even Otto and the older ones.

Polly took one look at the Eschalan and hurled her tub at him. Then she disappeared back inside, only to emerge again at once clutching the meat-knife.

'People of Luscany lay down your arms!' he piped.

'Let me have him!' she howled.

The madwoman's hand was huge, and so was the knife. Ranting she lurched past them so close Serin could feel the spray of her spittle. Her blade waved wildly.

The Eschalan gave a desperate cry and flourished his stick. It caught the woman on the wrist. She staggered aside, her hobnails striking sparks from the flagstones, but did not drop the knife. He tried to back off, almost fell over the tub, and thrust his stick at her head.

'Tripe and chitterlings!' whooped the potwoman.

'She's mad!' shrieked Marta, thrilled.

'They're both mad,' said Serin.

'They'll kill each other,' pronounced Otto.

The children began to scatter; all but Serin, who was fascinated. There was blood on the Eschalan's scarf. His ear-rings shook. He grimaced as he kicked at the potwoman's shin. Serin caught a glimpse of crooked, rotting teeth.

Polly dodged the kick. 'A pound of tripe and a pound of chitterlings!' she hooted. 'Hot off the bone!'

The Eschalan was remarkably nimble now he had room to move. Mad Polly carved the air.

They closed, stick locked with knife.

'Give 'im a 'aircut, Poll!' yelled Otto from the alley.

'Orange juice! Orange juice!' jeered Marta and Pig Rosse.

Faces watched from the scullery window. There were urgent shouts in the street, a whistle blown.

Serin was enthralled. The fight swayed towards her again. The meat-knife twisted this way and that. The man whined and panted, shoving at Polly's forearm with his stick.

'Serin?' shouted someone inside the inn.

Serin took a step closer.

Then there were running feet in the alley. The constables arrived, barging past the children at the gate. They grabbed the combatants, dragging them apart. Serin ducked, watching Polly aim a last chop at the man's neck as they overwhelmed her. She saw her jab the stump of her arm in a constable's throat; then, as the Eschalan tried to parry, saw the blade bounce off his stick and slice away his left ear as neatly as a wing of chicken.

Blood spouted black in the gloom. It splashed Serin in the eye as hands grabbed her under the armpits from behind. Alarmed, she jerked forward, throwing herself down among the jostling legs. But the hands were large and forceful and they had her still, and hoisted her clear.

'Serin, you little cat, come out of it!'

It was her Uncle Banner. He held her in a firm embrace of fur.

As they turned from the mêlée towards the stables, Serin wiped her face on his shoulder. He smelt of beer, and trees. She craned back for a last sight of the excitement. Mad Polly was being marched off. The constables were having trouble dissuading other patrons of the Bunch of Chives from attacking the battered orange man, who even now still cried:

'People of Luscany lay down your arms welcome your new lords!'

Then Serin was being wrapped in fur and set before Uncle Banner on his horse, to be jolted briskly into the shadows, away from the gathering crowd, and down the hill towards home.

'Uncle, why – '

'Hush.'

He caressed her head.

As they turned into Threadpole Street, all at once he asked, 'What did you want to do, uh? Get yourself a pretty wound?'

Serin didn't answer. Then, thinking of the woman from the inn and the seam across her face, she said: 'Mad Polly's not pretty.'

'She is not,' he agreed. 'You want to be a soldier? No, no.'

They went in the back way, leaving the horse in the yard licking stolidly at the damp cobbles.

Serin's mother came out of the kitchen and shrieked at the stains of blood on her daughter's dress. Her brother smiled broadly, and patted her on the shoulder cheerfully enough; but she flung herself at him and hugged him no less fiercely than if her child had been killed indeed.

'It's nothing,' he kept saying, in montano. 'Sh, it's nothing. She's not hurt.'

'There was an orange man, ma.'

'Where have you been?'

'At the Bunch of Chives.'

'What were *you* doing at the Bunch of Chives?'

'Watching the man.'

'What man, what are you talking about, what is this man?'

'It was an Eschalan, ma.'

Serin's mother gasped. 'Primary protect us.'

Her brother put his arm around her shoulders. She stiffened suddenly.

'Where is the coal?'

'In the alley,' said Serin. 'At the Bunch of Chives.'

'And what good will it do there?' demanded her mother, seizing Serin and driving her upstairs, to confront her with the grey remnants in the grate.

Serin looked at the worms of fire blinking and wriggling among the embers.

'I'll fetch it in the morning.'

'Stupid girl, don't you know someone will take it by then?' cried Amber Guille indignantly. 'Some beggar, some old drunk?' she added, as though the social status of the imagined thief made a difference to her loss. She shook her errant daughter by the arm, then wrapped her own arms about her and broke into sobbing.

'The Eschalans! They will kill us all!'

A moment later she sniffed heavily, then gestured at Serin's smock. 'What is this blood?'

'They had a fight, ma. Him and Mad Polly. I'm all right,' said Serin, trying to placate her.

But Amber couldn't take it in. 'The Eschalans come,' she moaned. 'We are dead. We are all dead.' She clung to her impassive daughter.

At times like this, when her mother was wild and unreasonable, Serin would withdraw into infancy, ceasing to care or make any effort. Nothing ever did any good anyway. From the cupboards and the shelves the sad old beasts called to her.

As soon as she could she disencumbered herself from her mother's embrace and climbed on to the shelf above the stairs. She was too big now to get right in between the cases, into their cave, but it made a good place to crouch while she took carefully out of her pocket what she had been clutching inside it all the way home.

Downstairs she heard Uncle Banner go into her father's workshop.

'Banner. What is all this noise?'

'Good afternoon, Tarven. I've brought Serin home. It's nothing. She got herself a little – dirty.'

'Dirty? Please explain.'

'A little blood. It's nothing.'

'Blood? Is she injured?'

'No, no.'

'Then what *is* all the noise about?'

'Some people were fighting. Serin was splashed with blood.'

'Where was this? I had no idea she was out.'

'At the inn. The Bunch of Chives.'

Serin sat motionless on the shelf as her father came snorting up the stairs. He stopped to glare at her, but shouted to her mother.

'Can't you even look after her properly? Must I do everything for you?'

Amber came rapidly to the head of the stairs and shouted at him, 'She lost the coal-basket and all the coal!' as though Serin were not there, within arm's reach, all the time.

'What *have* you been doing?' her father demanded.

'There was a fight,' she said again. 'Uncle Banner brought me home.'

'And what happened to the coal?'

Mute, Serin looked to Uncle Banner, lingering sullenly at the foot of the stairs.

'I didn't see it,' he said. 'I never heard of it.' A flicker of impatience crossed his face. 'I'll go and find it.'

'Don't bother, Banner,' said his brother-in-law, bitterly. 'We'll manage.' He turned again on his wife. 'Don't just stand there. Take her and clean her up. Give her some work to do. If you won't I will.'

Amber's bosom was heaving. In a soft and passionate vibrato she appealed.to her husband.

'Be kind to me now, Tarven. We must not quarrel. We have so little time.'

Leaning on the banister she took his hand and pressed it to her lips.

He turned his face away, retrieved his hand, and started downstairs.

'Nervous hysteria,' he said, to no one in particular. 'That's all it is.'

'Tarven,' said Banner, claiming him and walking him back towards the workshop door, 'one of them was an Eschalan.'

Tarven stopped.

'An Eschalan?'

'Orange as a carrot.'

'Are you sure?'

Banner scowled. Tarven returned to the stairs, to confront his daughter. His wife had gone to lie down.

'Is this true?'

She nodded, once.

'What was he doing?'

She shrugged.

Her father made an exasperated noise with his tongue, and went back down the hall, Banner following. 'An Eschalan? How on earth did he get there?'

'He was saying, Luscans, surrender,' said Banner.

'Who was it he attacked?'

'The cracked woman.'

'Mad Poll? Why her?' He exhaled, explosively. 'Why do I ask? Why does an Eschalan do anything? Vicious creatures. I tell you, Banner, I should like to have the dissecting of one of their crania. When I was in the army – '

Serin had no intention of listening to her father talk about himself. Fortunately, neither did her uncle. What he said by way of interruption made her attend.

'Tarven. Listen. What if it was an announcement? Maybe they are ready to invade.'

'Invade? Twelve years they've harried us. They've never got past Carphale. If they couldn't in '98, they never will now. Not with the new guns this Brylander's making.'

Banner had not heard anything about new guns. He was eager to learn. Dr Guille told him all he had heard about the new guns that would dispel once and for all the threat of invasion by Eschaly.

Serin pressed her nose against yellow glass. From the other side two ferrets grinned greedily.

Uncle Banner came upstairs and looked in at her.

'Little rat,' he said. 'Little thief. What do you have there?'

Serin liked her uncle. She wished she could live with him and his family in the forest, and go skimming across the snowbound meadows in winter. She opened her hand and showed him the orange ear, curled on her palm like some strange little animal from beneath the sea, its blind head still pierced by the ring of black iron.

As it happened, the Eschalan invasion was coming faster than anyone but Amber Guille suspected. Historians will never agree on the importance of the Luscan overcommitment at Carphale, or the precise movement of Eschalan troops in the final push, but no one would deny that Calcionne was largely unprepared. After the incident with the herald at the Bunch of Chives the Citizens' Defence Association enjoyed a brief revival, drilling with broomsticks in the park. There was much talk of evacuation; elaborate fortification of the whole northern outskirts was planned and, in some parts, actually begun. Clearly, it was not enough. Perhaps, like Tarven Guille, everyone was depending too much on the Brylander's guns, which failed to materialise. The fighting in the streets was bitter, brief, and hand-to-hand. The army was already in tatters; civilian resistance was swiftly routed and took to the hills. In no time at all, it seemed, the orange were in the royal palace, and an oppressive silence descended, relieved only by public executions. Amber would not let Serin go to them. She threw a tantrum when Tarven once tried to declare their educational value.

In a cell at the constabulary the Eschalans found the one-armed potwoman, and set her head on the end of a pike. It stood outside the gaol much of the winter. Though she had died for rage, Mad Polly's expression in death was of a dull kind of resentment. The birds had her eyes, first of all, then her lips and parts of her ears. Next she went black. The rest was a testament to the savagery of frost at that altitude.

The Luscan aristocracy, both civil and military, decamped in disarray. Some fled south; others took refuge across the border in Ducros. No one had seen Princess Nette for weeks, though a single bill had gone out over her name, requiring all loyal subjects of Luscany to submit to their conquerors and do nothing to endanger themselves.

The Eschalans strutted and wheeled in the Aspenpleyn, parading their lurid banners. Once in a while they performed some sort of ceremony with bowls of sand and burning cloths. Incomprehensible decrees were issued. They required every cobbler to begin making shoes to a specified pattern, and any who would not were run through. They commandeered all the carriages and exhibited a great passion for clocks. The gun foundry occupied them intensely.

Things did not begin to settle down until the beginning of the following year, when the prefect of the new administration arrived with much pomp and ceremony and set up quarters not in the palace itself but in the adjoining museum, to embark at once on a programme of pacification. Princess Nette appeared on her balcony, looking thin and pale but smiling. Several military divisions marched away, to be replaced by innumerable 'proctors' and 'overseers'. The Aveneda was reopened, and worship of the Primary permitted once more.

Despite their traditional loyalty to the crown, the hillfolk could only be angered by these palliatives. They became refractory. On Greylag's Eve the body of the head proctor's daughter was fished out of Payot Beck.

The prefect, not yet fully advised that the interests of the mountain communities could be distinct from those of Calcionne, responded inappropriately. The Greylag Masque, for the first time in fifty years, did not take place. A large number of the town sat around all afternoon, looking disconsolately into the empty streets and drinking more than was wise, as if attending the wake of all joy. This event, better call it a lapse, was the more poignant because Diaz Jonal happened to be making one of his infrequent trips into Calcionne. Madder than ever, the professor insisted on wandering about the Brinkway with a whore on each arm. His manservant, ridiculously mounted on the donkey, trailed after. It was the one bright incident of a disappointing day.

Next morning it snowed. Clouds the colour of pigeon feathers hid the mountains. Serin sat on her high stool behind the shop counter and wondered if the snow would settle, but it did not. Her mother had a headache; her father was occupied with something that smelled very strongly of tar. No one was speaking to anyone else.

Serin was dutifully dusting a glass-topped drawer faintly labelled THEWS OF THE MAMMALS COMPARED when the door opened and Diaz Jonal's diminutive companion came in.

Serin had never seen him before. She knew he was a servant by his cap. He had curly yellow hair, and funny pointed shoes. His coat had a big picture of a flower on it: Serin did not know what to make of that, nor of the fact that he was no taller than she, though his face was the face of a grown man.

'I know what you're thinking, little girl,' he said at once, as he brushed the snow from his sleeves. 'I've grown up as much as I'm ever going to grow up.' He grinned bleakly at her, then pointed to an ochre spaniel with green glass eyes. 'Who does this, your father?'

Serin nodded.

He stared at her, then rudely sucked his thumb; or perhaps he had a splinter in it, she supposed.

'Well? Go on; go and get him.'

Serin slithered off her stool and ran to the workshop.

'There's a customer,' she said. 'He's not very tall.'

Her father muttered imprecations, doused a flame and came out, wiping his hands irritably on a stained towel. Serin, who had not been told not to, followed.

'Are you the one who does this?' asked the dwarf.

'I am,' said Tarven Guille.

'My master is Diaz Jonal, whose name you know and respect, like the good citizen you are. He needs your skill. Our donkey is dead, alas. We left him outside all night and the Primary pinched him. His long ears are full of frost. Poor brute,' he said, and suddenly laughed. 'Ha! Now we must needs have him stuffed, would you credit it.'

Serin's father flapped his hands. 'How far is it? The pelt must be perishing even as we speak!'

He pushed past Serin and ran to seize his coat. She had never seen him move so smartly.

'This is work for a month,' he told the lounging dwarf. 'Your master is, I presume, wealthy?'

'You'll be lucky if you can get anything out of him. I never can.'

Dr Guille stopped; turned.

'Is this, then, some kind of joke? I thought the Greylag revels had been cancelled.'

'Don't look at me. He gives me these messages, I deliver them. What more can any of us do?'

The dwarf seemed altogether sober for an instant; then tired of the whole business.

'Look, I'm sorry. I apologise. All right? Don't worry about it. He'll probably have forgotten by the time I get home anyway. He's not that bad, really, it's me, I exaggerate. Tell them we'll send someone for the donkey.'

A thought seemed to strike him. 'I don't suppose you know where I can *get* a donkey, one for hire?'

'At the Cat and Canfrey,' said the taxidermist coolly. 'The third turning to your right.' He whisked off his cape.

The professor's manservant looked a bit red, Serin thought.

'Look. I'll take that, all right?' He chose the smallest item he could see, a canary in a tiny cage of brass. 'How much is the bird?'

'It's not for sale,' said Serin. 'It's mine.'

Her father noticed her presence for the first time. 'Serin, go and play,' he said; then to the dwarf, 'Wait. Put that down. I have something else that will interest you. Something you must tell your master about. Follow me.'

Serin ran ahead up to her room. Lying prone with her eye to the crack of the door, she could see her father usher the little man into the bedroom, where her mother was in bed again. Through the wall she heard her mother scream and her father say: 'I have been doing some work with separate ether, tell him. The process enables one to preserve the vital essence of the very youngest unfortunate. Amber, be silent.'

There came the sound of a drawer being pulled open, and Serin heard her mother wail with outrage and the dwarf say: 'Primary – ' and stop, just like that.

Serin had kicked off her pattens. She crept out in her stockinged feet and stood in her parents' bedroom door. Her father was showing the man Tomasina and Sybilla Kay. Her mother was sobbing loudly now and clutching the blankets to her chest.

'Their bodies are dead, but their spirits are caught halfway,' said Serin's father. 'I believe this is the case.'

The dwarf moved his head in a very queer way. 'Dead,' he replied, in a tight little voice. 'Dead, and embalmed. Look.'

'Tell your master I believe the astral portal to be at the site of the pineal gland, here, do you see?' continued Dr Guille, prodding Tomasina. 'With further funds, and his knowledge – '

'*No!*' yelled Serin's mother, and flung a tin candlestick against the wall. Her husband turned in anger.

'Amber, don't be foolish! This is our chance, you stupid woman. Diaz Jonal has audiences with the prefect.'

'Dead,' said the dwarf again, and sniffed. 'They look like wax.' He reached into the drawer.

The children's father pulled him back. 'No! Their eyes! See –!'

The dwarf uttered one of the six obscenities that Serin knew, and was sure her parents did not. Her mother saw her then, as if intuitively alerted to innocence in danger. 'Get out!' screamed Amber, and threw a shoe at her.

Serin ducked. Her father steered his customer quickly out of the room, though not out of the range of Amber's anguish.

'Sentiment and religious claptrap will not impede us,' he promised as they went downstairs. 'Do you think Jonal will agree? He must do.'

'It'll take his mind off the donkey, anyway,' said the mad professor's man. 'What are you asking for those two?'

'Do you think I would *sell* them? They are beyond price!'

'I hope I can bring him to have a look. If it's not inconvenient to your wife.'

'We should be honoured. Bring him this afternoon, tomorrow, at his pleasure. And here – ' He held out the tiny cage. 'Take him the canary. With my compliments.'

Dr Tarven Guille watched the man disappear along the glistening street, the dead bird in his pudgy hand. 'Serin,' he said, not turning, 'you may watch the shop.'

In the months ahead Diaz Jonal was to become a collaborator with Dr Guille. He would arrive at odd hours, often late at night. In the darkened yard the shed flickered with a green glow. The pair were rumoured to be able to reanimate dead matter; and in fact they had some modest success at first, notably with mice and bats.

When he heard of their experiments, the Prefect of Luscany marvelled. 'Not to die! To continue! What would we not be able to do?' he expostulated ardently to his moonshee, Charan du, who inclined his head.

—2—

Ceremony

It was a morning of thaw, but cruelly cold, and the sky still black. Princess Nette of Luscany was on her way to visit the Garden of Eternal Regret. She bid good morning to the Eschalan guard at the conservatory door and stepped out on to the terrace. From a frozen birdbath a hopeful bird inspected her as she passed, but her hands were empty.

Down in the grove that divided precinct and palace, lumps of frozen snow lingered amid the shrunken grass. The iron gate creaked; there was mud among the gravel, which sorely needed replenishing.

During the long, slow years of the occupation the cemetery of the elect had gone into a sad decline. Too many of the monuments represented the families of vanished dukes and exiled generals, with no one to keep them up; besides, it was no longer correct to continue honouring the dead. Unhindered, furry fingers of lichen had obliterated exhortative memoranda to generations that now had other demands upon their time.

The princess, however, was at liberty. Beneath her father's portrait in stone she stopped, her hands crossed on her breast; but she was not truly praying. She did not feel the Primary was attending; had not, really, for years.

She was remembering the dancing at her father's funeral. Nervous and clumsy she had been then, only a girl. Afterwards she had been taken sailing through the city on the *Capreole*, up the frozen river by the light of soda flares. They had lined the banks, caps in hand. No one had cheered.

Ten years later Prince Dolo looked blankly down on his daughter. There was a woodlouse on his left eyelid. That apart, she thought once again how noble he looked: much more than he had ever done in life, she was sure. And his nose had been bigger than that too.

It was here at the royal mausoleum, as she picked ice off the moulding, that the bishop came upon her.

'Good morning, Your Highness. You look a little wan. I hope you did not sleep badly?'

'The mines are haunted by dead miners, so they say,' replied Princess Nette. 'On windy nights their voices are heard across the east range all the way to what's-it-called. Begins with P.'

'Peirruich,' supplied the bishop, smiling. 'Surely, Your Highness, as the temporal ruler of us all, you could not forget the name even of so lowly a region?'

'I do forget things, Yvonne, you know I do. I used to get around rather more than I do now. I've walked the streets of Peirruich – '

'Really, madam?'

'Oh, very, very well! I *rode* the streets of Peirruich, was *driven* through the streets of Peirruich, probably, to be quite precise.' She fingered the hem of her sleeve. 'I probably could go there again, you know. With mother, Crespian Vittore, a couple of secretaries, an armed escort and a carriage full of astrologers. And Charan du. Not forgetting Charan du. He would tell everyone I was going out of concern for my people, to urge them to stop sulking and return to work.'

The bishop considered. 'Some might. Enough, perhaps. Will you put this to the prefect?'

'No,' replied the princess at once. 'And Primary forbid he thinks of it himself.'

'It could be useful,' the bishop advanced cautiously.

'Oh well then, it won't be allowed,' said Princess Nette conclusively. 'I may not do anything useful. I may only amuse myself with *this* ball and *that* breakfast. In between, there are simple private pursuits, like this walk to my father's tomb, and my bath. In future I shall take many more baths.'

She brushed flecks of ice from her gloves, examining them. They were already rather grubby.

'This machinery will be a great boon to us all, Highness,' observed the bishop.

'Let us hope Enginer Jessup is a little more handy with water than he has ever been with firearms,' replied the princess. She did not sound as if she expected he would be.

The women talked briefly of what the afternoon would bring; then Princess Nette bid the bishop good day and left the cemetery. She followed the path back to the gardens. Among the empty flowerbeds she saw Brant Carver, the head gardener, and smiled at him. He smiled in return; and tipped his hat.

Bundled in rugs on the terrace sat her mother the archduchess, accompanied, as so often, by the underscrivener Crespian Vittore.

As the princess approached he jumped to his feet and bowed.

'A good morning to you, Your Highness! See how the air brings a tint of springtime to Her Grace's cheek.'

'If you mean I've gone green, Crespi, say so.'

'Your Grace says such wicked things.'

'Morning, Nette,' said her mother, allowing herself to be kissed. 'Where have you been?'

'Talking to the bishop, mother. We were agreeing what a pleasure it will be to take more frequent baths.'

'You take all the baths you want now.'

'Indeed I do not. If I had my way, I should stay in my bath and never come out again,' declared Princess Nette.

'I too,' volunteered Crespian. 'There is no pleasure so convenient – '

'Poppycock,' said the archduchess. 'What good did bathing ever do me?'

'Perhaps it might do you some good, mamma, if you were to try it,' said the princess sweetly. 'Well, after today, we may see.'

'And how should *I* get into a bath?'

'I should be honoured to lift you, Your Grace,' offered Crespian.

'You'll do no such thing. We shall all be boiled like piglets, you mark what I say. It's most unnatural. Hot water belongs at Jordache Springs, not down here. What business is it of Mr Jessup's to interfere with the works of the Primary?'

'It's the prefect's answer to this continuous coal shortage, mamma. And the cooks and the launderers are very much in favour.'

The archduchess gripped the wheels of her chair defiantly.

'I'll disrupt the dedication, that's what I shall do.'

Her daughter sat on the edge of an ornamental urn and looked up into the clouds, swinging her legs.

'You don't believe me.'

'I've always been the first to own you capable of anything, mother.'

'Your Grace's will is indomitable,' put in Crespian Vittore.

'I can't walk,' said the archduchess. 'You forget that.'

'Your legs have a bad case of obstinacy,' said her daughter, rising to walk around behind her and release the brake of her chair. The dowager craned round to glare at her, suspicious she was being mocked.

Her escort rose with alacrity.

'Oh, allow me to take Her Grace's chair, ma'am, please do. It is a trifle heavy, as you know – '

'That's not what you said just now, Crespi,' said the archduchess loudly.

'But I meant, with respect to Her Highness, being a woman – '

'I could lift you, Vittore,' said Princess Nette, staring at him very rudely.

The underscrivener was left with no option but to bow once more and smile. 'As Her Royal Highness pleases.' He fell in a few paces behind.

'You may leave us,' said the princess.

'Oh, but ma'am, consider: should you need some aid – to open the doors . . . '

'Don't persecute him so, Nette,' said her mother. 'He's better company than you ever are.'

They walked awhile in silence. The sun appeared briefly through a gap in the clouds, and suddenly Princess Nette remembered what it was like to feel sunlight, in summer, on the skin. She looked down affectionately at the greying head before her and realised it was nodding.

'Would you like to return to your room before luncheon, mamma?'

'Crespian will take me,' replied the archduchess. 'This afternoon will be so exhausting.'

The princess stooped and kissed her mother on the top of the head. Her mother reached up absently and patted Nette's cheek. Then they parted, and the princess went into the palace, to a drawing room where Charan du was waiting to see her.

'Highness,' he said, with that odd, elbowy sort of bow they all had.

'Charan du.'

The princess thought, Every day seems an endless round of

conversations; and she wondered what she ought to feel about that. Then she took a cordial from the sideboard and went to sit in her favourite chair, where she prepared to be told how to do her job.

Today the prefectorial moonshee wore mauve satin with mica buttons, and a grape-scented pomade. He was immaculately gorgeous. He left her cold. She smiled attentively while he spoke to her of certain bowls of sand. He said: 'You will see that this is performed. You are so conscientious.'

There was nothing to do but pretend to take it as a compliment.

She had had Crespian Vittore look up Charan du in the Eschalan pedigrees one dull afternoon, in pretence of being terribly interested in his accent, but actually out of malicious inquisitiveness. The man had been born in Saltfan province, a third-generation colonial, and here he was daring to lecture her on protocol, all his precepts couched in flattery.

His visits were supposed to be an honour, she recognised that. That Prefect Lan olang should spare his personal interpreter to sit here rehearsing with her the duties of a civic event – a local matter, not an event to interest the Eschalan Empire – was a gesture of goodwill. The fact that the prefect was keeping a vicarious eye on her, and that the eye kept straying to her breasts, was a mere irrelevancy.

Princess Nette sat in the bath to which she had finally been free to flee, and considered: Did Charan du simply want to bed a princess, or did he want her, Nette zan Herlach? And did it make any difference?

'No!' she said aloud. 'He's repulsive!'

She lay down suddenly with a great splash, and giggled.

She wondered what it would be like to have a lover.

One man whom rumour had emphatically but erroneously associated with Princess Nette was Karel Jessup, the enginer she had personally fetched out of the low countries during the last stretch of the war. This Brylander was ten years and more her senior, but folk had seen something romantic in the princess's secret ride out of the beleaguered country, and her return with the husky foreigner who, they learned, had promised to make guns for her.

The reality was, as usual, more prosaic. Jessup had hired

workers and set up at Stretenmul, near the falls. Princess Nette had given him what was really a considerable sum of money, then heard nothing but repeated stories of explosions and other setbacks. She had visited him and found him swearing at the hands in Bryle. The guns had not been ready to meet the Eschalan when they came.

There were those, wise after the event, who said the establishment of the foundry had precipitated the invasion; claimed that Karel Jessup was an agent of Eschaly foisted upon the princess for just this end. Princess Nette could not think the orange capable of such subterfuge. Nevertheless, Jessup had remained in charge of the foundry, under the weighty advice of a trio of Eschalan supervisors. From his vats now issued a stream of the weapons with which the Eschalan Emperor was gradually subduing the west.

A stream it was, but not a great or smooth one. Seizures lasting a week were not uncommon, usually owing to the Brylander's recurrent inability to make himself understood in either Luscan or Eschalan. The supervisors would surely have replaced him long ago, but for their own race's complete incapability with machinery of any kind. Instead, they kept him out of the way as much as possible, distracting him with this bizarre notion of bringing the hot springs to the town.

His gangs had had the roads up for months. For the great pump that would serve the prefecture, the palace and – generosity of generosities – the primacy, a previously unregarded courtyard had been selected. When Princess Nette had peered down into it one wintry day she had seen men smothered in icy mud wrestling with huge pipes of black iron while, on the edge of the pit, an orange foreman barked insistently.

This afternoon it was a scene of optimism and splendour, polished brass and painted white wood, lit erratically by the thaw sun. The public were admitted. They milled around the platform that had been constructed in front of the open doors of the pumphouse, craning their necks and generously sharing their ignorance. Into the Eschalan enclosure, while the band made protracted squealing noises, the guilds filed in strict order of precedence, each trying to outdo the others in glossy representatives.

The prefect arrived with his entourage and climbed on to the platform. Everyone applauded, and cheered when the princess stepped up from the other side to meet him in the middle. Symbolic things were done with coloured eggs and gravel. The Eschalans looked suitably solemn, the Luscans tittered and yawned.

Then came the speeches. First the prefect, through Charan du, offered a miscellany of thoughts on a theme of prosperity, congratulated Karel Jessup, and complimented Princess Nette.

Then Bishop Yvonne commended the pump to the attention of the Primary, comparing it favourably to that divine provision whereby water rises into the sky and falls again on to the land. She wished that one day the society of prefecture and people might be so harmoniously ordered, and prayed for the particular welfare of Princess Nette.

Next, by some mistake, Professor Jonal came trotting up with a paper megaphone, claimed all the credit, then revealed that he was talking not about Jessup's mighty pump, no, but about one of his own, which he called his Hydraulic Expurgefactor. The Eschalans smiled, not understanding a word. Jonal sang part of a ribald song, then called for a cheer for the beautiful Princess Nette.

Last of all, the princess herself recited the short speech that Charan du had thoughtfully suggested, and announced Enginer Jessup, who was to pull the decisive lever. Everyone onstage gathered around the doorway, gazing expectantly inside. Jessup, looking most unnaturally starched and brushed, was striding about rapping on dials with his knuckles.

Over the heads of the crowd the princess saw that Under-scrivener Vittore had wheeled out her mother, who sat squinting peevishly in the brash sunlight. The archduchess, as her daughter had foreseen, did not do anything to create a disturbance. It was a skinny boy in an apron who did that, lunging up to the platform with a pistol, shouting, 'Long live Princess Nette!'

Perhaps he should not have shouted. If he had not shouted, perhaps he would not have been so immediately jostled. As it was, there was a bang, and a clang, and a sudden dent in a piece of brasswork. No one could have said whether he had meant to hit Prefect Lan olang or, less explicably, Enginer Jessup.

He had no opportunity for a second attempt. Howling, the prefectorial guard leapt into the crowd, thrusting everyone aside in their urgency. They were upon the boy in a trice and clubbed him to the ground.

Suddenly there was uproar, and orange constables everywhere. Surrounded, Princess Nette caught a glimpse of Vittore briskly pushing the archduchess back indoors. The soldiers were carrying the luckless pistoleer away by his arms and legs.

Bishop Yvonne stepped forward, calling for everyone to be calm, but the marshals were forcing the crowd back out of the arena. There were yells of anger, cries of panic.

Inside the pumphouse Diaz Jonal was fussing around Karel Jessup, who was most determinedly continuing with the operations to set his machinery in motion. A sudden loud booming, accompanied by a thunderous rush of subterranean waters, redoubled the noise in the courtyard. Startled and excited, obstinate sections of the crowd turned again, cheering and tussling with the marshals as they tried to go back towards the stage. The marshals retaliated, striking out at heads and arms. The last thing the princess saw as the orange guard moved her offstage was a group of people breaking the cordon and trampling the white ropes of the Eschalan enclosure, which was utterly deserted.

In fact, looking around the crush in the lobby where they fetched up, the princess noticed that the prefect, Charan du, and all the other Eschalan dignitaries had also vanished completely, bundled off to safety while she and the rest of the Luscans were herded in here. She gestured for the attention of a wild-eyed officer and spoke above the hubbub.

'The reception will continue.'

'Highness – not possible – '

'Nonsense,' she said.

'The risk – ' he said.

'What risk?' she asked. 'You have the boy.'

'Perhaps the boy was not alone.'

'You can post men at every exit, in the corridors and at the windows, if you like,' said the princess. 'Nothing will happen now. It's all over.'

She led the party into the reception hall, smiling reassuringly at the stewards and flustering the soldiers, who wanted an order to prevent her. Other guests were finding their way back around the courtyard, and had begun to cluster at the doors.

'Let them in,' she directed.

Anxious consultations were made, but before long flagons and little cakes were circulating at speed. Charan du reappeared, without the prefect.

The rebel shot had punctured the calm of ceremony and loosed a bright, unstable hilarity in the air. Karel Jessup, pent in a corner by admirers, gruffly accepted congratulations, muttered effortful explanations. Children ran back and forth along the polished corridors, reporting on the progress of the first hiccups of hot water from the royal taps. The soldiers stood aside, glowering. The princess directed that they should be offered refreshments.

Crespian Vittore appeared to inform Her Royal Highness, apologetically, that Her Grace the Archduchess was most insistent she be brought to the party.

'Let her come, Vittore, she'll never give me peace if I refuse.'

Meanwhile, Diaz Jonal had gone missing. It was already late when he returned, looking flushed. He had polished his head and put on a flannel jacket marginally less filthy than his usual one. For the occasion, a crooked bolt of lightning in gold brocade had been awkwardly tacked down the front.

'Do you like it? A brilliant touch, eh, ha ha! Came to me in a dream. Had my man up doing this at two in the morning!'

As furtively as one of his bulk could, he wrapped crudités in a napkin and stuffed them into an inside pocket.

'You never know!' he cautioned, sheepishly, then brightened. 'Have you met my collaborator, ma'am?'

'Mr Jessup? Many times.'

'We are here today in his honour,' said Vittore, stiffly. Jonal was always an embarrassment to him.

'No, not *him*. Jessup and I don't see eye to eye at present, I'm afraid,' confided the professor, glumly. 'I rarely work with Jessup these days, very rarely. No, no, I mean Guille. The man's astonishing. Pioneering work, ma'am. I'll fetch him for you. Excuse.'

He raised a finger and stepped aside.

'Who is this we are to meet?' demanded the archduchess.

'His new protégé, I assume,' smiled the princess.

'I'm afraid the man's a dealer in dead animals, ma'am,' shuddered Crespian Vittore, who always knew everything, and knew it first.

From the corner back came Jonal, leading a bony-looking individual in black with his hair in the most conservative of pony-tails. He had a poor complexion, pitted by the fumes of his trade, but his eye was piercing, and his voice rapid and urbane as he said: 'An altogether auspicious evening, Your Highnesses. Tarven Guille, Doctor of Necrobiotics, waits upon you. May I present my family?'

These were two: the wife an obvious montano, formerly handsome, now tubby and, if the archduchess was any judge, a laudanum-tippler; the daughter an underfed fifteen with lank hair parted in the middle.

The archduchess shut her eyes tightly and announced in a voice of extreme boredom: 'We recognise them.'

'Do you?' said Professor Jonal in surprise. 'Oh, I see what you mean. Where's the moonshee? We must apprise the prefect of our latest findings!'

Having put in his official appearance, the prefectorial moonshee had left early. The weather had taken a turn for the worse and sleet stung his face as he passed through the slype to the prefecture. The flags were ruffled, the faces of the old buildings slick with an acid light.

In the windy penetralium of the Hall of Accomplishment, Charan du spoke to a porter, then ran lightly up the ticking stairs to the prefect's office.

When he had first inspected the Hall of Accomplishment at Calcionne, where he had been advised to house the Eschalan prefecture, Lan olang had been pleased to find a different kind of clock on every landing. This he took as a good omen. Now there was a clock of some kind on every stair. Lan olang would have preferred them all to show the correct time, according to the northern system, but the cadets to whom the duty inevitably fell simply rewound them when they were told, not otherwise, and without reference to the funny signs on the front.

Lan olang was satisfied that he was a kind and considerate governor. He was proud of the intent, resourceful people in his charge. To be shot at, after all this time, without having offered the slightest provocation, was rather distressing. He had sought solace, in the brief absence of his interpreter, by rearranging the Luscan historical treasures that decorated his office. Charan du found him directing the hanging of a mounted pair of tusks, both quite badly chipped.

'A little to the left . . . to the left . . . Ah, Charan du, you return. How was the reception? Do you know, the beast who wears these horns dwells either in the hot forests on the south-west frontier, or in a marine form, under the frozen seas of the north?'

He hovered by his desk, stroking one corner, as if afraid to move too far away from it. 'Exactly so,' he called.

When the labourer had climbed down from his ladder and been dismissed, Lan olang touched his interpreter on the arm. 'Come, Charan du, and tell me: Have you seen the boy? Why should he wish to kill me?'

His eyes wandered back to the tusks, as though he expected to find an answer there.

'Ingratitude can smoulder in the ashes of complacency,' observed Charan du. 'But have you not examined him yet yourself?'

'He is with the questioners now. I should not wish to interfere.'

'I must advise Your Estimability otherwise. To confront him with his intended victim, still joyfully alive, may provoke some illuminating reaction from the wretch.'

'As you say, as you say,' admitted Lan olang. 'Perhaps one might look in on them in a while.' He moved over to the window and gazed sadly into the brutal sky. 'What a distressing end to a charming day. Why was this not *foreseen*?' He might have been talking about the weather.

'The Minister of Oneiromancy has an old woman from Criorne who dreamed three times of a boy that spat lead,' said the interpreter casually. 'And just after you left the palace, the haruspex said something about a tortoise. But I have expected this.'

'You?' echoed the prefect.

'Not in such a way, but generally. A drift in events.' Charan du tilted his hand gently from side to side.

Lan olang looked worried. 'Good Charan du, you always tell me I am too trusting, too innocent.'

'All must take more care from this afternoon,' said Charan du, his voice suddenly full of iron. 'I have left instructions for Crespian Vittore to seek me here. I trust this is not incoherent with the prefect's wishes?'

'Who? Oh, your man, of course, of course. I wonder what they are doing to that boy ... Ah!' cried the prefect suddenly. 'The astrolabe! I had forgot! Wait here for me, Charan du,' he said, and hurried out, clucking over his lapse.

Frozen rain gusted against the roof. Charan du perused a pair of landscape paintings. Even in these absurdly literal renditions, there was something violent about the mountain scenery. He himself would have preferred a subject more healthy, more balanced.

In a while Crespian Vittore arrived, somewhat out of breath. 'I'm sorry to be late, minister. I had to take the archduchess back and see her comfortable.'

'Your dutifulness does you nothing but credit, Crespian Vittore,' said Charan du. He could never bring himself to adopt these people's custom of addressing each other by half the name only. 'How did this lamentable incident appear from your vantage?'

'I didn't see the boy, minister, only heard his cry, and then the front of the crowd began to sway. The prefect threw up his hands to shield himself. I heard the report of the gun. Her Grace made a – a vulgar exclamation.'

'Indeed. But Karel Jessup, what did he do?'

'Stood stock-still for an instant, then turned again to his machinery.'

'So it was. Does such absence of fear argue some premonition, some collusion, even?'

'I cannot see that he would put himself in danger, in that case, minister. As it was, he was almost hit.'

'I muse aloud merely, Crespian Vittore.' Charan du brushed a finger across the top of the glass dome that encased a brown wax figurine, as if checking for dust. 'What assessment might you make of the princess's response?'

'Her Royal Highness could not be expected to look with anything but abhorrence on such wild treachery, even if done in her name.'

'Her Royal Highness is a model of all that is virtuous beyond reproach,' said Charan du smoothly.

'She is the flower of women,' affirmed Vittore, and he went pink.

The eyes of the moonshee flickered on him an instant, then returned to the doll in the bell-jar. 'Such a paragon must be zealously protected,' he averred.

The prefect had come back into the room, followed by the workman and his ladder. He looked at his interpreter and the Luscan, then turned rapidly to inspect the tusks.

'How gruesome those great teeth look! They make the whole room seem positively gloomy. Take them away at once, would you.'

As the man set up his ladder again, Lan olang addressed the moonshee.

'Charan du, I have made up my mind. I shall see this boy. His plight concerns me.'

'I shall accompany you, prefect. And I should recommend that Crespian Vittore be permitted to accompany us both.'

'Ah yes, your faithful observer,' said Lan olang, smiling favourably at the Luscan, who greeted him formally in Eschalan.

'I rejoice to see you by daylight, Your Estimability.'

'Yes, yes, your pronunciation is flawless, Crespian Vittore,' replied the prefect. 'But look: the light is gone already from this day.'

It had stopped sleeting, but the clouds had not broken up. Undetected, the sun had slipped below the mountains. Soon, for a few minutes, all the birds of the wild wood would sing.

The Prefect of Luscany led the way down a back stair to a cell where a naked native boy sat whining on the floor between the thighs of a burly woman in a black-stained leather apron. It was a curiously intimate scene. A small man, similarly clad, stood watching with a pair of pliers in his hand.

The boy had fouled himself. Blood was pouring from his nose, and running down his right hand, which the woman was holding firmly. She was engaged in peeling back the second of its fingernails.

Charan du nodded. Crespian Vittore stifled an exclamation.

The woman paused in her task, looking up at Lan olang and beaming widely. The condition of her teeth was lamentable. The peculiar little noise the boy was making continued unabated.

'Can he stand?' asked the prefect.

The man darted forward and kicked the boy's foot.

'Rise, dog, and beg His Estimability's forgiveness!'

Since the man spoke this in Eschalan, the boy made no response. The woman made to stand up, heaving him up by the arm; but his head slumped forward, his eyes unfocused.

'Let him be,' said the prefect with distaste.

'What stories does he tell?' asked Charan du.

'Just one, minister,' replied the man. 'His name is Otto Meringer. He is devoted to his princess, and cannot bear the honouring of the barbarian who, according to him, has known the pleasure of her bed.' The man ducked his head, deprecating the indelicacy.

'The boy meant to shoot the enginer?' asked Vittore in surprise.

'He meant to shoot Karel Jessup,' confirmed the questioner.

'These primitive passions!' said Lan olang, caught between pity and admiration.

Vittore glanced at Charan du, uncertain how to react, but the interpreter neither moved nor spoke, gazing steadily at the bloodied face of the unsuccessful assassin.

'I cannot say I am not relieved,' confessed the prefect, heading for the door.

'Go on until you get the truth from him,' said Charan du to the questioners. 'I shall myself return – '

'Interpreter, you are too exacting!' cried Lan olang. 'Has he not suffered for his folly, whatever it was?'

'Your Estimability, I believe this boy was not alone in his villainy,' said Charan du, quietly.

'Well, he is alone from now on,' replied the prefect petulantly. 'I banish him. There! Leave him until he wakes, then give him food and water, dress him and take him to the border. Let him think there what befits a loyal subject of Luscany!'

So saying he swept Charan du and Crespian Vittore from the room, and let the door slam on the stench of sweat and excrement.

'The next thing for us all is to have a good bath,' declared Lan olang as they mounted the stairs. 'Do you know, in all this uproar I haven't even been to see how they're getting on with the hot water.'

—— 3 ——

Two Pale Figures Ache
in Silence

It was night in Calcionne. The owls had left the pinnacles of the Aveneda to hunt the Cory Waste. Above the dark city the mountains lay under a fine glaze of moonlight. In their bed Tarven Guille slept with one arm flung out across his wife's body, and his mouth open. He dreamt he stood on the banks of a great river while a congregation of dead people went floating by, their white bodies intertwined, weeds draggling their limbs. At one point he seemed to hang suspended over a flux of pale faces, coming and going in a yeasty mass.

Amber Guille, meanwhile, was dreaming men encircled her, shouting at her to dance. But Amber was sulky, and would not. She felt a great offence, but could not name it to demand redress.

The Guille's firstborn, Tomasina, lay swaddled in musty-smelling russet cloth. Beside her Sybilla Kay, in yellowed lace, stared impassively at the bottom of the drawer above. Doubtless they too dreamt, but of what wraiths, what vapours, it is bemusing to conjecture.

Next door their sister Arethusa was not dreaming. She was awake, listening to the mice in the attic. A pendant rag of cobweb stirred in the draught. She could not see it, but it had been there as long as she could remember. So had the badger with the broken leg on top of the cupboard, baring its perfectly preserved fangs as if it wished to be up above the ceiling, among the drifts of dust and bones of sparrows, hunting mice.

Serin wondered whether she needed to pee, and decided she did. She got out of bed and groped for her pattens. She would never use a chamberpot unless there was snow on the ground.

Serin made no sound as she left her room, but a stair creaked, and she heard her father call out something in the hollow language of sleep. She passed the workshop, where someone's favourite rat had been pegged, and let herself out into the yard. Cold moonlight silvered the flags. Serin hurried to the jakes, wishing she had brought a shawl. As she squatted, she whistled under her breath an old tune of her mother's.

> We gathered in the meadow
> On that day, on that day
> There were no tears falling
> On that day.

Those were not the words that they sang here, in the city, but the real words, the montano words.

> We gathered in the meadow
> On that day.

On her way back indoors she stopped to peer in at the window of the shed where her father worked with Professor Jonal, and where she was forbidden to enter. Nor did the light of the moon permit her to see very much: a glint of glass, a gleam of brass, and, on the table, a long bulky shape completely swathed in oilcloth. It was all very still, as if nothing would ever move again in there. Serin came away.

She jiggled the handle of the pump and set her mouth to the resulting trickle, then sluiced her hands. With numb fingers she worked the latch, then stood in the kitchen, hands on hips, still thirsty, wondering whether her mother would miss it if she took some milk.

> There was no milk missing
> On that day.

She lifted the beaded muslin from the jug. There wasn't much left. She scarcely touched the rim with her lips, so as not to leave a mark.

She didn't think she'd had more than a mouthful, but the level was now alarmingly low. Perhaps the shadows had deceived her. She stood awhile hesitating, but there was only one thing she could do. She eased up the back-door latch again and carried the milk jug to the pump.

Holding the jug to the spout, she nudged the pump handle. Nothing happened. She shook it. At first there was again nothing; then, with a gurgle so loud she feared it would wake her father and mother, a gout of water splashed into the jug and out again all over her hands and face.

Serin gasped. She put down the jug and wiped her face. The sleeves of her nightgown were soaked. She squeezed water from them, shivering. Then she looked into the jug. It was almost brimming.

Grimacing, Serin carried it carefully back inside. She didn't close the door, but stood in the shadow and set to to drink the jug down to where it had been in the first place. It hardly tasted like milk any more, and she feared it was probably brown, because the water so often was.

Gently she stood the jug back on the sill, with its spout pointing the right way, fumbled in vain for a towel, then pushed the door silently closed and stole upstairs to bed again.

The cobwebs were still fluttering, the badger still snarling, but the mice had fallen quiet. Serin wriggled down under the covers, wrapping her wet sleeves tight about her thin arms and clutching them to her chest in the hope the warmth of her own body would dry them. Before she slept she heard somewhere the sound of a triangle, and soon the weavers clattering past on their way to work, murmuring in dull, companionable voices.

Then at last Serin Guille too dreamed. She dreamed of a strange thing that had happened on her fourteenth birthday. They had made the obeisance and were just leaving the Aveneda. Serin, ahead in the throng, had become separated from her mother. Looking back, she had seen her caught up in conversation with a neighbour. Serin had gone on into the open, where she had wandered aimlessly about, whistling.

The sun shone on the common boneyard that lay between the Aveneda and the river. Everything looked very tranquil and drab. Serin had almost screamed when she spotted the scrawny white figure sitting on top of one of the scrubby hummocks. His face had been turned towards her, his head nodding gently.

That morning she had turned and fled, and finding her mother immediately, had mentioned nothing. In her dream, Serin stood transfixed as the spectre repeatedly cast a fishing line into the freshly dug earth and drew it up again and again, always empty. *'Nothing yet!'* he chirruped. *'Nothing yet!'*

At breakfast Serin's father and mother did not greet her. Her father glared coldly, her mother pointed to the sill.

'Who took the cloth from the milk?'

Serin frowned, looking vaguely where her mother was pointing.

'A cat,' she suggested.

'There is no cat here,' said Dr Guille with suppressed emotion.

'A rat, then.'

'What rat, you little mongrel!' he growled, out of patience, rising from his seat and almost knocking the chair over. He came around the table in two strides and gripped Serin by the shoulder, wrenching her to her feet.

'Ow! Ah!'

Tarven Guille marched his daughter out of the room and into his workshop, where he banged the door and began to rummage in a drawer until he found what he was looking for: a stick of willow.

'Get your skirt up,' he said. 'You know by now.'

Serin stared at him.

He struck her hard across the buttocks. 'Do as you're told!'

Expressionlessly, Serin reached behind her and raised her skirt a couple of inches. She bit her lip as the switch cut the back of her thighs, twice. At the third she yelled in pain and staggered forward, but her father had her by the arm, and hit her again.

Then the door burst open and her mother rushed in.

'What are you doing, you mad man?'

'I'm finished,' he said loudly. 'Take her,' and he gave Serin a shove. Her mother reached for her, but the girl pushed past without looking at either of them and fled for the stairs.

'You treat your daughter as an animal!' Amber was shouting.

'She behaves no better,' declared Tarven. He threw the rod into a corner. He was breathing hard.

'You are so cruel!' heard Serin from her room; and, 'She has your dark blood!' While they raged she sped downstairs again, snatched her coat from the peg and biscuits from the table, and fled out into the day.

Overhead the sky was a soft and even blue, with one small, slowly twirling cloud. In the alleys old women shuffled with pitchers of water and nets full of eggs. Up a ladder, a boy was cleaning the ash out of the cressets, while below a young girl sat with a little trolley, binding fresh faggots for the night to come. Her fingers moved sleepily, her eyes said that she was not properly awake yet.

A cat stood at the edge of a manhole, peering down. A boy with a flag waved at the leader of a party of Eschalans riding out from Melkonnen in pink coats with metal wreaths on their heads. Serin decided to go the other way, up Rowe, where the market was starting to do business.

'Roots and berries! Roots and berries!'

'Tassatan, tassatan, tan tassatan. . .'

Serin had a few pence, but was not in a mind to buy a honey apple or a string of buttons. A potter shouted something as she raced past his stall, and his neighbour, a seller of oils, laughed unkindly. Serin ignored them.

Chewing biscuit, she slowed to a walk. The road grew steeper. People shook bedding from their windows and infants tormented barking dogs. Serin heard nothing, saw nothing but the dark mouth of the forest, calling her in.

Across the high meadows she went and into the trees. It was shady there and green. Through the bristly haze of branches morning could be seen creeping up the far side of the valley.

The hard earth was thickly carpeted with dry grey debris. The undergrowth was sparse, except along the length of a fallen tree, suffocated in moss, where columbine and kindleweed crowded into the slot of sunlight. Birds were chattering, a breeze hushing in the firs. Serin found the one that was black with lightning and went up to the right of it, over the rocks. As she climbed, the fact that the backs of her legs were throbbing finally caught up with her. She twisted around to look at the weals and hissed at them through her teeth. Then she clambered on up, her mind full of knives.

In the clearing, something twitched in the grass ahead. Serin knew at once it was nothing to fear. She crouched down to watch, but whatever it was got away unseen.

Across the clearing, on top of an outcrop, there was a derelict hut. Her mother said it had been a hermitage. The roof was buckled and bowed. Fungus dripped from the eaves. Shutters drooped across the lightless window.

Serin had wondered before whether the clearing below the rock had once held the anchorite's garden, with beanpoles, radishes, perhaps a tethered goat. There was nothing here now but grass and thickly mouldering needles. To one side, in a cleft, was a spring with watercress growing.

The steps went up the side of the rock. They were full of dust. Bright green beetles scuttled across the broken slab in front of the door. Serin pushed; the door jarred open a little way. She went inside.

No one had been there. Good. One day Serin had found a smear of grease and cinders on the floor. Some of it was still there.

Ferns sprouted in the corner where the roof was broken. The only furnishings were a wooden cot and a rusted dish. Serin sat down on the cot and rubbed her legs. She thought of a timber wolf leaping on her father and knocking him down, going for his throat, over and over again. She thought of him falling into a great pit of spiders, snorting as they entered his nostrils, choking as they skittered into his mouth. She said nothing; nor did her face betray any emotion. She squatted, seemingly at peace, hugging her knees.

It was unclear to Serin why she did not run off with the gypsies; why she persistently went back down to the shop, to her parents. Why should the brute fact that two people originally made you mean they had the power to run your life, to decide what you did, where you stayed and went, when and with whom? If the Primary had consulted her, she would have advised the creation of some other pattern to human existence, whereby you could stand after a couple of hours, walk after a couple more, and make your own way thereafter.

Serin sat alone in the vacant seat of piety, thinking rebellious thoughts and listening to the birds and the frogs and the bubble of the hermit's spring. She could live here even, as she had done, that forgotten saint, on mushrooms and berries and watercress, and the flesh of small creatures. She would be alone with her thoughts; she would never have to look at another Esch; and she would *never* go back to that dismal house, not until her father was dead indeed, and her mother, and the neighbours came with lanterns to keep the wake. Not even then. She would spurn her own mother's funeral. She would spurn all occasions, and abjure all human society.

Satisfied with her gloom, the girl lay down on the dusty cot, her hands under her head. Her thoughts recommenced in a different key. She thought of Otto Meringer, abandoned in these woods. It had been out by Piecap, the place where the Esch had dumped him. His family had broken the law, going there afterwards, but had not found him. Perhaps he had made it over the pass and into Ducros. Or perhaps he was gone wild, covered with hair, living in a cave. Sometimes the wolves rescued people and took care of them, not just babies.

The sky above the hole in the roof was an intense blue. Serin heard a woodpecker knocking at a nearby tree. The forest murmured continuously, and Calcionne seemed very far away. Still she did not want to come out of the dingy cell. Its dimness had settled comfortingly over her, its coolness seemed to sooth her rage. She saw herself then, dispassionately, as a creature of contrary forces, running away like a child in a temper, trailing back every time because nothing else was really possible. She would not want to be here alone at night, for example, and in the winter it would be a terrible place, fit only for God and the mad.

Serin sighed and rose. She dragged the door open again, and stepped out into vertical sunlight.

Her father was coldly and mildly righteous, as he always was on such occasions, making no allusion to her crime, her punishment or her absence. He passed her her portion of lentils. Her mother had somehow, in the course of the morning, turned against her, muttering and sighing over the dishes and wiping an imaginary tear with her sleeve. To Serin she spoke curtly, with dark, reproachful looks. Serin was glad to retreat to the shop, where she sat all afternoon, studying, as her father prescribed, texts of anatomy and compendiums of disease.

The light was already failing when the door banged open and an Esch walked in. He had on a black tunic and dark blue leggings, and a square hat. He carried a satchel which showed he was a page of the messengers. He was only a boy.

'Stand up,' he said.

'Why?' said Serin.

'There is a letter from His Estimability Lan olang, Prefect of the Eschalan Administration.'

'You've got squinty eyes,' said Serin, indistinctly. Often they couldn't understand you if you didn't speak clearly.

'Stand up,' said the boy.

Slowly Serin got down from her stool and came around the counter.

'Doctor Tarven Guille,' said the boy. 'He is here.'

'No,' she said, just to be contrary.

'You will give him the letter.'

'I might.'

He gave her a paper. She unfolded it. It was written in Eschalan, in shiny black ink.

'I can't read this.'

The page grew very agitated. 'No! Not to you! To Doctor Tarven Guille!'

'He won't be able to read it either,' she lied.

'His Estimability Lan olang Prefect of the Eschalan Administration will visit! In three hours!'

'Tonight?'

He held three fingers up stiffly. Then he turned on his heel and left. Refolding the letter, Serin watched him jog back up Threadpole Street and out of sight. Then she went to tell her father, who was in his workshop. He was aghast.

'Tonight? But Jonal has said nothing.'

'Perhaps he doesn't know anything.'

'Don't be stupid! Give me that.'

He snatched the letter and devoured it with his eyes, then looked at the clock.

'But that's only three hours! What can I do?'

He pointed out of the window.

'Go and sweep the shed. No, wait.' He seemed to recall something. 'I'll do it. Where is Jonal? Does he expect me to cope with this on my own?'

'Should I go and close up then?'

'What? Yes, yes.'

She had done no more than reach for the top bolt when he came rushing in after her.

'He must see Sybilla. Not Tomasina, but Sybilla at least.'

'Ma won't like it.'

He made an impatient gesture. 'It doesn't matter. She's unwell. She fails to appreciate – Serin. Listen to me. This is what you must do.'

Serin continued to bolt the door.

'Leave that,' said her father sharply. 'Go and make the infusion for your mother.'

Serin sat in the kitchen and waited for the kettle to boil. She toasted two crumpets and spread the last scrapings of honey on them. Her mother didn't like honey, but there was little chance she'd be awake enough to eat one, or to notice what she was eating if she did. Serin put the tray down on the landing and opened the bedroom door.

Amber Guille lay back on several pillows, her cheeks flushed, her long hair tousled.

'Come,' she said, patting the bed. 'Sit and talk to me.'

'How are you feeling, mamma?'

'I dreamed of the south again . . . but there was ice there too. Ah! How could that be? We must fetch a scryer to tell us what all these things mean.'

Serin, pouring out the tisane, said nothing. She kissed her mother on the cheek and felt her forehead. No matter how long she dozed, there were still black circles around her eyes. Their pupils were shrunk to tiny dots.

'Was it a busy afternoon in the shop?'

'No. Papa said to tell you some people are coming later.'

'Jonal! That devil . . .'

The taxidermist's wife gave a groan. She had taken bitterly against Professor Jonal and the secretive work he and her husband performed in the shed after dark. At first, Tarven had been able to sweeten her opinion with the promise of prosperity that waited upon their success, but as the years went by and nothing material changed, she had soured absolutely.

'He wishes to make me sick,' she clamoured, and clutched at her heart.

'Do you want a crumpet?' asked Serin in a small voice. She had already eaten hers.

'They plot to poison me. I heard them talking. It was not a dream.'

'I'll eat it for you if you don't,' offered Serin. Her mother reached vaguely towards the tray and seized the steaming cup. 'Careful, it's hot!' said Serin, but she drank it down regardless, and belched.

'I feel so much better today. This tea will cure all pestilence,' Mrs Guille declared brightly.

'Can I have the crumpet then?'

Her mother seemed to focus on her for a moment. 'You were a wicked girl,' she recalled. 'Wicked, wicked, oh! He beat you.'

'Yes, mother.'

'Show me.'

'Mother . . .'

'Show.'

Unwillingly, Serin lay on her stomach and let her mother caress her legs with a feverish hand.

'Stay with me now, Serin, don't rush away. Stay with your mother . . . I don't feel strong enough to get up. What is your papa doing? Is he hungry for his dinner?' She made a face. 'Let him eat with Jonal. Let the mannikin cook for them both. See if he can! But lie here beside me, just a little while, little bird, then I get up.'

Serin curled up on her father's side of the bed and ate the cooling crumpet. Her mother seemed to relapse, singing very quietly a montano song about pumpkins and babies while she swilled the dregs around in her cup. Serin retrieved the shawl from where it had slipped down behind her, tidied the pillows, then, tiring of this elementary nursing, sat before the broken mirror and tried out the various paints and powders, pursing her lips and sucking in her cheeks.

She did not know the professor and the dwarf had arrived until she heard the sound of excited argument coming from the shed. Then she recalled her errand. As quietly as she could, she slid open the heavy drawer and took out her elder sister.

Papa was right to favour Sybilla Kay, Serin thought. Tomasina had been looking a bit peculiar lately. Serin suspected she was beginning to turn green. Sybilla, though, seemed as fresh as ever, if a little glassy-eyed. Standing there at the foot of the bed where their mother lay sleeping now, Serin rocked the rigid baby in her arms, pretending. Under her breath she murmured a lullaby.

Out in the shed someone began to hammer something vigorously. Amber stirred, but said only: 'Goblins down below.' She muttered in montano: she was dreaming of the past again. Serin took her sister downstairs. In the yard there was a sharp smell, like charred meat.

Her father came rushing from the shed in quite a frenzy. 'Give her to me, quickly.' He seized Sybilla, then peered at Serin's painted face by the light of the window.

'What have you been doing?' he cried. 'Now of all times! Idiot girl!' He lashed out at her. 'Go and clean yourself up.'

Jonal's dwarf appeared behind him, grinning in the doorway. 'I think she looks very nice,' he said.

Ignoring him, Tarven stood glaring at his daughter. Un-
attended, Sybilla Kay began to slip from under his arm.

'Mind the baby, doctor,' wheezed the dwarf. He was clearly
enjoying himself. The taxidermist nearly knocked him down,
charging back into the shed with his burden.

At that moment Serin heard the shop bell clinking; and, almost
at once, whoever it was began to batter at the door.

'The prefect!' cried Dr Guille. 'Serin – go and let him in! Tell
them I'll be there instantly. Instantly, do you hear?'

Indoors it was quite dark now. Serin lit a candle and went
through to the shop. The candlelight twinkled in a galaxy of glass
eyes. She stretched up to jiggle open the bolt, peering as she did
so around the edge of the blind.

It was not the prefect. It was the enginer, Mr Jessup. He
pushed past Serin with scarcely a glance.

'Is he here? Jonal, is he here?'

The burly man was through the shop and into the passage
before Serin could react. He glanced in the kitchen, then
walked into the workshop. He saw the pegged-out rat and
grimaced, then looked suspiciously around the dark room
before coming back into the passage and cocking his head to
Serin.

'Is he upstairs?'

'No,' she said, suddenly frightened of him. What did he want
with Jonal? His violence distressed her.

'There's nobody up there,' she said.

'Where have they gone? Have they gone to the Aveneda?'

'No.'

'Where is he, girl? Are you simple?'

He seized her by the shoulders.

'In the shed.' She indicated the kitchen door. 'Don't touch my
father!'

Jessup was gone. By the time Serin reached the kitchen, he
was in the yard. By the time she reached the yard, he was in the
shed. She heard angry exclamations. She went nearer.

'We need you,' Jessup was saying. 'What are you playing at
here?'

'The secret of mortality is at our fingertips!' exclaimed Professor Jonal. 'A fellow like you knows nothing of these things,
Jessup. Don't touch that, you oaf!'

'Be careful man!' cried her father.

'I haven't time to cross wits with ye, professor. For the last time, will you come and help us?'

'No!' His voice was shrill. He sounded annoyed, afraid.

'We need wire, professor. Wire and cable. More tools.'

'Take anything you need! My man will carry for you. Now leave us alone.'

'We need your mind too, Jonal. But you've sold that to the orange.'

Serin was about to take a look inside the shed when the dwarf forestalled her, hopping out.

'Hello, little girl. What a to-do, eh?' He rubbed his hands.

Serin was taller than him now. She could see his yellow hair was black at the roots.

'Do you really like it?' she asked. 'My face? Like this?'

'Very nice,' he assured her. 'Very colourful.'

Her father came out, almost dragging Jessup by the arm. Serin noticed that the enginer had dust in his beard and on his shoulders. His trousers and his fingernails were filthy. He looked more like a miner than the man she had seen at the pump ceremony in his stiff, formal clothes, grappling with the lever while they carried Otto away. He was hairy and sweaty, his belly stuck out.

'Please,' her father was saying. 'We're expecting a most important visitor. It's the girl's fault. She should not have admitted you. The shop is closed.'

'Closed?' Jessup growled. 'Closed? Ye're dead and buried, the pair of ye!' He sounded disgusted, his accent very strong. He summoned the dwarf. 'Here, you.'

The shop bell jangled.

'Not that way!' cried the taxidermist. 'The back way!' He thrust them towards the gate. 'Serin, the shop!'

The prefectorial party had come to Guille's discreetly, in a shuttered carriage. The only ceremony the Head of the Eschalan Administration had allowed himself, on this occasion, was the woman who preceded him across the threshold to announce his arrival by bonging a modest gong. He entered then, the top of his great hood brushing the lintel.

Serin looked curiously at the old man in his gorgeous plum-coloured robes with their thick quilted sleeves, his face like a parched cheese wrapped in fur, the stringy white beard spilling down his front. He leaned with both hands on his silver-topped stick and uttered something majestic and incomprehensible in a high, creaky voice.

The man who followed him in was his interpreter, the moonshee. He was tall for an orange, and severe looking. His mane and his eyebrows glistened as he stared down at Serin, translating.

'His Estimability Lan olang, Prefect of the Eschalan Administration of the Imperial Annexe of Luscany, bids you greeting.'

'All right,' said Serin. She felt a bit nervous, but not inclined to show it. She led them abruptly out the back.

'Hello, Prefect! Hello, Charan du!' Diaz Jonal came striding across the yard in overalls a size too small, his bald pate smirched with soot.

'Professor!' said Lan olang. The two old men embraced, gingerly. The attendant banged her gong.

'Honoured,' said Serin's father. 'Most honoured. This way. Please. This way.'

He ushered them into the shed, then caught sight of his daughter loitering in the dark yard. 'Go to bed now, Serin.'

'I'm going for a piss,' she said.

A spasm of annoyance crossed his face. 'Go on then,' he said. 'Hurry up.'

He shut the door behind him.

Serin wandered over to the outhouse, and back again. A cold light was flickering from the window of the shed. She stood on tiptoe and peeped in.

Sybilla Kay was lying on the bench under the window: Serin could just see her feet. Nobody else was looking at her. They had a dead sheep in there, lying on the slab with its feet tied up, its head in a puddle of pink water. The fleece had been hacked away around its neck, and iron skewers inserted into the flesh, with wires trailing from them. The professor was trying to shove some kind of funnel into its stomach. Their words came faintly to her.

'Professor Jonal is of the opinion – '

'With respect, Dr Guille, it was you who ascertained – '

In the fizzing, flaring light they all looked wan and ill, huddling intently about the carcase of the sheep as though expecting it imminently to open its mouth and bless them with a cure. Whenever the moonshee spoke, the prefect bobbed up and down excitedly and gestured to the woman, who banged her gong and scribbled on a little tablet. He poked the sheep. It did not respond.

The interpreter asked Serin's father something, and he swung round to pick up Sybilla. Serin ducked. She went to listen at the keyhole instead.

Their voices buzzed and mumbled; the machines crackled, pumping their erratic green glow into the yard. Serin began to yawn. The professor was engaged in some tedious, half-audible explanation.

'. . . the partition of the materia, here, d'you see, from the base fluids . . . inspissation . . . it's as if you had a man running backwards up an infinite staircase . . .'

His tone grew more and more desperate. An engine whined complainingly. There was a bang. The light went out.

There was an awful pause; then the prefect spoke.

'Thus the past disdains all summoning,' she heard the interpreter translate equably, as if it were all the same to him. Serin crept back to the window. They were bumping into each other, groping for lucifers in the dark. Nothing interesting would happen for hours now.

She gave up and went in to bed. Lan olang had sounded very disappointed, she thought. She wondered if it was so terrible, being old.

—4—
Another Festive Compromise

I dwell once again by water, as I did when I woke. Here there are trees all around. Birds fly to and fro. The Primary is bounteous. Yet I recall how I used to lie, under a bush, in the mud beside the river, knowing nothing. My name had deserted me, also my history.

The first thing I remember hearing was the crying of the owls. I did not know then they were owls, but I knew they called me. I knew their tongue, and soon competed for their food. That was before I knew I did not have to eat. I still can eat, after a fashion. It is a compulsion that comes upon me once in a while, to eat.

There were people along the riverbank, dead ones, with ropes around their necks like rotted halters. They poked up, one here, one there, out of the mud, their bodies bent oddly about. They had no eyes. Some of them had their heads full of little eels. They meant nothing to me.

I followed the voices of the owls to the great building. I wandered about, looking up at its dark windows. I was afraid, and did not go in. I crouched among the humps of earth and watched. When the bells rang, I think I suffered some sort of fit, and fell to the ground. When I woke the second time it was day. I could feel no pain.

I went back to the great building with its metal doors. They stood ajar. Inside it was all lit up with lanterns, and filled with a crowd of people listening to a woman. These people were alive, I could tell that at once. They were the first such I had seen. I think I began to know I was more like them than I was like the owls, or the bats, or the mice. But they wore clothing, and rejoiced in lights that hurt my eyes. Their congregation was not for me. Also they had dogs, which I shunned as a fearsome enemy, and still do.

Whenever people came to dig holes and replenish the earth with dead, I used to hide myself in the mud with the old ones on the riverbank, my

*head or my legs in the cold water. I would hear the buriers in the
distance, some of them groaning and weeping. I would hear their voices
as someone paralysed on the brink of sleep hears words spoken over him,
knowing sounds but not sense.*

*She was the first I heard making that other sound, and it was because
of that I let her see me. They were all inside the building, none walking in
the ground of the dead, and I was sitting in the sun. She came around the
corner, alone, making that sound, and enchanted me. I who before had
always hid, sat like a stone to watch her mouth and try to seize on the
thing that was going in and out at my ears.*

It was her whistling that drew me to her, that and nothing else.

*It began to make my head sway, and that was when she saw me. She
stopped the whistling and ran away; and I fled to the river, afraid she
might fetch the ones with dogs, but no one came. I lay in the water with
all the dead ones and tried to feel as empty and nerveless as they; but
now I could not, and never have since. There was a preoccupation, a
congestion I felt gathering beneath my breastbone.*

*It was later that same day I took the fur skins of the creatures that I had
killed and fixed them together about me.*

The archduchess chuckled.

'Do you know what he said to me? He said, "Madam, you have
the respect and admiration of the whole realm." So I told him,
"Chancellor, there is nothing more likely to incline one to vice."
Which reminds me, they will be waiting for me at the table. Are
you coming, Nette?'

'Mother, you know I hate playing cards,' said the princess.

Her mother pursed her lips. 'Have I told you what Mancini
says in *On Cartophily*?'

'A hundred times, mother,' replied Princess Nette, knowing it
was futile.

'*The well-ordering of a deck of cards much resembles the good
government of a people, –* '

' *– the setting of a realm in just array,*' Nette concluded for her.
'Which is why it is proper for me to fold my hands and let it be
done by those much more able than I.'

'And what will you do instead, polish the silver? Practise your
pavane? Do a little something in watercolours?'

'I was considering visiting the old soldiers at the hostel,
mamma.'

'Ha! What do *they* do all day? Play cards!'

'Then you must come with me, mamma, and give them a game. Poor things, they would be overjoyed. After all, you do have the respect and admiration of the whole realm. They might even let you cheat, if you were discreet about it.'

'Nette, you're being absurd.'

'Then tell me, mamma: why *is* it you prefer a bad hand of tacou with orange functionaries to a good one with brave men and women, your own people, who would die for you and once very nearly did?' Nette heard herself becoming irate. No one but her mother could anger her so quickly.

'Sometimes, my dear,' said the archduchess seriously, 'I can't be sure whether you're extraordinarily innocent or extraordinarily stupid. The orange talk. One listens.'

'As to that, the old soldiers would *love* to talk to you!'

'Indeed. And what would we talk about?'

'Oh, some of them have the most wonderful stories of battle, mamma . . .'

'The reminiscences of the defeated are of no interest or use to us, Nette.'

'How can you be so callous?'

'How can you be so dull? These people sit and gossip in your own palace, and you don't want to hear what they're saying.'

'They're extremely boring, mother. And petty.'

'It is they who decide what is petty, just as they decide what is trumps.'

'Oh, I'm tired of arguing with you,' cried Nette, who had begun, as usual, to feel obscurely in the wrong. 'I shall accompany you, since you insist, and judge for myself.'

'Your most sensible decision of the day,' said her mother. 'Will you ring for a footman, please?' Crespian Vittore, her self-appointed guardian, had gone at last to his own office.

'There's no need, mamma. I can push your chair.'

'It would not be seemly, Nette.'

'A display of affection!'

'Which you feel very little at the moment, one might think, from the way you shout at me. I should become nervous with you at my back. I like to have you where I can see you.'

The archduchess said nothing further until a man had been summoned and they were on the way to the card-room. Then she remarked suddenly: 'I don't know why I play without Crespi. I'm certain it's bad luck.'

The princess ignored her.

Once, of course, the archduchess had had her circle, and favoured them in turn with invitations to cards. Now it always seemed to be the same three, all orange. As one by one the Luscan nobles had made their excuses and fled for the border, the Eschalans had sidled politely into the vacant seats and picked up the discarded hands. They were permanent now. Princess Nette was angry because her mother did not dare get rid of them.

The royal party entered the room. The company rose. Deliberately, Princess Nette took a seat aside, and sent a page for her embroidery.

'Will Your Highness not grace our game?' asked the ageing haruspex, Movan ilor.

'Her Highness is above our folly,' said the archduchess as the footman pushed her in at the table.

The Eschalans tittered politely.

'I deny that it is folly!' Pan oc waved her hand. 'Your games are most instructive.'

'Precisely what I was just trying to tell Her Highness,' the archduchess replied. A bottle and a glass were placed at her elbow. 'We live and die in a hand of tacou.'

'You may consider, Your Highness,' said Pan oc, a historian, 'the cards are like a book so old it is ageless. Everything is told within its pages – each time a new story!'

'Always with the same outcome,' said the archduchess. 'I lose money.'

Ara jast, the third of the party, ventured to console her and deny it, at the same time. Princess Nette wondered if he was stupid; or if they all were.

The archduchess shuffled.

'Now we shall see something!'

'Cut?'

'Three and eight. Eleven.'

The princess nibbled some strips of dried pear.

'Ti-pom, ti-pom, pom *pom*.'

'Tss, tss, tss.'

'Ah! I don't believe it!'

A footman trimmed the lamps.

'What is she scheming, I wonder?'

'Your Royal Grace has the luck of the wise!'

'Now *I* remember a game . . .' began Movan ilor.

At last the princess could stand it no longer.

'Is there any news from Nairi?' she asked, casually.

'They cannot prevail,' said the old man immediately. 'It will be over in a week. Mark it.'

'Nairi is an old wound in the body of the Empire, Your Highness,' observed Pan oc.

'Fever and confusion!' exclaimed Ara jast distantly. 'Has *no one* a seven?'

Princess Nette took her leave. 'Please don't get up,' she requested, but they did anyway.

Her mother cornered her before dinner. 'You see?' she hissed, proudly. 'They are losing in Nairi.'

'They did not say so.'

'You can tell, if you know them as well as I do.'

'In any case, I heard that three days ago from Thisbe my maid.'

The archduchess was not to be dissuaded. 'Rumours and dust,' she opined.

'And how do you know this is anything more?' Nette demanded.

'Augurers and historians do not trade in rumours.'

'I should have said they do nothing else,' said the princess through the teeth of a radiant smile at Movan ilor as he passed with his retinue. 'I believed my maid. I still do.'

'Ara jast is a senior messenger,' added the archduchess.

'All the more reason he would not have admitted anything to Pan oc and Movan ilor. Anyhow, he said nothing all afternoon but "Peril and confusion!" and "Does anyone remember what I scored last hand?" '

'Don't be arch, my dear. Ah, Crespian, thank goodness you're here! She's taking advantage of my senility again.'

'Good evening, Your Royal Highness,' said the under-scrivener. He wore a new steel pin.

'Good evening, Vittore,' said the princess. 'Tell us, won't you, your opinion of tacou.'

He frowned judiciously. 'I believe it's a gambling game, madam. The orange have rather taken to it. I fear I should not. I am deficient in the mathematics, as well as in, ha ha, the money.'

'In those too?' said the princess quietly, and then at once: 'You know, I'm sure, that Her Royal Grace the Archduchess is a devotee of tacou?'

Vittore smirked at his elderly patron. 'I, ah, have once or twice had, ah, the occasion – '

'Do you think *I* should take to it, Vittore?'

'Her Grace is the one you must ask, madam. Though I should be honoured to help her instruct you.'

'Should you, Vittore? How kind you are. What a pity you are deficient in the mathematics.'

'Study would make good that deficit, madam.'

'I fear that would waste your time, Vittore.'

'Why, madam, no minute spent in a study of your commending could ever be counted waste.'

Nette smiled graciously, without replying, so that he had to scurry to fill the pause.

'It would help consume the long winter evenings ahead.'

Nette wrinkled her nose. 'All that reckoning for a handful of pasteboard.'

'Good reckoning is its own reward, Highness.'

'Ah, another disciple of Mancini!'

'Highness?'

'Mancini on Cartophily. A noble treatise. My mother will tell you about it. She knows it by heart, I think. You will excuse me.'

Princess Nette turned away and left him bowing.

Later, in private, her mother said to her: 'You must stop baiting Crespian. You disgrace yourself; and you embarrass me.'

'You disgrace yourself, mamma, by letting him fawn upon you. He's a sycophant and a parasite. Don't make me say worse.'

'You have an ungenerous nature, Nette, I've told you before to mind it. Crespian is worth ten of your baronets. He dotes on you, you know. Why, if he weren't a commoner, I dare say – '

'You dare say many things, mother. You dare say that I should elevate Crespian Vittore because you enjoy his flattery.'

The archduchess had not enjoyed her dinner, which had been cooked as everything was these days in the peppery mode of Eschaly. Dyspepsia made her uncivil.

'I'd rather receive such flattery than another's flowers,' she declared.

The princess was astounded. 'And what has *he* to do with this?'

'It was you who mentioned disgracing oneself by associating with inferiors.'

Nette closed her eyes. 'Brant is the best gardener the palace has ever had. He takes pride in his work, and so do I.'

'He's a gypsy. And you spend altogether too much time talking to him.'

'He tells me news of his people, who are good people, mother. The montanos are courageous and loyal, which is more than I could say of certain underscriveners. This is a stupid conversation. I'm not going to continue with it. We should both lose our tempers and gain only a disturbed night's rest.'

Princess Nette rang for the archduchess's bedservants and, courteously wishing her goodnight, left her glaring her displeasure, sitting stiffly upright and gripping the arms of her wheeled chair like a throne.

The bad news from Nairi had a most palpable effect in Calcionne. As if in fear or mourning, the Eschalan community stayed indoors. All along Melkonnen, blinds remained drawn. Suddenly a carriage on the Apronway was an event.

Why were they cowering, Princess Nette wondered. They could not reasonably have thought themselves in danger. The fighting in Nairi could never spread to the high countries, nor was its example likely to inflame the phlegmatic folk of Luscany. Even in Peirruich things were quiet that season, though she knew that in the hills whole families of farmers were flouting the curfew to ride to their midnight bonfires. The sword was up on Tallenbrach; but in Calcionne everything just ground to a halt. Gangs of idle apprentices stood in doorways, eyeing the prefecture, but its windows remained unbroken.

No, it was in a ritual of withdrawal, a remarkable racial self-abnegation, that the Eschalans disappeared from the streets that autumn. They were feeling exposed, out on this remote and unfashionable northern limb of the Empire. Tropical Nairi had enjoyed Eschalan administration for years. To hear that the heartland was up in arms was discouraging for the occupants of a much younger frontier. They felt cut off. Why, the Great Road East itself was imperilled! In unlighted rooms, the Eschalans fasted, listening mutely to the termites in the foundations of their existence.

'The ice fair will bring them out of it,' said Charan du; but his voice did not sound so confident. He set down the sickly little drink he had been toying with and began instead to smooth his mane, though it was immaculately plaited and oiled as ever. Charan du was not in retreat.

'That's a good while off yet,' Princess Nette observed, frankly. She was relishing his access of anxiety, especially since he carried it with a kind of shocked innocence, as if he didn't know what it was. There was the Imperial Destiny; there was no alternative plan. Opposition made no sense.

'And Nairi will be secure again by then,' he said rapidly, as if dismissing the subject.

'If the Primary permits,' said Nette lightly.

He looked affronted, then gave her a thin smile. 'Of course,' he said, and stroked his hair.

'The prefect requires me to tell you,' he continued, 'that preparations for the fair may begin as usual – this permission is a mere formality by now, as you know. Our people also enjoy this junket! It is not our way to require our subjects to weep when we weep; rather, to borrow from them the gift of merriment.'

The princess laughed, quite merrily. Charan du was pleased to accept it as a display of sympathy.

'The hams shall be hung and the apples set in pickle,' she said, 'by gracious forbearance of His Estimability. I shall have it proclaimed.'

'Please do.'

The prefectorial moonshee seemed still to have something on his mind. Princess Nette smiled receptively, but made no attempt to help him. He came to a decision then, and leaned forward in his armchair.

'I believe you should know this. You are wise enough not to disclose it until the time is right.'

He hesitated just long enough for Nette to say, blankly, 'How shall I know when it is?'

'I shall tell you.'

'Of course,' she said. 'Forgive me. What were you saying?'

'It is this. We are suing for the visit of an imperial herald.'

'How impressive.'

'A personal envoy from the emperor himself might do much to encourage our people.'

'But you don't want to tell anyone just in case he says no.'

'The time is not right,' said Charan du.

He was being evasive. What was it? Was he afraid of losing face should his petition be rejected by the emperor? Nette thought not. She put her hands together and said: 'What glory for His Estimability if the emperor says yes!'

'It will not be necessary to bother the prefect with this trifle straightaway.'

Ah.

She pressed it home. 'I'm sorry, Charan du, I must have misunderstood. Who do you mean by "we"?'

'The Council of the Guild. The messengers.' He ducked into officialdom. 'It is, still, a guild matter. The imperial heralds are our most senior and distinguished associates, elevated by decree. There is a protocol. The prefecture, of course, does not concern itself directly with – '

'Your hair looks lovely today.'

'Your Highness?'

'It's quite perfect. Your hair,' Nette nodded.

Charan du smiled; removed his hand; and ran the tip of a finger along each eyebrow. 'Your own also,' he said.

The princess got to her feet. He followed.

'I wish your wish the Primary's favour,' she said formally.

He was back in control now, and standing perhaps closer than was correct. 'Will you say, for all my wishes?'

'No, Charan du,' said Princess Nette, 'for then what should become of us?' She held his gaze. 'What should become of any of us?'

She left him then, and went to her own apartment.

That evening, on impulse, the princess wrapped a blanket over her head and slipped out into the darkened streets. She kept to the shadows and tried to walk slowly. The light was burning late in the window of the postmistress's office: perhaps she had the entire upper council of the messengers in there weaving plots. Or perhaps they were playing tacou.

Princess Nette stood awhile on the Brinkway, looking down at the cold river. She wished she had the courage to go into a tavern, somewhere where there were people.

She saw a man. She thought he was looking at her. She decided to go home.

Cloud lowered upon the mountains. A line of trees stood out in silhouette, then disappeared, like a rampart overwhelmed by smoke. The snow had come early, as if to hasten festivity. The forest paths were obliterated; washed clean by a day of sun; obliterated again. The montanos sat on the edges of white meadows working with wood and laces, wax and grease. Their breath steamed. They were happy.

The orange brightened up too, when it was finally announced that the messengers were assembling a roll of sponsors for the route of a Heraldic Progress. Names were unofficially circulated; officially denied. Obscure committees held musical rallies in the park. Lan olang rode about the city, beaming at everyone indiscriminately and throwing comfits to the children.

Inscrutable symbolic extravaganzas proclaimed the merit of this nominee, that nominee. Hastily printed broadsheets were circulated, and money changed hands. Movan ilor of the haruspices was much involved. The princess's maid had heard he was getting all his equipage up in masks that resembled the heads of giant insects; or perhaps it was fish.

'Heraldic Progress seems to move an inch at a time, at a crown an inch,' the princess observed to her mother, the archduchess. 'What is it, Stevon?'

Her secretary bowed. 'The Enginer Jessup awaits your pleasure, madam.'

'Oh how boring. Tell him, tell him I'm in the bath.'

'Nette,' said her mother sharply.

'Well, by the time it gets to Jessup, it'll be true.'

The princess made to leave the room, but her secretary did not immediately step aside.

'It is about the baths that he is here, madam. There has been an interruption in the supply of hot water. Apparently a valve has frozen.'

'Well, what can I do about it? Does he want money?'

'It seems he is here to apologise, madam.'

'Splendid. Tell him the princess accepts his apologies, is sorry for his trouble, and hopes the Primary will speed his work.'

'See him, Nette,' said her mother.

'Oh, very well. Show him to my study. And *then* I shall have a bath. Tell the housekeeper: hot water.'

Jessup was looking haggard. She addressed him in Bryle, she thought he would like that.

'Damage to the piping, Mr Jessup? Do you suspect sabotage?'

'No, ma'am, frost.'

'But surely the water is hot?'

'Not all of it, ma'am.' He smiled, slightly shy.

'Explain it to me,' she said.

'Ma'am, I'd be glad to. I'm glad you want to hear. But you just wouldn't know the words.'

Between his great brows and his great beard he coloured, fearing to give offence.

'Not that you don't know Bryle, ma'am; but you don't know plumbing.'

Nette began to feel more friendly to the man. 'At any rate, you can, presumably, deal with frost.'

'Yes, ma'am. They're to it now, but it will be a while.'

'Don't worry, Mr Jessup. We managed before your piped water, we'll manage again now. Is the prefect without hot water too? That will inconvenience him. Do you know, Mr Jessup, I swear the orange spend more time in their bath than in their offices? It must be their habit of bathing in company.'

The princess bit her tongue and smiled brightly, grateful that her mother was not there. The remark had been improper; but this time the enginer was not embarrassed, apparently.

'They come from a warmer country, ma'am. It's only natural. But it's their own fault,' he said, rising, 'if they're finding it a bit chilly today.'

The princess was intrigued. She was also amused. Jessup still had his lowland manners. Anyone else would have asked her permission before getting up to go.

'Their fault? I thought you said it was frost.'

'Yes, ma'am, but the frost shouldn't be there. Or rather, to be exact, the ice shouldn't be there, even when the frost is. The valve shouldn't have frozen,' he said, sitting down again.

'Surely that's your responsibility, Mr Jessup. It's your work – a marvellous work.'

'That's just it, ma'am. I can't *do* my work. There's too much of it. And if the orange want guns, they can't have my eye on the hot water system. I can't be in two places, not at the same time.'

'They're imposing upon you at the gunsmithy,' presumed the princess.

'They want twice as much of everything, and all for Nairi,' he answered.

'Of course. Can you do that?'

The enginer shook his head. 'Twice the work with the same tools? And the bad iron. The miners are against us.'

'What if you refused to make the guns?'

'Someone else would.'

'Would you not – prefer that?'

Something closed in his expression. 'I like my work, ma'am.'

'Yes, Mr Jessup, of course you do. I should like to do mine. I too do what is – permitted. Not all of it is for my people, not all by any means.' She looked at him with solicitude. 'Forgive me, Mr Jessup, I do not speak personally, but I should have expected you to be a much more unpopular man than you are.'

'There are quarters in the city I'd not walk through alone,' he said.

'No one else has shot at you?'

'Not yet.' Unexpectedly he smiled and flicked his chest with his thumb. The sound was metal, muffled.

'Armour?'

'Woven steel.'

'Is it not dreadfully heavy?'

'I've the back for it.'

She was about to speak again when there came a thud from outside.

The enginer raised a finger in warning. Once more he rose, and with surprising stealth and speed crossed to the door and flung it open. He looked out, not speaking.

'Is there someone?'

Karel Jessup came back into the room, saying nothing, leaving the door open.

'What is it?'

Nette got up and hurried to the door. Across the hallway on a high stool at a bookcase sat Crespian Vittore the underscrivener.

'Your pardon, Highness,' he said clearly. 'I regret disturbing you. I dropped one of these ledgers. They are infernally heavy.'

'No disturbance, Vittore. We were merely curious.'

Princess Nette closed the door and returned to Enginer Jessup with a smile of satisfaction.

'Your Highness, you must beware,' he muttered. 'I know that man. He works for the interpreter. He was listening to us.'

'I doubt very much he understands Bryle, Mr Jessup. Let him listen.'

'Ma'am, don't trust him. He is a spy.'

'I know.'

'You should get rid of him!'

'No, no, I prefer to have him here, where I can keep an eye on him. Besides, he's company for mother.'

—5—

How to Bring a Blush
to the Snow

The argument had gone on, in a desultory fashion, for the best part of an hour. The rumble of their voices was like a storm trapped among the mountains. It rose and sank as they came back again and again, circling around, both of them exhausted, neither of them able to let it rest.

Serin sat upstairs, hunched over a candle which she was mutilating with burnt-out lucifers. She was quite content for them to go at it forever. As soon as they were finished, she would have to go out to the shops.

(This one she had started herself.

'There's nothing to eat,' said her mother. 'Serin.'

'Money,' said Serin, not looking up.

'Ask your father.'

And Serin had, but not in private; she had sat and waited until he came in, then said: 'Mamma wants me to go shopping, father.' If there was any tone in her voice, it was one of resentment.

'Well?'

'Well, I need some money, don't I?'

Tarven Guille swore, not looking at his wife; but Amber, unable to resist the provocation, snapped back at him. Quietly and coldly, Tarven replied. Equally quietly, Amber insulted him. As he embarked on a rejoinder, Serin rose to leave them.

'Where are you going? You sit down!' cried her mother, but Serin ignored her.

She was a prisoner of their war. Her helplessness was her shield; her weapon too, when she chose.)

It was getting cold. They had already had some snow. With the money her mother had extracted, Serin traversed the damp streets in a corridor of self-absorption. The only things she saw were two ravens fussing around down by the shambles.

Late afternoon was a good time to go to Rowe Market, especially on a dull day. Serin started at the top and bought, more or less at random, what was being cried up as the cheapest: frilly black mushrooms, a skewer of trotters, a bundle of rather limp chard. At the bottom she stopped for a cup of brandy tea, to fortify her for the trip home. While she drank, she looked about for the first time at her surroundings.

Lank ferns hung over a black wall at the end of the tannery. Two urchins poked bits of refuse through a crust of snow into a drift of wet soot. In a doorway sat an old woman bundled up in ten coats, her face crumpled and warted like a monstrous tuber. The air smelled burnt and sour.

Serin did not go straight home. Almost without thinking about it, she turned right beneath the arches, whistling loudly for the pleasure of the echo.

> On that day, on that day
> We gathered in the meadow
> On that day.

The Hyacinth House was down at the end of Leech Street. This walled mansion, with its profusely efflorescent architraves, had belonged to the Margrave of Tourmalix. Millie Traker's mother had worked there, in the kitchen. Towards the end they'd been holding orgies there, Millie's mother said, according to Millie. After the family left it had been turned into a brothel, which the orange had closed down. It had stood neglected ever since, its splendid paint flaking, its woodwork down to the grain.

The house itself had defeated Serin. It was shuttered and locked. But the garden, that was hers.

She squeezed through the side gate where there was a stanchion missing. Under the black horse-chestnuts the lawn lay white, undisturbed but for the scribble of birds' feet. The statues of naked people were wearing caps and mantles of snow. Their pensive eyes gazed away over Serin's head as she went whistling by.

She went down to the summer-house, which was built on a

platform overhanging the river. Dukes and people used to fish
from it. In fine weather she would sit and dangle her legs
through the railing into empty space, over dark water moving
quick and cold below. Not today. There were icicles.

She climbed the steps anyway. As she reached the platform
she heard a noise behind her: a soft, crunching noise.

Serin turned round.

Something was coming across the lawn. It came on all fours
through the snow, so she would have taken it for a dog; but it
looked like a man. When it swayed up on its hind legs and
staggered upright to the steps of the summer-house, she saw
that it was almost entirely hairless, its skin white and covered in
purple blotches. It had a man's shape, and a man's face.

Serin screamed.

The man clapped his hands over his ears. 'Don't do that!' he
cried.

He seemed so frail and pitiful that Serin only gaped at him, and
forgot to be afraid.

He was old, bald, wet, and obviously very ill. He wore nothing
but otterskins, in a kilt and about his neck. His lips were highly
coloured, his eyes startlingly bright in the collapse of his face.
'Do – the other thing – again!' he said.

'What?'

'The – ' The lunatic waved his fingers agitatedly in front of his
mouth. 'Like a song.'

'Whistling?' said Serin, and did.

'Whistling, of course! That!'

'I was only whistling,' she said, unnerved by the intensity of
his response. 'I didn't mean anything. I didn't know anyone was
here.'

'I'm here,' he said. 'I – live here. I – ' he said again, as if
correcting himself, 'I stay here.'

He was shivering horribly.

'Are you all right?'

He had to think about this for a while. 'No,' he said finally,
troubled, as if reaffirming a conclusion he had reached before.
'No, something's wrong. Things are different. I forget – things,'
he said.

He wiped his hand slowly down his face.

'I'm sorry I frightened you,' he said. 'You were whistling. You
were whistling, so I came. Do it again.'

She had to laugh. His wits were out. He was only a poor mad loon. She whistled again for him.

Now there comes a time to every man –

'I saw you once, whistling,' he told her.

This meant nothing to her. 'It's only whistling,' she said. 'Can't you whistle?'

'There it is,' he said unhappily. 'I'm sure I used to. But it's gone.'

'Aren't you freezing? You haven't even got anything on your feet.'

He looked down at himself, plainly seeing nothing wrong. 'No,' he said. 'I know I should wear clothes, I know you do, all of you. Are you cold? Should we go indoors?'

'Can you get in?'

'Of course!'

'I've got to go.'

'Will you come back? I don't know – anyone. You're the first one I've spoken to, do you know that?'

'I don't know,' said Serin, getting ready to flee. 'I'll see,' she said.

'Then you could show me how to whistle,' he said.

She laughed again. He was just like a little boy. 'I could show you that now, if you like.'

She stood at the top of the steps and the naked lunatic stood on the ground, shivering, and she showed him how to whistle. 'That's it. Now blow gently. Breathe out. You're not breathing . . .'

'No,' he said, in a voice like the wind in the wood, 'no. I think I used to.'

Serin's spine froze.

'You're – not – b – '

'Please don't scream again. It hurts my – my – '

'Ears,' she said, with a gulp.

'Yes.'

'You're a ghost,' she said. 'I'm seeing a ghost.'

'No, I don't think so,' he said. 'Here: feel,' and he stepped up to her, holding out his arm.

Serin touched the back of his hand, took his wrist, dropped it again. His flesh was firm, but very cold. The purple stains were like bruises, some of them very dark indeed.

'You've – escaped from somewhere, haven't you?'

'Yes!'

'You're very ill. You've had some sort of accident, a bad accident. You've got to go back there.'

'No! I – live – here! I'm no trouble to anyone!'

'Where did you come from? Do you remember?'

'Yes, I used to be at the place where the dead ones are.'

'The graveyard! I saw you there. Did you live *there*?'

'Between there and the river.'

'But there's no shelter.'

'I don't mind the cold, or the rain. When it – this – '

'Snow,' said Serin.

'Yes, when it snowed, I came here. Snow – gets in the way. But it shows up the tracks of things wonderfully!'

He wiped his face again.

'Are you hungry?' she asked.

'No, no.'

'I've got some food,' she said, pushing her basket at him.

He looked inside it. 'I don't need these things.'

'Suit yourself,' she said, miffed.

'You are kind,' he told her.

'You really live here?'

'Yes!' he assured her. 'Come and see.'

He led her back across the lawns. He had his own way in. She stood and watched him swarm up the wall.

He clung to the top of a shutter, gazing down at her, his head on one side.

'I can't do that,' she said. 'You'll have to come down and let me in.'

He disappeared beneath the eaves and reappeared, some while later, at a low window, which he opened.

Negotiating the sill and a heavy curtain, Serin stepped down into a large, dark room filled with a great many trunks and crates stacked one on top of another. The air was not pleasant.

She squeezed her way around piled furniture to the door, which proved to be locked. She couldn't see any other way he could have got in. Now he was squatting in a small clear space in front of the cold fireplace. In one corner was a shapeless white heap that looked as if it were covered in feathers: something bundled up to make a pillow, she supposed.

'What's in all the boxes?' asked Serin. Her voice sounded funny in the dead room.

'I don't know,' said the creature. He seemed to have no curiosity about them.

Now her eyes had got used to the dark, Serin could see there were big, dim pictures painted on the walls. Two showed people in very old-fashioned clothes sticking spears into wild animals. The only other one she could see was a woman in chains, standing on a tiny rock in a stormy sea. They were all painted badly, Serin thought. The anatomy was all wrong.

There were cobwebs everywhere, furry ones. The smell was getting worse.

'I've got to go home now.'

Her companion smiled up at her, an empty smile, which frightened her for a minute. He sat with one hand on the feathery cushion, which was, she suddenly realised, a dead swan.

'I've got to go.'

'Whistle again,' he hissed.

Serin whistled, picking her way back to the window.

'Yes!'

'I'll come and see you again one day,' she said. It didn't sound very convincing.

'Whistle when you come, so I know it is you.'

Scrambling out of the window with her shopping, Serin promised.

'Wait!' he called. 'What is your name?'

'Arethusa,' she said, safely outside and peering in the crack. 'What's yours?'

He shook his head.

'Arethusa,' he repeated. 'Don't tell anyone about me, will you?'

Again he looked like a little boy, all alone in the big old house, meaning no harm.

'No one,' she said, wondering who would have believed it anyway. 'Goodbye!'

And screamed with laughter on the way home.

In the days that followed, she kept thinking about the old tramp. While she dusted the parlour, he would suddenly occur to her, how he had looked, his face so damaged, and eager, and pathetic. He was completely mad. She smiled. Then she thought, whatever his sickness was, he should not be alone in that decrepit old house, not with winter upon them. But what could she do about it? Nothing.

Then it snowed in earnest, and she had to go and see, if he was still there, if he was all right. She thought and she thought, and then she waited until her father was in his shed and her mother in the jakes, to go into their room and take a bundle of things from the wardrobe. Then she put on the furs that Uncle Banner had given her, and her skis, and off she went down into the shadowy heart of Calcionne, down Leech Street to the Hyacinth House, whistling all the way.

> And if that maiden had a horse
> And if that horse could cross the sky
> Wouldn't the stars be surprised?

At the open window she lost her nerve. She would not go in. She knocked on the pane.

'Hello?' she said cautiously, and whistled some more.

He was not there. He was gone, or they had caught him. He was lying dead in an upper room. Perhaps he had never been there at all, and *she* was the one who was mad. Then soft and silent as a cat he edged into view.

'Arethusa! Come in, let me help you.'

He stretched out his bony hands. She drew back.

'No. I just came – to see if you were all right. To see if you wanted anything.'

'Talking,' he said.

'Pardon?'

'Talking would be nice,' he said. 'That's what I want.'

She laughed. He didn't seem to mind her laughing.

'I'll come in for a bit,' she decided. She held her skis in at the window, and he hastened to help her with them. 'Now get out of the way,' she said as he hovered. 'I can manage.'

'Skis!' he proclaimed, jubilantly. 'I remember more all the time. I've made the door open, and explored upstairs.'

He had pushed back some more of the obstructions, Serin saw. The swan had gone, which was a bit of a disappointment. Her father never got swans.

The air in the room was no sweeter.

The pallid creature had enlarged his clearing to make room for two chairs, set facing one another.

'That one is yours,' he told her. 'This is how I make myself remember. Sometimes I have talked to you! Sometimes I think I believed you were truly here. I have had dreams,' he said, 'or something of the sort. Distant noises; other voices.'

He crouched by her chair, rubbing his shoulders.

'I dreamed two men lifted me out of a hole in the ground. It was dark: night-time. They pushed two spikes into my neck. I saw a great, hurtful light. Then they dropped me back in the hole. I woke . . . or slept. One or the other. My neck still hurts,' he said, conversationally.

'Let me see,' said Serin.

The pelts he wore were stiff with frost. She shifted the one at his throat, and saw two little round puncture marks side by side.

'You have got a wound there,' she said. 'It looks like a bite. Probably fleas in this fur. You really ought to wear proper clothes.'

'I don't think I should like that,' he said, huskily.

'Of course you would. People have to wear clothes. It's not decent otherwise.'

'I'm not – ' he began; but she held out her bundle.

'Here.'

It was a pair of boots wrapped in a pair of breeches.

'Whose are these?' he asked, turning them over wonderingly.

'Yours. Put them on.'

He frowned, trying to work something out. 'No,' he said. 'There was a man who wore these already, wasn't there?'

'My pa,' said Serin. 'Second-hand not good enough?'

Doubtfully, he put his foot into a boot.

'You'll have to put the breeches on first,' said Serin, 'or it'll be a bit difficult later. Hold them up. Which is the front? That's right. Can you put them on?'

Clumsily at first, but with increasing confidence, the man drew on her father's breeches, buttoned them at her instruction, then pulled on the boots.

'They're a bit small,' said Serin doubtfully. 'Are they comfortable?'

'I don't know,' he said helplessly.

She had to lace the boots for him. His skirt of skins hung over the top of the trousers. She had seen his genitals, pale and shrivelled.

'I didn't dare take a jacket too,' she told him. 'Are you all right? Can you move about?'

Stiff and self-conscious, he toddled out of the room and up the stairs. Serin found him gaping at himself in an old tin mirror.

'Oh . . .' he murmured, overcome. His damp eyes seemed to wander in and out of focus.

'We'll have to get you something. I wonder if there's anything here?'

The old man's 'explorations' had not gone far. All the rooms were locked. Serin pointed out the door with a key still in the keyhole.

They went in. It was a bedroom, or had been. The bed had no mattress, and the carpet had been rolled up. Peculiar things had been drawn on the walls.

'Here's something,' said Serin, 'but it's not much good to you!'

On the bed was a white torso stuffed with straw: a tailor's mannequin, or perhaps a bayonet target. It had been taken off its stand and dressed in a corset of rotten pink silk, with purple laces.

'Should I not wear that?' he asked.

'That? No! That's not for men, it's for women.'

'Ah. Arethusa. That's one thing I thought of to ask you. I'm not a woman, am I?'

He asked so seriously she was touched, and could not mock him.

'No,' she said, 'you're not a woman. Oh! We've got to find you a name!'

'I thought I wasn't one,' he went on. 'But you are.'

'I'm just a girl,' she said, embarrassed. 'Don't take any notice of me.'

'Oh no, you teach me so much. You are my friend, aren't you? You bring me – these.'

'I wanted to bring something,' she said, 'but I hadn't anything to bring. And I didn't know what you wanted. You don't eat, you don't feel the cold – but you must have clothes. It's only proper.'

'I shall remember,' he said positively. 'I'm not going to forget any more.'

'And a name,' Serin went on, 'so that I can call you something. Barnaby. Maluk. Talleyrand. Oh, I'm no good at this!'

Try as she might, the amnesiac would accept nothing but to recall his own name; which he could by no means do.

'One day,' he promised, 'you and I shall be talking, and something will snap, just like that, and I shall remember it. "Tomalin!" I shall say!'

'Why Tomalin? Tomalin, is that it?'

But he could not tell her.

'You should get out, walk about,' she advised him. 'Something might remind you. I know – you could come to the fair. No one would notice you there. No one could tell if you wore a coat and a big hat. You could see everything!'

His eyes suddenly grew very wide, and he opened his mouth. His teeth and tongue were stained, as if he had been chewing berries.

'To walk amongst you, unknown!' he exulted. His fingers seemed to clutch shadows.

Serin left him at once and ran back downstairs. Her heart hammering, she skied across the Maltleather Bridge and went home a different way.

There was a motley camp on either bank days before the river froze. Hauliers and builders set up pitches early, plying for the favour of the hiring-man. Sausage stands and dowdy sideshows appeared: The Rat Maze; Tombola; Aurora Borealis the Painted Lady. At the iceboat yard braziers were burning all hours as they made ready the royal barge *Capreole*. The bone-plated tips of its mighty runners were cleaned and polished; its chains were brushed and oiled. Even the Eschalans, who hated snow, were cheerfully bustling around: a corpulent dignitary from the fatherland had arrived at the prefecture.

The montanos appeared at four in the morning, the coldest part of the day. The ice fair was the only occasion in the year when they would put off their accustomed shyness and ride down into the city with their whole families. The women burnished their teeth. The children fought together with extraordinary passion, like young lions. Some of the men even took jobs, for no montano could be short of money at the ice fair. There would be stalls where they would sell game, and articles of weaving, and cunning implements in wood and horn.

On a silty spit the ice gypsies built a small lodge, which the chief came down to occupy. The river was black as a portion of night, and showed no sign of freezing. But even if the townspeople had misjudged, the montanos were there, and they were never wrong about the weather.

Tarven Guille discovered the disappearance of his boots and breeches, and interrogated his wife Amber; but she was too busy with her own clothes, letting out old skirts and darning faded hose.

'These leggings I have had since I was your age, Serin!'

'You said that last year, mamma.' Amber Guille always roused herself and became vigorous and happy when her people came to town. Serin could only resent it, knowing it would not last.

'Let me see now. Yes, this necklace is a lucky one. I dreamed the other night of a whole ham. Come, Tarven, dance with me as we did at the hop-picking . . .'

Grimacing, the taxidermist waltzed his wife stiffly about the bed. Touchy as he was on the subject of her relatives, he could not be dour and grumpy while she chattered and sang.

'I feel so much brighter these mornings! I swear it was that old remedy, the squirrel's tail. Did you not tell me, love, that the winter kills off all disease?'

The temperature dropped; struggled up again; dropped; and dropped. Serin and her father came down one morning to find Amber's brother Banner seated at the kitchen table, gobbling porridge.

'The river is frozen from Tirree to Seger's Acres!' said Uncle Banner by way of greeting. He spoke with his mouth full, making Tarven wince. Amber was leaning on her brother's shoulder, beaming and rolling her eyes.

'Good morning, brother Banner,' said Tarven. 'I trust you are well. Is there any tea to be had here?'

Banner turned his red face to Serin. 'How's my young chicken? Got your skates sharp? All the young chickens are on the ice, out to get themselves a young cock. Don't you be last, Serin, you'll get an ugly one!' He laughed heartily. Serin only looked sullen. 'Cheer up, chicken,' chided her uncle. 'Hearts are won and lost at the fair.'

The Guilles were the only family in Threadpole Street who set off that morning by dog-sled. Neighbours stared from upstairs windows and hooting children threw snowballs. Amber kept calling out to her brother in montano, embarrassing Tarven who understood not a word and found it undignified, though Serin knew her mother was only asking for news of people and clucking excitedly over every titbit.

The bunting in the Aspenpleyn hung frozen from the lampposts. There were hot dampers and chestnuts at Five Spires and toboggan races down Brinkway and across the bridge. All Calcionne was up and about, jostling and sliding towards the river.

Careless of Dr Guille's discomfort, Banner drove his team right into the midst of the gypsy encampment, where Amber was at once mobbed by chirping, clamouring women in traditional costume no less colourful than her own. Her husband sat smiling stiffly on the sled, refusing flasks of akvavit thrust into his face by jovial bearded giants with swords at their belts. Serin's eyes flickered from side to side, taking in everything: the covered sleds; the brawling dogs; the fires everywhere that smouldered with dung; the boys, arrogant and shy, who stood apart in huddles, looking at her and whispering.

Her uncle Banner helped her from the sled. 'All the girls are at the skating,' he said, giving her a purpose.

'Be back at noon,' her father instructed her.

The river was frozen from side to side, with snow thick upon the ice. It seemed impossible that the booths and the tents, the trestles of food and the drays of ale, and all the milling crowd, were supported only by water; but the water had forgotten its nature. The skaters, mostly women and couples, went around in a great loose circle while an orange band trumpeted from the Bennedock. Inside and outside the circle younger children cut shakier figures, pushed one another and went sprawling. Serin Guille sat apart shivering with her skates slung about her neck, but made no move to put them on. She saw some girls she knew, but did not greet them, and nobody greeted her. Horns blew; people cheered; dogs barked and barked and barked.

She wandered in a while to the sideshows, where for three-pence she saw a huge black woman sitting on two chairs side by side; an eight-legged calf; a green donkey; a man who swallowed live eels and brought them up again still wriggling; and another man who chewed up wood and glass. Diaz Jonal was there again with his Electrical Calliope, which gave no more sign of making music than it had the year before. The best the professor could coax from it was a deep hum that made the teeth ache. Eschalan proctors and fair constables stood remonstrating with him, afraid the vibrations would damage the ice. They edged around the contraption, trying to avoid the heavy blue vapour that eddied about it and would not disperse. Jonal, his head deep inside the casing, called muffled instructions to his dwarf, who seemed to be suffering from the cold. His long nose was quite blue. He hopped from foot to foot, grimacing at the officers and slapping his arms. Serin moved away quickly, hoping he hadn't noticed her.

She came by the royal barge, moored until the grand procession. Parents were vainly trying to keep their children from playing underneath it. On deck there was no sign of the princess or any of the royal household, only a gaggle of nobles cheering their champions in the ice joust. Serin joined the crowd watching the heavy sleds being trundled up the lists and back again, careering to violent collisions.

'Hurrah!'

A man touched her arm. She turned and looked into feverish yellow eyes.

'Arethusa! I have been searching for you everywhere.'

It was 'Tomalin', wearing a huge velvet tam o'shanter and a voluminous black coat. 'Look,' he said, opening it to show her a doeskin waistcoat over a yellow jersey, and under that a powder blue chemise. He still had on his tippet of otters' fur. 'You see? I remembered! In clothes, no one notices me at all. And they are not uncomfortable, not a bit.'

He was very excited. His face was powdered and brightly painted in scarlet and black.

'Hush.' Serin buttoned his coat to cover her agitation. 'Where did you get them all?'

'Oh, I have been everywhere, up the city and down. Such places! Such people! I even spoke to some, and do you know, they paid me no more regard than if I had been another just like themselves.'

'You be careful,' she urged him, but he had wriggled out of her hands and was leaning forward in the press about the tourney, crying 'Hurrah!' as another pair were unseated, and waving his hat in the air. His grotesque head bobbed around like a white bladder.

Serin tugged at his sleeve. 'Come away.'

Obediently, but with much fidgeting and looking back, he let her lead him through the fair to the edge of the river. His feet crammed into her father's boots slithered this way and that, but he kept upright after a fashion, and followed Serin towards the spit where the gypsy chief kept his hut. She wanted at all costs to avoid being seen by her parents, but she had a vague idea that he would be less conspicuous there; that in his extravagant costume he might be taken for some zany of the montanos.

He chattered all the way. 'I feel I am growing stronger. Shrill noise still bothers me; and dogs. But I am remembering things: certain streets; the sound of a hurdy gurdy; the smell of burnt almonds – '

'Come along!' said Serin; then stopped so suddenly he collided with her and they both went sprawling.

Amid angry cries Serin struggled to her feet. There were half a dozen of them, gypsies, armed with swords, behind the chieftain's lodge, where a gypsy woman crouched wailing in terror by the body of a fat Eschalan. His legs were kicking, his puffy orange fingers scrabbling in the snow. As Serin stared aghast, his eyes rolled up in his head and he spouted blood, sticky and bright, over his chins and all down the front of his fur.

They laid hands on Serin, and she screamed; and the woman screamed too. Serin's companion, just rising to his knees, yammered in agony and pitched over face forward clutching at his ears.

'No! No!' shrieked Serin, kicking and struggling with the men who held her. 'Don't hurt him! He's – '

But one of them hefted a sword, still wet with Eschalan blood, and thrust it into the nameless one's back. He squeaked, and choked, and lay quite still. His ridiculous hat fell off.

Serin screamed again and gagged on a leather sleeve. Then she felt herself falling over, and something hard struck her on the back of the head. There was a flare of blinding white; and that was all.

—6—

Waiting in the Cold Light

Towards the end of the morning Princess Nette decided she was drunk. She decided this when she realised she'd been staring for a fifth of an hour at page 27 of the Eschalan Nuncial Bill on Loganberries and hadn't read a word.

'Thisbe,' she said to her maid, 'I think I'm drunk. What do you think?'

'It's possible, madam,' Thisbe replied.

'Possible,' Nette repeated, thoughtfully. 'Probable,' she said. She dropped the bulletin carefully on the floor, and peered into her empty glass.

'You have had four of those,' Thisbe pointed out.

'Four?' The princess nodded slowly. 'It's possible.'

'It's so!' laughed Thisbe. 'I think you are drunk, madam.'

'Good,' said Princess Nette. 'That will help. Being drunk makes it less of an – effort.' She poured another.

She had come down to the river directly after breakfast, given her little speech and received her official tour of the fair, as always, but cut short because it was already snowing again. It might have been less uncomfortable if she could have had a slide (as she'd been allowed up until the age of twelve) or gone skating (as she could do, but not until much later, at the ball), or tried scrambling for a pig (which she could never, never do); but instead she'd been led around under an enormous tasselled umbrella, seeing less than she could now out of the window. Outside tumblers tumbled, carollers descanted, and tourneyers battered one another with tree trunks, while Princess Nette had merely to sit in her tiny cabin on the *Capreole*, waiting for noon and the procession. Her duty then would be to sit on deck, under a canopy, and smile. She would be cold, she knew, despite the furs, because she was not supposed to move about; but there was nothing that said she had to be sober.

'Wouldn't you rather be out there, Thisbe, larking about in the snow, instead of stuck in here with me?'

Thisbe glanced down at the revellers and shook her head. 'It's a lot of folly,' she said. 'And what will they have to show for it but bruises?' Yet there was something wistful in her voice, whether she knew it or not.

'Well I should,' said Princesse Nette. 'I'd win something. I'd win a pig.'

'You don't want a pig, madam!'

'How do you know? How do you know I haven't cherished a lifelong desire to have a pet pig of my own?'

'Who would feed it for you then?'

'You would. Or no, I know, I know who.' The princess snickered. 'Crespian Vittore! I should make him Master of the Royal Swine. He'd do it, too. I'd tell him, Feed my pig, and he'd do it.'

She took a sip of her drink. 'You may laugh, Thisbe. It's a comical notion.'

'You're very hard on Vittore, madam,' said her maid.

'Well he shouldn't be so soft on me.' She drank some more. 'Actually, I've already got some pigs, I think. Didn't someone dedicate a flock to me once?'

'Herd, madam.'

'Herd, then. More than one, probably. They're still out there somewhere, squealing and stuffing themselves, I suppose. Unless the palace has eaten them all already. Perhaps we're on the second generation by now. A generation of pigs.' She thought about it. 'How long's that, Thisbe?'

'Madam, you're rambling,' Thisbe admonished her.

'No, really, Thisbe, what would you say?'

'I'm sure I don't know, madam.'

The princess looked sour. 'Then go and find me someone who does,' she said. The maid rose. 'No, Thisbe, don't bother.'

They sat awhile without speaking.

'Did you know,' said Princess Nette at last, 'that pigs can't swim?'

But whether Thisbe knew or not, or even if she knew better, her mistress never learnt; for at that moment came footsteps and a knock on the cabin door.

'Oh, Prime,' swore Nette softly, burying her glass beneath cushions and composing herself, after which Thisbe opened the door.

'Vittore,' said the princess.

'Your Royal Highness,' replied that worthy, and bowed.

'Is it time?' asked the princess, slightly hazily. 'Time to process?'

'Not yet, madam. There is some commotion among the Eschalans.'

'Ah,' she said. 'Do you know, Vittore, how many Eschalans it takes to bait a fishing hook?'

'No, ma'am, I don't believe I – '

'Fifteen,' she said. 'One to hold the worm, one to hold the hook, and thirteen to give their consent.'

'Hahaha – very droll, ma'am. One for the worm, one for the hook, and thirteen – hahaha – I must remember that.'

'Yes,' said the princess. 'So you said last time.'

'Your Highness is so bounteous in wit – '

'How long is a generation of pigs?' she asked.

He tilted his head up and smiled. 'Now this one I honestly don't think I've heard . . .'

'Never mind,' she said.

The swinemaster designate hesitated a moment, apparently uncertain whether to laugh or not. He brushed absently at his coat.

'I think the day is not as cold as it was last year,' he ventured. 'What a shame Her Royal Grace is not well enough to attend.'

He was plainly nervous in her presence without his usual protector. In fact, alone it could be said he had no business on the royal barge at all, having neither rank nor duty. He strove to distract her attention from his superfluity.

'I spoke to the master and he predicts a good smooth run,' he said. 'If we get started at all, that is.' He turned awkwardly to the window. 'Goodness me, how it snows. Where are all those fellows going, I wonder? Can you see what's happening over there, Thisbe?' he asked the maid with patronising familiarity, craning to see over her shoulder.

'There's some bother with the gypsies, by the looks of it,' Thisbe reported.

'No doubt someone's infringed a crucial orange regulation,' said the princess languidly. 'Buttered her tea, or put her left snowshoe on before her right snowshoe.'

Crespian Vittore looked quizzically at her. 'The left snowshoe before the right? I had not heard of any such ordinance . . .'

'Hadn't you, Vittore? Well, I suppose you can't be everywhere at once.'

Thisbe was still looking out of the window. 'They're turning the sleds about!' she said. 'They're sending people away.'

Nette closed her eyes. 'Primary have patience, what's the matter now?'

'I'll find out for you, Highness,' offered Vittore with alacrity, and hurried from the cabin. The princess, not waiting for his report, took a final hasty swig from her flask, stood up and rearranged her furs, then went out on deck with all the sober self-possession that could be required of her, and Thisbe following after.

Charan du decided that he did not, after all, like Tumak coh. The man was stupid. He had shown more interest in the mulled ale and the skating women than in the symbolic and flattering tableau the Messengers' Guild had prepared for him. Then he had bribed his escort to go away.

Now this. Violence. Weakness inevitably led to violence. Charan du felt almost ill with resentment. He was covered in snow. He stamped his feet slowly as they brought the man across the empty campsite.

'This is he, minister,' one of the proctors announced. 'Dr Tarven Guille.'

He was a skeletal man in a long grey fur; not a montano. His face was white as chalk. Lines of anger radiated from his mouth. 'You are the one who found the body?' asked Charan du.

'What body?' replied the angry man. 'Those ruffians have carried off my daughter. What I want to know is what you are going to do about it?'

Charan du closed his eyes. These people. Why was nothing ever straightforward?

'Your daughter will be found, doctor. This is not my concern. I wish to hear about the last hour of the imperial herald, Tumak coh.'

'I don't know what you're talking about,' said the pinch-faced doctor. Charan du had recognised him now for an associate of that fool Diaz Jonal, the shepherd of Lan olang's fancies.

'The imperial herald has been stabbed three times in the back,'

Charan du informed him, 'and his body hidden in a bank of
snow. There.' He indicated the crudely made hut, and the gaggle
of constables below it, standing glumly by the frozen river. 'And
you know nothing of this.'

'They'd all gone by the time I got here!' the man protested.

'And taken my daughter with them.'

'You saw nothing, then.'

He shuddered and gesticulated widely: at abandoned hurdles,
black smudges where fires still smoked, footprints filling swiftly.

'There was nothing to see!'

'Yet you called the constables.'

'I want my daughter back, Eschalan. I want you to send a
search party. They could be anywhere by now. They've got holes
and caves all over the east range.'

Charan du did not wish to be reminded of this. He nodded,
dismissing the man from his attention even as he stood there. He
was of no use. But a stray thought flitted through the interpreter's head as he watched the constables tramping disconsolately back up the bank. He pursued the thought and caught it,
and voiced it as a query.

'Why did you look here for your daughter?'

'We told her to meet us here. She did not arrive. The montanos
have all disappeared. Isn't it obvious?'

'To meet whom?'

The man's head gave a little jerk. 'I beg your pardon?'

'Whom did you instruct your daughter to meet?'

'Myself,' said the man. 'Myself, and my wife,' he amplified
grudgingly.

'Where is your wife?'

'Gone,' said the man. 'She has gone home,' he said.

'Did she see anything of this monstrous – '

'No. Nothing.'

'Perhaps daughter also has gone home,' one of the proctors
suggested.

'The gypsies have abducted her,' the man said tightly.

Charan du left them to it. There was some commotion up by the
bridge. A proctor came to fetch him. The riders had caught up with
a couple of the gypsies in flight; they were being brought back now.

Charan du hurried to the spot. This was more promising. He
was keen to see them confronted with the evidence of their
crime. He would make them writhe.

Half a dozen Luscan constables were coming down the road, conducting with many a rough buffet the reluctant progress of two bulky figures. Their hands were tied. As if in imitation, Charan du clasped his hands behind his back to watch their stumbling arrival.

The man was gross. His lip was split. There was blood matted in his snowy beard and in the fur of his hood. The woman was no less large, especially swathed as she was in layers of gaudy shawls. She was snivelling.

'We caught this pair trying to escape, sir!' said a young constable proudly to a serjeant of the proctors.

The Eschalan serjeant led the prisoners to the travois where Tumak coh lay strapped like a beached walrus, snow falling into his mouth. The sight provoked no visible response from the man. The woman merely began to whine more steadily.

'Take them to the prefect,' ordered the serjeant, losing patience.

Charan du stepped forward.

'Wait,' he said.

He looked at the glowering man. 'It was you that killed him,' he proposed.

Still the oaf did not react.

'What do you say to that?' asked Charan du.

'Never saw him,' said the man thickly.

'You are lying,' Charan du replied.

The gypsy glanced up at him from under shaggy brows and shook his head, more out of weariness, the interpreter thought, than denial. Such stolidity was a challenge. He would enjoy having it broken out of the man, systematically and thoroughly.

He spared the woman a look: one of the emotional sort, obviously, who would say anything. There was little amusement to be gained from such a creature. She would, however, be the appropriate way into the man's sensibility.

Lan olang would not appreciate this pair; would in all probability fail to extract the truth from them.

'The messengers will take care of this matter,' announced Charan du, in Eschalan. 'Deliver the prisoners to the duty officer at the posthouse.'

The constables looked at the proctors. The proctors looked at one another.

'I have full responsibility,' said Charan du. 'I shall make the report of this arrest to His Estimability myself, including special commendation of the efficiency of your men, serjeant.'

He said this very loudly. It revived all the Eschalans. They took it as a dismissal, permission to go away, in out of the snow. They all shouldered their staves and left at the double, before the moonshee should change his mind. The prisoners' escort looked at them going, while the officer began to translate the orders.

The montano took advantage of that moment of distraction. She lurched forward out of the hands of her guards and butted one in the face. She turned, yelling in montano, and kicked another on the shin and in the crotch.

Her man gave a great shrug, to wrench himself free; but the constables hung on to him tightly. Incredibly, though, the woman had evaded them and was running on to the bridge.

'Stop her, you imbeciles!' cried Charan du.

Unnerved, one of the departing proctors spun around, drawing a pistol. There was a crash and a cry. The woman hit the roadway with her face.

'Amber!' bellowed the man.

She lay quite still. His companions congratulated the marksman.

The montano began again to struggle mightily. The constable whose nose the woman had broken punched him in the stomach, and then in the face. They led him away.

Efficiency, thought Charan du bitterly. He slapped snow from his shoulders and followed.

Behind him he heard a hoarse cry. It was the thin citizen, still looking for his lost daughter. He was stooping stiffly over the body of the dead gypsy.

It had stopped snowing by the time Princess Nette arrived back at the palace. She took luncheon. Charan du called and spoke to her briefly. She thought he seemed preoccupied, as if thinking of somewhere he would prefer to be. When he left she called for her wrap and went out into the garden.

An icy wind fingered her hair. Grey clouds stirred heavily overhead. The grounds were thick with snow, but the paths had been shovelled clear.

As she went, the princess looked back over her shoulder. Her mother the archduchess was watching from an upstairs window.

It couldn't be helped. She walked on, more quickly.

In the glass pavilion she startled an undergardener, who turned white and dropped a pot on the flags, where it smashed.

'Y'Royal Highness – '

'Fetch Brant,' she said.

'Yes, Y'Royal Highness,' said the undergardener, crouching to gather the debris with shaking hands, her eyes not leaving Nette's face.

'Leave that,' said the princess sharply.

The glass pavilion was warm, but barely. There was still frost on some of its panes. While she waited she looked out at the blank garden, where snub twigs poked out of the snow. The brandy had worn off, leaving her dull and sore.

Brant came, pulling off his gloves and hat.

'Put it on,' she gestured, but he would not.

'Tell me,' she said.

'It was not planned,' he said.

'Do you expect me to believe that?' she said, displeased. 'You hated him.'

'He was hated, yes,' said the gardener. 'But they would have done the same to any of them. The spirits of the young men ride high at the fair.'

'High spirits,' she said bitterly. 'And it just happened to be the imperial herald.' She rubbed a gloved finger on the glass. 'How did it happen?'

'He had a woman. One of our women.'

Nette groaned. 'What did they do to *her*?'

He looked at her feet, stubborn, saying nothing.

'Never mind, I don't want to know. Go on.'

'He took her behind the chieftain's lodge. Some lads saw them and followed. He tried to order them off and that made them worse. Quite a crowd of them had gathered. He took hold of the woman again and they did for him.'

'In the back,' said Princess Nette.

Brant glared at her. 'Some say that was too good for him! He should have seen it done!' He realised he was shouting and backed down at once, muttering apology, crumpling his hat to his chest.

'Stupid man,' said the princess, and he looked at her in alarm; but she was cursing the ill-fated Tumak coh, who had already paid the cost of his folly. She said a word then that Brant was shocked to hear from her.

'What about the girl, the one who disappeared?' asked Nette.

'They took her,' he said. 'She saw them, so they took her.'

'Is she safe?' the princess wanted to know.

'That depends on her, I should say,' he answered.

'You do realise that will turn the town against you?' she said.

'It was none of their wishing,' he said.

'And if anything happens to her,' she went on, ignoring that, 'it'll be worse. There are plenty of people who'll help Charan du for the sport of it. He's going into the mountains. I shall not be able to stop him.'

Brant looked up through the glass. 'Weather's with us,' he pointed out.

'When that man's hunting,' she said, 'I shouldn't want to be the deer.'

The gardener bridled, and Princess Nette realised she had insulted his people. 'Or the bear or whatever!' she said, impatiently. 'What about this man, the one the messengers are holding? What does he know? Was he there too?'

'Now they say there was a man with the girl. They say he was a clown from the fair.'

The princess frowned. 'Her uncle?'

'I don't know, ma'am.'

'Where is he?'

'Under the snow. One of them says he left a blade in the clown when they ran away.'

'Oh, wonderful. There's another body out there the orange don't even know about yet.'

'Young men's spirits ride high, fall soon and brag later,' Brant opined, dismissively.

'Be that as it may,' she said. 'I want you to take some people down there and look for it as soon as you safely can. Hide it,' she said.

'If it's there it's fair hidden already,' he said.

'And chance they'll find it before we do? No,' she said firmly.

'They won't be digging in the snow,' he said. 'They hate the snow.'

'And when it thaws?'

'There's more of this coming,' he told her, positively. 'He's safe till week's end, I'll warrant.'

With that, the princess had to be satisfied. It annoyed her that he could stand before her with his hat in his hands and refuse to obey her; but if she didn't respect his knowledge, why consult him at all?

'Probably it's just as well,' she said. 'Otherwise there would be crowds to see the bloodstains. Oh, why did this have to happen? It's the worst possible thing.'

He took a step towards her.

'You can go any time, Highness,' he said gently. 'You have only to send word. My sister will take the message when she goes up ministering. Give me leave to tell her you're ready to go.'

Princess Nette sighed, and shook her head. 'You'll forgive me, Brant, if I confess that your people are not altogether my favourites today. Nor, I think, are the mountains such a safe place to be.'

'Highness – '

'No. I must stay and see this through. They must be pacified.'

'Highness, pardon, but what if it's not that way? I see folk rejoicing. Not just hill folk. And the orange don't know what's hit 'em. Maybe this is just the tip of the blade.'

'A blade that'll be snapped off and trampled underfoot, then.'

'A blade of good Luscan steel!' he retorted.

They stared at each other, neither yielding.

'Have heart, princess,' said the gardener softly.

But she said, 'It will take more than high spirits to remove them, Brant. More than pride and vengeance; more than swords.'

She turned from him then, seeming to have said the last word and given judgement. She ran a finger down the stem of a potted sapling with a bag tied over it. 'How deep do roots grow,' she asked, 'in seven years?'

In an inner cellar of the posthouse, preparations had been made for work on the gypsy. He had been stripped to his breechclout, yet he was not shivering but sweating, because of the proximity of the brazier where the irons were heating. He was spread-eagled on the wall, saying nothing to the moonshee, who was sitting on the sill of the hole in the wall that was the only way in to this low room. He was petting his white rat.

'What is your name?' asked Charan du, in Luscan.

There was no reply.

'I know you can understand me,' continued Charan du.

The man said something in montano: it had the vehemence of

an oath, and probably was one, given the circumstances. But who could tell?

'Is that your name?' asked Charan du.

There was no reply.

'A beast does well enough without a name,' observed the interpreter. 'I expect the questioners will find one of their own for you, shortly.

'I shall remind you, before they return, of three things we intend you to tell us. These are they: one, who killed the imperial herald, Tumak coh? two, where is he? and three, where is the missing girl Serin Guille? Think about these points. You will answer all of them, in whatever order you prefer. When you have answered all of them, we shall leave you alone.'

'I'll tell you nothing, you murderer!' roared the man suddenly, in Luscan. 'You shot my sister. You spider.'

'That was regrettable,' admitted Charan du, getting down from the ledge. 'It was premature. But it was not I.' He secured the rat to a leg of the table by its leash.

'Kill me, why don't you, get on with it. KILL ME.'

The cellar boomed with his rage and despair.

Charan du waited until it had grown still again.

'Three things,' he said, holding up the middle fingers of his hand. 'Who killed the imperial herald? Where is that man? Where is the girl? Bear those in mind.'

He reached for a flail.

'Interpreter turned questioner,' said an ironic voice behind him. 'Under the ground, how things change.'

Charan du stepped aside. It was the imperial nuncio, Aten lo, stooping to enter. 'Is this your place, Charan du?'

'This man is about to tell us who killed the Emperor's Tongue,' said Charan du boldly.

'Is he? Then you won't need that,' replied Aten lo, taking the flail from him.

'Best o' the day, Charan du,' smiled Ap riuli, following the nuncio in. 'Thought we'd find you here.'

'Quiet, please, Ap riuli,' requested the nuncio mildly, as he laid the flail back on the table.

They all looked at the suspended gypsy.

'He doesn't seem to be telling us anything at all,' said the nuncio. 'Perhaps he is confused. Perhaps he wonders why the witness to a crime finds himself thus in a cellar of the Messengers' Guild. As do I.'

He turned to the signaller. 'I was not aware our guild had powers of restraint, Ap riuli, were you? I thought those were reserved for the army, the proctors and the prefecture.'

He gestured at the montano.

'Since this is not your prisoner, Ap riuli, and he has patently passed out of the hands of the proctors, he must be on his way to the prefecture, must he not?'

'He's stopped off for a bit for a rest,' said Ap riuli, enjoying this, as he enjoyed everything that ever happened.

'Of course, honoured colleague. We shall see to it, Ap riuli and I,' said Charan du politely.

'Splendid,' said Aten lo. 'I shall go at once and tell His Estimability to expect the witness forthwith. By your leave, gentlemen,' and smiling pleasantly, the imperial nuncio returned the way he came.

Behind his back Ap riuli gave a fatuous smirk.

Charan du's face was completely expressionless. He picked up his rat and stroked it.

The montano, not understanding the exchange, was nonetheless amused to see Charan du discomfited.

Charan du reached for the flail. Ap riuli laid a meaty hand on his arm: 'Leave it, Charan du.'

Charan du did not withdraw his hand.

'Confusion,' swore the signaller. 'Leave it. Have done. Come and have a drink.'

The men went up to the buttery and drew bowls of tea, into which Ap riuli dispensed generous measures of akvavit. 'Filthy local stuff,' he said, as he always did.

The rat was snuffling crumbs. The signaller looked around. 'There's a page,' he said, and was about to call the girl over.

'No,' said Charan du.

'Are you going to cart him there yourself?'

'No.'

'I'm not helping you, if that's what you think.'

'Not that either.'

Ap riuli looked disbelieving. 'Do you really want to fight Aten lo?'

'Lan olang shall not have him,' determined Charan du.

Ap riuli blew on his tea and took a swallow. 'What are you hatching?'

'We'll send the gypsy over on horseback,' said Charan du.

'If he's half the man he looks – '

'He'll get away.'

Ap riuli drank tea. 'Spite,' he said.

Charan du grimaced with impatience. 'Think, forthright colleague. You will set a man to track him.'

'Oho . . .'

'A good man,' added the interpreter, rising in the posture of valediction. 'And find some upperman to take the blame.'

'And where are you going?'

'To bathe,' said Charan du.

He went along the hall and out of the posthouse by the alley door.

In the alley he shivered. He would never get used to the cold. At least it was not actually snowing, though the odd flake blew past him as he walked.

Charan du had first encountered cold as an intern in Ducros. He had been unable to believe it could be so cold, ice gumming the dormitory window closed until one of the idiots, in a display of muscular health, had forced it open; in which position it had immediately frozen again, and not even the idiots could budge it.

In the daytime Charan du had stayed away from the idiots, studying – not the language especially, which was pitifully degenerate, but the politics of ascent. Ducros had been his first opening in the colonial service, and he had jumped into it, never mind that the north-western frontier was even less civilised than his natal province of Saltfan. The mentality of these highlanders was as disorderly as their intemperate terrain. This lamentable ice fair, for instance. Cavorting upon frozen water! Drinking strong liquors and kindling fires! Ducros had been as bad, with its bear-running and complicated vendettas. It was the duty of all Eschalans to instil order in the chaos of primitive lives. Sometimes it was a burdensome one; and sometimes not.

The young Charan du had been pleased to find that the guild enjoyed more power in these remote corners of the Empire. Messages could be steered, delayed, withheld, reinterpreted to advantage. The army always left confusion everywhere behind it. Victory had to be subsumed into order; and the Messengers' Guild controlled the channels down which the orders flowed. A clerk who paid attention to the currents, who made himself useful to people who mattered and showed intelligence and initiative in the maintenance of that particular little conduit that flowed across his desk: such a one could begin to enjoy small tips and favours. He could be quietly advised to be in such a place at such a time, perhaps with a copy of a certain letter which he might leave, for a few minutes only, lying on the mantelpiece. He could be entrusted with extra commissions out of hours and out of sight; while his colleagues were getting up early to go running, or brush up their irregular subjunctives. He could find himself included in certain confidential dispatches. In short, he could align himself with the currents and induce power to flow through him.

For such a one, attachment to a prefectorial administration was either the end or the beginning. To continue to rise in the guild while being efficient and loyal on behalf of, as it were, a rival establishment required true flair and often nerve. To distinguish himself in service and receive promotion to the prefect's household was about as much as one could achieve.

Yet Charan du was still dissatisfied; very much so. Perhaps because that was his disposition now, and he couldn't lose the habit of it; perhaps because it was frustrating to have been appointed to an inept and cloudy old fool like Lan olang, who couldn't even exert control over the metal that was the only thing of worth this uncongenial spot had to offer.

And then there was Princess Nette.

Charan du had desired many white women, and enjoyed some of them; but none had ever fascinated him like Nette zan Herlach. Other admirers praised her eyes, her hair, her stature. For Charan du it was not so much any feature of her, but rather a condition, an attitude, that drew his attention. It was extremely attractive to see so strong a woman in a position of powerlessness. She had the hearts of her people, and a noble mind; yet she was a puppet of the Eschalan will. Lan olang failed to exert proper control over her too.

Charan du knew exactly how such a woman was to be treated. He knew it in his blood. Under the silver and fine satin, she was a woman, with a woman's body. Sometimes he would invent a commission from the prefect just to go and look at her. Sometimes, even while she was attempting to sharpen her wits against his, he would look at her sitting there opposite him and imagine

her naked. This afternoon, when he had begun to threaten her
beloved mountaineers: that had been a whisper of what it would
be like to take possession of everything of hers: her principality,
her property, and finally her person.

Perhaps it was a fantasy, something to warm him through the
long, freezing Luscan nights. But perhaps this dream was of the
sort that it was the purpose of power to make real. And perhaps
the princess did not altogether dislike him.

He felt the rat stir against his chest, where he had tucked it out
of the cold. He put his hand inside his coat, letting the creature
gnaw a little at the leather of his gauntlet, and realised he too was
hungry. Entering the vestibule of the Luscan Hall of Accomplishment, he ordered food to be sent down to him at the bath.

This facility was a solemn reminder that on the frontier it was
necessary to make do. The public baths in civilised countries
were tranquil, calming places where business and sociability
flowed inextricably together. This was little more than a metal
tank. Three people made it feel crowded. The room where it
stood was dank and clammy. Peculiar moulds sprouted from
behind Karel Jessup's black iron pipes. The hot water, when it
was working at all, ran green and cast a flat, sick light on the
walls and on the bodies of the bathers. It seemed to Charan du a
sure venue for guilty assignations of a sexual kind.

However, that same atmosphere of damp seclusion also made
it a suitable place for a conversation with Crespian Vittore, who
arrived shortly bearing a covered tray.

'They asked me to bring you this, minister. I must say it smells
rather fine.'

From the tank, Charan du waved an arm. 'Help yourself,
Crespian Vittore; then do step in and give me your account of
this assassination.'

'Is that what it was? I'll put this here, shall I, where you can
reach it. Is the water hot?'

'Of course,' said Charan du, to all three.

'My informers tell me,' said Vittore, coiling up his plait with
long fingers, 'it was an accident in drink, and the gypsies have
run away for fear of retribution.' He paused a moment to pet the
interpreter's rat, straining on its leash from a convenient nail.

'Consider, my friend; we may take what was done by one
montano as done by all.'

'You seem – remarkably sanguine, minister,' said Vittore. He took off his clothes, padded shivering to the side of the bath, and climbed cautiously in. 'Oh! Ah!'

'I'm furious,' said Charan du. 'Nevertheless, the thing is done, and I had far rather have Tumak coh's skin pierced than my own, say, or that of any other guild member.'

He scooped up a handful of millet from the tray; smiling, Vittore did the same. They chewed companionably.

'Then,' resumed the interpreter, 'there is the consideration, as you say, of *retribution*. This His Supremacy will undoubtedly require, however much His Estimability the Prefect dislikes to obey.'

'You'll need to find them first, minister,' Vittore pointed out. 'They are veritable mountain creatures, you know. You won't assail them successfully till spring.'

'You think like a soldier, Crespian Vittore, with insufficient flexibility.'

Offended, the underscrivener smothered his irritation by ducking briskly under. He came up with water streaming from his nose.

Charan du proffered the dish. 'Have a hot roll, and say, how do you find Her Royal Highness after this shocking disturbance?'

'As soon as you left she went out in the garden.'

'Her interest in the work of horticulture remains keen even in the dead time of winter.'

'Do you know,' said Vittore, 'that's almost exactly what Her Grace said.' He bit into the roll. 'Minister, my favourite! You remembered!'

—— 7 ——

Fear and Shadows

Serin dreamed.

She dreamed that something small and cold lay across her face. It was trying to pull off her skin.

Curiously, this was not painful. Serin stared upwards into its body, which was flat and taut like flesh, but bluish-white, translucent. She could feel it pulse on her cheeks. It was suffocating her. She did not mind. Once her face was destroyed, she felt, she would be able to get out. What she meant by that, in the dream, was that her soul would be able to leave her body through the ruined head. Father is right, then, she thought; and woke.

There was nothing on her face, but she could not move her arms or legs. She lay in smoky darkness loud with stir and murmur, under a ceiling of rock. She had been bound in stinking leather, and put in a nest of something prickly and dusty. Dead leaves, she found, turning her head a little, but could see nothing else.

The dream had left a peculiar chilly afterglow, neither pleasant nor unpleasant. Serin lay in a stupor awhile before it came to her that she was high up, with people and animals gathered below her. In a cave, on a ledge, she thought. The crumbled bracken made her sneeze. At that she saw a head appear, a face, looking up at her.

It was a brown face, seamed and creased; a woman's face. She wore a sort of tight-fitting cowl. Her eyes were rimmed with red. She opened a mouth startlingly lacking in teeth and said, in montano, 'Birdie wakes.'

It was a moment before Serin understood she was referring to her.

'Where's my mother?' asked Serin. 'Is she here?' The effort of thinking and speaking made her aware the thing that was hurting her head was actually inside, a clawing headache.

Shrivelled lips stretched into a smile. 'Birdie wants her ma!' crowed the old woman; and there were answering voices below, cawing with laughter.

Serin pushed against the restricting bands, beginning to be angry.

'Let me out! What have you done to me?'

'Sing, birdie!' cried the old woman.

'I didn't do anything!' yelled Serin.

'Oho, sing! Sing!' Still cackling, her visitor sank from view.

With a wrench Serin jerked around on to her side, blinking leaves and twigs out of her eyes. Below she could see large animals in a pen, dogs running around, firelit faces grinning up at her.

'Uncle Banner!' she shouted. 'Uncle Banner!'

Then a large woman pushed through the press, cursing as she came. She hauled herself up on the ledge, breathing hard. It was Aunt Cary.

Without a word she rolled her niece over. Serin felt something at her back unfastened, and the bands being unwrapped. Two turns, and she could free her hands, though they were numb. Aunt Cary loosed her legs, and the first darting pricks of returning circulation began.

Somehow Serin sat up, rubbing herself clumsily with hands that felt like clubs.

'Is ma here, Aunt Cary?'

But her aunt said only, 'Come on. Hurry up,' and started down the ladder.

More because her aunt had told her to than because she felt ready, Serin knelt and fumbled her dead feet on to the rungs, screwing up her face at the fierce needles in her limbs, the thudding in her head. Aunt Cary's hands grabbed her waist and she was lifted down into a world of straw and charcoal and matted fur, thick with the reek of dung and bodies. People everywhere, huddling, leaning on others, kneeling, sprawling. Dogs yelping excitedly, lunging at her.

'Come.' Roughly Aunt Cary seized her wrist and half led, half dragged her a short distance away to a fire where wide-eyed children with dirty faces crouched around and stared. Two young boys shoved each other. An older girl smiled maliciously to see Serin. Cousins.

Serin didn't care for them. She stumbled to the flames, stood hunched over them, trying to rub some life into herself. Slit-eyed men stood about smoking and passing remarks.

Aunt Cary hunkered down heavily and snatched up a lap loom which she began to work with automatic fingers, glaring all the while at Serin as if everything were her fault.

'Where's Uncle Banner?' asked Serin, sullenly. It was the first time she had been with any of her mother's family without him being there at least.

'In the city,' said Aunt Cary angrily, as if this were a great disgrace. Her fingers flew, up, across and back, up, across and back.

'What for?' said Serin.

'For your sake,' her aunt snapped, 'and theirs.' Her eyes flicked sideways, but Serin couldn't tell who she meant. It was clear that whatever her husband was doing, Aunt Cary did not approve of it.

Serin thought suddenly of an old man falling to the ice with a gypsy bravo's blade in his back, and of what danger she might be in.

She turned to hobble out of the circle. 'I'm going home,' she said.

They laughed at her. It was a huge cave, too dark and smoky to see how huge; and it was full of people. All around, people were amused by the sight of Serin stumbling towards the daylight. For a moment she glimpsed the open sky around a corner of rock; but the gypsies got in her way. They hooted and whistled. They pinched her and poked her and elbowed her. A boy stuck out his foot, and she tripped and fell into the lap of an old man. This was funnier than ever.

'*Aha . . . !*'

'Let me go!' she yelled, rising. 'I've got to go!' For she realised that she had indeed, in another sense: her bladder was demanding to be emptied.

They tripped her again. Scrambling over bodies, careless whom she kicked and trampled, she turned about and struggled back towards her aunt. She was amply kicked and trampled in return.

'Aunt Cary, I've got to go!' she cried, and clutched herself so her meaning would not be mistaken. Her voice sounded strange to her, high-pitched.

Aunt Cary looked at her with disgust, as if this were an extreme indignity, and all hers. She motioned roughly to one of the girls who sat by her.

'Show her,' she growled.

The girl who rose unwillingly to lead her outside was one of about Serin's own age, called Muir she thought, and already possessed of something like her mother's shape. They jostled her too, but she shoved them roughly aside, and Serin followed her out into the daylight and the cold.

Squinting, she had a swift impression of great height. The ground fell away sharply between the trees. The air was very still. The cave mouth was a narrow triangular recess in the rock, with no hint of the vast spaces behind. Only a litter of equipment and a couple of dogs nosing about gave any sign of human presence.

'Up here,' said Muir, taking a steep path through the trees. The trodden snow was ice underfoot, but it was not far. The pit was shallow, and stank despite the cold. 'This is the girls',' said Muir. Serin unbuttoned and squatted.

Directly a handful of packed snow hit her on the ear, and she almost overbalanced. Another hit her on the leg, and one on the chest. She yelled in alarm, and then in anger, and looked fiercely around.

There were boys among the trees, at a distance, whooping and balling up more snow. Serin grimaced at her cousin, but instead of defending her, Muir jeered at her and shouted encouragement to the boys; who, however, had reached the limit of their daring, and after their second volley ran lithely away, shrieking and warbling in triumph.

Serin dashed snow from her face.

'Why am I here?' she demanded, but cousin Muir would say only:

'You're in trouble.'

'I didn't do anything!' said Serin again, but Muir just folded her fat arms and stared in the opposite direction. Then something seemed to occur to her, and she set off to go back down the path.

'Wait!' pleaded Serin, making haste to button up her flap.

Muir addressed her over her shoulder. 'Ma di'n't say I had to bring ye back!' Then she spread her arms and slid expertly away.

Serin swore and tottered after her.

Down outside the cave the dogs were investigating a chunk of blackened bone. There was no sign of Muir or the boys. A dim sun shone in a blank sky.

Serin blinked, looking across the slope, wondering where she was and reluctant to go back in to face the mob. She suddenly realised she was looking at a pile of skis.

Escape.

She stole past the dogs, pulling off her mittens.

She knew her size by eye, and the lacings were no problem, being exactly like her own. She flexed her fingers.

The dogs contemplated barking, stretching their necks and eyeing her sideways.

Which way the gypsies had come up from the city was plain to see. Serin seized a pair of ski-sticks and pushed off, weaving uncertainly through the trees.

The ground was very steep. Her sense of height was right, she saw, though everything was under snow and nothing was recognisable. From beyond the trees the glare was bad. Her head started to ache again. She had to squint. That didn't make any of it easier.

She had to slow down to get under a branch; then there was a fallen one lunging up at her like a frozen snake. She dodged and faltered, wishing she could go faster, but concentrating on staying upright. She didn't dare look behind her.

Her father would be looking for her. Her mother would be going frantic, cursing him, then sobbing into her shawl. Papa would blame her, then turn on Serin when she got home. They would not be pleased to see her. This would all be her fault, somehow.

A low bush suddenly spread itself before her. She made a desperate swerve around it and overbalanced. Her feet went from under her, skis crossing, sticks flying.

Her head hurt too much to know if anything else did. She gasped, sobbing, struggling to sit up.

Was that someone? She thought she saw a dark shape slide smoothly by. She made herself get up, but by then there was nothing to see but trees.

Serin wiped the snow from her face. She had an ear full of it. She decided to go on.

She found herself remembering the old man again, the madman. She saw the knife go into his back once more, saw him buck. Behind him she saw the fat Esch, gargling in his own blood.

Death had never been like that before. Death was not violent. Death came with an odour of almonds, in a glass jar, in a sack. Or there were little dogs that had been run over by carriages. Blood was dark and treacly. It dribbled, it didn't spew.

Then she remembered the Eschalan's ear. She hadn't thought of it for a long time, not since Mad Polly's face had fallen off. Her father had caught her trying to embalm the ear, and thrown it out.

The track ran clear for a way. The cold air buzzed in Serin's own ear, the wet one, as she picked up speed. To her right the ground fell away sharply, and showed her snow-capped trees below, and a ragged, frothing stream. If she slipped here, all her problems would be over together.

She wondered whether anyone was out after the montanos, or whether Papa had sent anyone to find her. She doubted it. Anyway, there would be bad drifts on the road by Seger's Acres. Dully, she wondered how she would get past. The pain began to play a tune in her head.

And then the track disappeared entirely under the snow. Serin sped on, looking left and right. She thought she glimpsed a building, further down the far side of the stream; then more, over the trees.

It couldn't be Calcionne. But farm, hamlet, village – whatever it was, it would be somewhere to rest, and find out where she was. They might even help her.

There was another building on her left, some way ahead: a round tower, it looked like, in silhouette. For some reason, she thought it was a church. More after that, this side the water: a narrow spire, built of struts, supporting a large wheel. Other buildings, long and low. And nothing but boulders all the way down to them.

The place looked deserted as Serin went by: nothing moving, no tracks, not a sound to be heard. It was a mine, she realised foggily, the workings shuttered and frozen in midwinter. There would be plenty of dark corners to hide in, if she *could* get down there.

Then she thought of the church, and went on to it, her heart complaining at the effort.

It was a chimney, Serin discovered, sticking straight up out of the ground, and topped by a huge wooden cowling against the wind. She took off her skis and trudged urgently around until she found a door, closed by a simple bar. The door was heavily blocked by snow, but it was old and not very solid, and she managed to prise it open at the top with a ski, just enough to squeeze in her head and shoulders, and then the rest of her when she had made sure that there was not simply a sheer drop within.

In fact, a ledge a yard wide ran around the shaft, fenced with black iron. Serin tried to look between the bars, but couldn't see anything. Scraping a spot clear of snow to sit down, she found a rusty bolt and kicked it through the bars. She did not hear it land.

The grime and shadows would have made this a forbidding place at any other time, but now it was a Primary gift: a place to stop and catch her breath, and think what on earth to do next. She sat, and panted, and ached, and shivered, hugging herself. Part of her wanted to cry, but the tears seemed frozen in her eyes. Gazing up into the cowling at the tilted white circle of sky, she could see huge icicles jutting from the rim. She blew her nose. Darkness and silence surrounded her, drawn from the well of darkness beneath.

And then she heard the voice.

It was a creaky whisper, floating up out of the shaft.

'Can you hear me?'

A miner, she thought. But the mine was closed, there were no miners working. She held her breath.

It spoke again.

'Can you hear?'

Serin hugged the wall.

There was something about the voice, as if it belonged to something not perfectly human, a tiny subterranean creature of metal and ore.

'We can hear you very well,' it squeaked. *'You don't sound any distance away at all.'*

Serin had not made any sound. She crouched without moving. Any moment she expected opal-eyed goblins with grins of brass swarming up over the fence to devour her. But when the creature spoke again it said only: *'Bit of snap in a fifth.'*

Apart from a click, like a metallic talon striking a stone, that was all.

Serin began to move again, began to shiver violently. Then she pressed her head to the railings, trying to hear if there were someone, or something, clinging to the side of the shaft.

The silence was so complete she began to wonder if she'd imagined it all.

'Hello?' she called. 'Is there anybody down there?'

Echoes fled spiralling down into the void.

'Hello?'

No answer.

She reached for one of her sticks and rattled it along the railings. The black air clattered.

No response.

I'm going, thought Serin. She went back to the door, still wedged at the top with one of her skis. She thrust her sticks and the other ski through the gap, then hauled herself up and squeezed through after them.

She dropped headfirst into deep snow. Struggling upright, she saw two young men on skis standing watching her.

'Did you find anyone?' one called, conversationally.

Serin didn't reply.

'We was looking for you down there,' he said, pointing towards the minehead. 'It's a good job you gave us a shout.'

His friend sniggered.

The youths wore moustaches, and carried swords. Serin recognised them from the fair. The montanos had sent two people who would have the greatest interest in catching her.

'We wondered if you was going to take a jump.'

'Do our job for us.'

Serin tried to make a dash for it. One of the gypsies kicked a ski between her legs and brought her down. He came over and lifted her up by one arm twisted painfully behind her back. He offered her to his friend. 'Slit her belly,' he said.

The first one came closer. 'We could rape you and throw you down the hole,' he observed.

She struggled in the grip of the second, who was breathing hotly in her ear. 'You'd like that,' he gurgled at her. 'You're so ugly no one but him would want you.'

His friend flew at him, so he threw her into the snow.

She lay and watched them pelt each other with handfuls. 'My Uncle Banner – ' she began.

They stopped their fight.

'Your uncle's not here, little girl.'

'Where is he then?'

'He wouldn't come.'

'He wanted to talk to your Mummy and Daddy.'

'To tell them about you.'

'To tell them not to talk to the oranges or else.'

Serin glared at them. 'You hurt me, he'll get you.'

'You reckon.'

'You don't know nothing,' said the first youth, the curly one. 'He won't be getting anybody. The oranges will get him.'

They grabbed her.

'They'll twist his arms – '

'Ow!'

'And his legs – '

'Ow! Ow!'

But she was sure now they would do nothing worse to her. Some higher authority forbade it; and this was not the ice fair, where apple brandy and anger spoke louder than prudence. She backed off and leant against the chimney, nursing an aching knee.

'You killed the Esch,' she accused. 'He'll tell them.'

They laughed at that. 'You *don't* know nothing.'

'You killed my friend too.'

'The old moke in the big hat?' They smirked at each other. 'Funny friends you got.'

'His people will be after you,' she promised them, knowing as she said it that him there would be no one to avenge, no one at all. 'The Esch will come and get you too. Don't think they won't find you. They'll find you.'

They ignored her.

There was a noise in the wood, a harsh squawking like a startled crow. As one, the young montanos threw back their heads and gave a throaty howl. They were answered by yelps and more howls. A dog sled came out of the trees.

The curly youth gathered up the skis while his crony bound Serin's hands roughly behind her back. They tied her to the sled, and sat beside her.

The driver said only: 'You walk.' The lads got up. The driver roused his dogs with a guttural shout, and dragged Serin back feet first all the way up to the cave, jolting her painfully at every bump and hollow.

Aunt Cary took her back into the family circle, but would not speak to her, or untie her hands. Serin was weak with hunger and fatigue, yet a mealtime came and went; everyone else gobbled bread and stew, but no one gave her so much as a spoonful. Serin spoke to Muir, but her cousin avoided her eyes and would not listen. Serin lay on filthy rushes in a daze of misery and exhaustion.

All at once there was a murmuring and a turning of heads. Knowing better than to ask, Serin looked inquiringly at Aunt Cary. She had gone grim, her broad face set like stone.

With difficulty, Serin got up and looked where everyone else was looking, towards the front of the cave. A young woman had come in, evidently out of breath. She was reporting to a thickset old man with a great bush of white hair, who was nodding impassively while all about him younger men were getting to their feet. The woman wore a longbow slung over her shoulder, and a quiver of arrows. She kept pointing out into the snow. After a brief consultation three of the men hurried out. They came back shortly, leading a horse on which a man sat slumped.

A noisy crowd pressed about him at once. Hands lifted him down. Aunt Cary stood her ground, fists on her hips. Serin darted across the cave and shouldered into the throng.

'Uncle Banner!' she called.

He was not, as she'd feared, unconscious, though he looked bad enough and thoroughly weary. He heard her and raised his head. 'Serin,' he said.

At that people unwillingly stepped aside and let her through.

Banner Marchan sat on a legless chair draped in furs. He reached up to her.

'Still tied?' he said, when he saw.

'She ran off,' said the old chieftain.

Banner turned her about and roughly undid the knot. 'Stay put,' he told her.

She sat at his feet.

His face was battered. One of his eyes was purple and closed, and there was blood on his scalp, and on his chin. He was wet where the men had tried to clean him up with snow. Now Muir brought a wooden bowl of steaming water and a rag to finish the job.

'Give that to me,' said Serin.

Muir looked at her father. He didn't say anything. Muir set the bowl down and thrust the cloth at her cousin; and though the girl glared, and though her hands were stiff and clumsy, Serin made shift to wipe her uncle's face.

'Nothing food and sleep won't cure,' he said, hoarsely.

Two of the men who had brought him in were having a discussion. One of them squatted down and put his hand on Banner's knee.

'Did they not follow you, Banner?'

He moved his head from Serin's hand to smile at his questioner.

'Just one of them, Streaky. I left him in a ditch. His horse ran away, more's the pity. I was going to bring it you.' He laughed huskily, and stopped with a sharp intake of breath. 'Mind the eye, girl.'

'Sorry, uncle.'

'They won't come today,' said Banner Marchan.

'They daren't go out in the snow,' said someone.

'Over their heads.' It was a ritual joke.

Another spoke up. 'My daughter is in Calcionne,' he said. 'In service.'

There was a brief chorus of additions: 'My brother.' 'My wife.'

'How will it go for them now?' demanded the first man.

Banner Marchan closed his other eye, saying nothing, taking his ease. Serin wrung out the cloth and began to rub carefully at the blood caked in his beard. He reached up a hand to pat hers, but did not speak.

'We must go down and get them, Banner. Every man his own.'

'Better to sit tight,' said another, shaking his head. But their exchange had the air of something already argued to a standstill.

Banner grunted and opened his good eye. 'Am I pretty enough yet for mixed company?'

'Uncle?'

He stretched cautiously, and spoke to the chief. 'With your leave, Entenmann, I'll go and greet my family.'

The chief nodded. 'They said you were mad to stay,' he said. 'We're stronger with you here.'

Some of the chief's men helped Banner rise; then, leaning on Serin, he limped off through the throng, people greeting him as he passed. Muir led the way.

'Uncle Banner?'

'What, chicken?'

'Did you tell mamma I'm here?'

Something flickered across his face.

'I told her.'

'Can I go home now? I won't tell anyone.'

He sighed. 'No, little bird. You stay with us awhile. You'll be safe here.'

'Won't the Esch come after you?'

'They won't find us here. Don't fret.'

'Did they beat you up because you wouldn't say?'

'They beat you up first, then ask questions after.' He smiled groggily to see Aunt Cary standing waiting for him, monolithic and unmoving in the congratulatory crowd. 'Then they give me a horse. There's no understanding them.'

'Is papa cross?'

'Is he cross,' repeated her uncle ruminatively. 'He called the constables,' he said.

'And mamma, is she – '

Her uncle lurched ahead suddenly, reaching out to clap a hand on his wife's shoulder. 'Good evening, my dear. Is that stew I smell?'

His wife looked mutinously at him, refusing to welcome him. She signalled brusquely to one of the girls to bring him food. Serin's other cousins relieved her of their father's weight and lowered him on to his pallet. He put the bowl of stew on his knee and stirred it clumsily.

'This smells good,' he said, and looking up at Serin, reading her face in the gloom, asked her, 'Have you had some?'

Serin shook her head.

'Feed her,' he said to Aunt Cary.

She did not react.

'Feed her!'

Another bowl was brought. It was gamey, and thick with roots and grain. Serin ate ravenously.

'More,' said her uncle soon. 'More for your cousin too.'

Children hurried to obey. Aunt Cary lay on the other side of the fire, her face turned away, her dark bulk unmoving.

'Have you been looking after your cousin?' Uncle Banner asked.

There was a pause. Then Muir's voice came in the darkness.

'She run away, pa.'

'Did she now.'

'Weren't my fault.'

'Well, that's something to be thankful for,' he said. He sounded stronger already with a meal inside him.

Sitting unfettered with her uncle's family, eating their food, in at least a semblance of hospitality, Serin felt obliged to explain herself.

'I didn't see why I should stay,' she said, somewhat stiffly. 'I took some skis.'

'Handy,' was his only comment.

The talk and the coming and going in the cave were ceasing now. Fires were being banked, giving place to lamps that burned with a dim yellow flame. Serin scraped her bowl; and found a little boy at her side ready to take it from her.

'They made you bring them back,' said her uncle at last. 'The skis.'

'Yes.'

'Who was that?'

'Two boys – young men,' she said. 'The ones I – saw. At the fair.'

She wished she hadn't mentioned that.

'Lukas and Ned. They've had practice.'

Serin didn't understand.

'Carting you about.'

'Oh. Yes.'

There was another pause.

The children had begun to spread rugs and lie down around their mother. Serin thought it seemed early to be going to bed, though she realised she had no idea what the time was.

'How far did you get?' Uncle Banner wanted to know.

'I found a track down to the valley. There was this mine. I hid in a sort of chimney for a bit, but they heard me.'

She wanted to mention the goblin voice, to ask her uncle if there were ghosts in the mines, but it seemed silly; and she didn't want to frighten the little ones.

'You'll stay with us for a spell,' her uncle said.

The conversation seemed to be over. Uncle Banner moved slowly around the embers and settled down next to his wife, who immediately began to harangue him in an undertone so soft Serin, a couple of yards away, couldn't make out a word. She wondered where she was to sleep. She even thought of trying to pick her way back across the cave to the ladder and the leaf-strewn ledge where she had woken up, but was afraid of blundering into people in the dark. She stood once more on the frozen river watching the blood fly, the bodies fall; and came to with a start. The camp was stirring again, torches and lamps being lit. The chief was speaking.

'What is it? What's happening?' Serin cried out unaware. They hushed her.

Over by the chief's circle a woman was standing with torches about her. She wore the dusk-grey robe of the Sisterhood of the Primacy.

'Who is it?' asked an old woman Cary Marchan was trying to wake.

'It's the minister,' they told her.

'I bring bad news,' announced the sister in montano. 'Bad news from Calcionne.'

—8—

The Point of Departure,
the Eve of Despair

When I came to my senses and managed to kneel up it was quite dark. All the people had gone, even Arethusa. My clothes were wet through with the snow that had lain so thickly over me, and which was still drifting down through the darkness like blossom from some vast invisible tree.

As I stood up, the sword fell out. I picked it up and stuck it through my belt, for that I had seen to be the proper way to wear one. My fine great hat had vanished utterly, which grieved me much. What a simpleton I must have been in those days, to take pride in such vanities.

Profoundly I wished Arethusa were there to explain this unexpected and unpleasant turn of events to me. I called her name aloud again and again, but there was no one. My voice sounded foolish to me, like the wail of a disconsolate calf. I desisted, and began to poke around in the snow. I thought my friend might perchance be sheltering inside the small wooden house, but there was nothing within but some cold, charred bones, dirty beakers made of clay and, in one corner, beads from a broken necklace. I stepped outside again and slithered down on to the ice.

The great fair was half dismantled and all deserted. Among the snowy remnants I saw but a single light shining, so made for it at once. I conclude I was not yet quite in my right wits.

In possession of the lantern were two of the small people with orange faces, who, I surmise, being set to watch over the spot, had heard me holloa-ing and come to see. They spoke somewhat together in their own tongue, seeming not well able to understand mine, or to speak any of it save a few curt and peremptory insults and instructions. They searched in my pockets, leaving alone what they found there as though disgusted; but readily they took my sword and confined my hands, then led me up into the city, to a great grey building. The snow came in through the rent the blade had made in the clothes upon my back. I thought it best to bear this, and all things, patiently, as when I was taken to a small room in the depths of that building and locked behind a wall made all of iron bars. I disliked to be detained, but held my peace. Soon a woman brought me a mess of food and a mug of water. The former, as was my custom, I let alone; the latter I sampled but as always found thin and insipid, quite insufficient to my needs.

An hour, it may be, passed in unhappy thoughts of Arethusa. It occurred to me now most forcibly that she too might have been attacked and lain all that while pinned under the snow by the river, unable to rise or reply to my feeble cries. She might even have been made dead. I paced my tiny room, anxious to get out and resume my search for her, until two orange fetched me up to the prefect. Either of them alone I might have risked, but feared, sensibly enough, that two would surely be more than I could manage.

The prefect was an old man in fur slippers and a heavy robe. With him was a younger, taller one with shiny hair who asked me who I was, where I lived, what I had been about in the snow, and so forth, repeating each of my answers to the prefect in their own tongue. At first I was cautious and I lied to them, saying my name was Riorty, I lived in Maltleather Lane (or some such) with my young daughter Arethusa who would surely be most anxious for me; but then I understood that they had found the fat orange I had seen stabbed and bleeding, and wished to know what might have befallen him. Out of compassion then I enlightened them. When I agreed that the swordsmen had been of the tribes called montani, that is, mountainfolk, the younger man looked triumphant and spoke earnestly to his master, who nonetheless grew glum, it seemed to me. They conversed thus awhile ignoring me. I heard the younger mention the name of the princess, urging, I thought, some consideration, some course of action, to which his superior seemed loth to agree.

On a sudden, without apparent instruction, my interrogator said to me:

– You had a montano sword about you when you were brought in. How came you by it?

– I found it in the snow, I said, and picked it up.

– There is a cut in your clothing, he said.

Peering solemnly over my shoulder as if to verify his words, I had to own that there was. I supposed it had been made when I was struck down. This he conveyed to the prefect as before, then said:

– His Estimability wishes to see this cut for himself.

For this I was unprepared. When the prefect ascertained that the vent *was not in my clothing alone but equally in my person, he grew excited, and gave out many more questions which I was unable to answer. In incontinent spirit he set a man upon me, to strike me about the face; and when I still did not satisfy the curiosity I had unwillingly aroused, ordered him to take me out of the chamber and back, I feared, to incarceration. When the soldier goaded me downstairs I knew my fear for certainty.*

Weakened and miserable as I was, this I could not stand. At an unlit corner of the stair I turned on my guard. He was, I believe, surprised, and even more so to find me indifferent to his blade. His eyes opened wide and he began to yammer most piteously, gazing into my face. I was easily able to persuade him to cease his jabbing and succumb.

Being used to rats, birds, the occasional infant, I was surprised how long an adult lasted, and how rich was the savour of his juices. Nervous for the danger of discovery, I was yet unable to leave him unfinished for the intoxicating delight of it. Moreover, I was presently glad I had at last obeyed this natural appetite, for when he did grow lax and limp in my embrace, I felt myself more invigorated than at any time in my remembrance, scanty though that was. I disencumbered myself of my erstwhile escort, pausing only to relieve him of his sword, which was longer than the first, but slipped as smoothly into my belt. Then I took to my heels and raced away out of the building, losing myself straightway among cloisters and snowy courtyards. Heedlessly I fled, turning to right and left at random. The darkness was complete; yet now I could see everything as clear as day – clearer, for my eyes are not at their best then. The Eschalan's sword banged uncomfortably on my thigh, and I wished for my own back again, which was shorter by a handsbreadth. Nevertheless, when I heard footsteps running and the barking of dogs, I at once leapt up and over a high wall with a speed and agility that astonished and gratified me. My greatcoat billowed at my back like black wings!

Behind the wall I found myself in, as I thought, a small wood, all set about with lettered stones and stones carved into the likeness of people. The darkness under the trees soothed the irritation of my nerves, and I felt its motionless inhabitants more congenial than the company I had just left. While I sat crouching on a low, black branch, the ululation of the hounds came faintly to me, as if from another world.

'We need courage now,' said the bishop. 'We shall all need courage.'

'You fear reprisals,' said the princess.

'Grief makes all creatures cruel,' the bishop said.

'Grief,' said the princess, 'doesn't seem to enter into it.' She scratched a fingernail along the grain in the arm of her chair. 'Charan du wants to go charging off into the mountains and drag back someone to hang.'

'What will you do?'

'What can I do? If I do not co-operate, he will say I am protecting the guilty. If I do, I forfeit the loyalty of the hillfolk.'

'You have no obligation to protect them from the consequences of their own crimes. If it had been a Luscan killed – '

'The malefactors would have been handed over to the city constables,' said Princess Nette. 'Formerly, at least. That's what my father always required. He granted them immunity from city law on their own land, and sanctioned their own judgements there. Sometimes I wonder if he had any choice.'

'Sister Annina must know how to find them. Tomorrow early let me send her to remind them of their duty,' said the bishop. 'If it please Your Royal Highness,' she added quickly.

Princess Nette caught her eye and smiled. 'Thank you, Yvonne,' she said. 'Your suggestion will have weight in my considerations. But the montanos, you see, don't consider this a crime; according to Brant, anyway.'

'It is a crime against God,' the bishop reminded her.

'And that should be my text.'

'There is no other. All lives, all lands, belong to Her.'

'The Eschalans deny it.'

'The Eschalans are in error.'

'The Eschalans are our enemies,' said the princess, slapping the chair-arm lightly. 'We have grown used to their faces; we have grown lazy and complacent in their keeping. We forget, but they are still our enemies.'

Bishop Yvonne was waiting for her to finish speaking. She said, 'The war was over and done, lost and won, seven years ago.'

'Not in the hearts and minds of the montanos,' the princess replied. 'Brant tells me this was the first stroke of the last battle.'

'Three blows in the back of an unarmed man,' said the bishop, 'is murder, madam, not war.'

'Are they not armed? There are other weapons than swords, Yvonne. Do they not attack us daily with their papers and their provisos, and with their phalluses too? Don't look so shocked, bishop. Tumak coh had a woman with him; not an orange woman either.'

'I had heard that,' said the bishop gravely. 'I had also heard she was not unwilling.'

'Then she was unwise. And so was he. It does not make either of them innocent.'

'This is all hearsay, madam,' said the bishop a little coolly, 'and it would be ill advised of you to judge on the strength of it.'

'Oh, suspend judgement, by all means,' said the princess at once. 'I meant only that we may have to reconsider what is war and what is not. But you are right; I should like to be well advised. I should like that.'

'Turn to the Lady, ma'am. Open your heart to Her.'

Nette brooded a moment, her jewelled fingers absently pleating and smoothing the fabric of her gown.

'If it comes to hearts,' she said, 'my montanos have a claim upon mine far superior to any Eschalan's. Did you ever meet the deceased, this Tumak coh?'

'He made some inspection of the Aveneda.'

'Did he vouchsafe any comment?'

'Oh, yes, we had a short interview. Our faith seemed to – amuse him.'

'And what impression did he make on you?'

'I could not presume to judge . . .'

'Could you not,' said the princess. 'Well, I can. He struck me as a man who had been given too many free dinners and too few responsibilities.'

Bishop Yvonne made to turn her face aside, then looked straight at Princess Nette and smiled frankly.

'I thought you'd like that,' the princess continued. 'It's mother's observation, in fact, but for once I agreed with her entirely. A wretched man to break a peace over.'

'Then you have decided that the peace is not an illusion.'

'I have decided nothing, Yvonne,' said the princess, and she sighed. 'Nothing at all.'

The bishop leaned forward in her chair, the soft sound of her shifting robe audible in the silence that had fallen.

'Madam,' she said, 'the Entenmann will appreciate the predicament. The chief is no fool. He will not be disloyal.'

'But shall I be disloyal to him? Shall I ride up to his tent at the head of a party of Eschalans and demand he give up the brave men who struck this blow against the usurpers? Will he be disloyal to his tribe and hand them over? And if he refuses, how long will his tribe remain loyal to me? You may say I should not calculate; and yet I must. I must.'

Princess Nette could see that Bishop Yvonne was sorry for her, and would try to comfort her. She wished there were someone who could.

'All the hillfolk have your welfare in their hearts, Highness,' the bishop said. 'Send plain words calling upon them to do what is right. Let my minister go to them. If they will not, send a pair of constables. If they return alone, send eight or ten. Do not allow an orange face to be seen approaching their camp. Let them know this is a matter between them and you their ruler. By these steps you may pace out the rest of winter and approach spring, when passage into the mountains becomes easier, and all prospects appear more hopeful. Time may – '

There was a knock at the door.

'Enter,' called Princess Nette.

A footman came in, and held open the door for Charan du. 'The prefectorial moonshee,' announced the footman; but Charan du was already advancing, not waiting to be recognised.

'Charan du, good evening,' said the princess, as Bishop Yvonne rose and was ignored. 'I did not realise we had a second appointment today.'

'The troubled day recedes, Your Royal Highness,' said the interpreter. 'There was indeed no appointment made. I regret the intrusion.' But he made no move to step aside.

He was alarming. He was about to confront her with something. Suddenly she did not want to know what it was.

'The bishop and I were just finishing our business,' she admitted.

'Bishop,' said Charan du, with an inattentive little bow.

'Good day, Charan du,' replied Yvonne. 'May I say how shocked and distressed all our sisters are by the terrible death of your esteemed colleague? The Sisterhood of the Primary is at prayer for his immortal soul.'

With an effort he brought himself to listen to her. 'Your attention to these matters is most consoling, Madam Bishop,' he said, a trifle impatiently.

'May I ask what provisions you will make for his funeral?' continued Bishop Yvonne.

'His remains will be burnt, no doubt, after a few days, with all due honour,' he said, 'according to the custom of our nation. Your officiation, madam, will not be necessary. Nor your presence now.'

He gave her a vicious smile.

The air in the room suddenly seemed icy as the night outside. Then the bishop, swallowing the offence, commended her sovereign to the Primary; 'and Her to you.'

'You have given me good counsel, bishop,' said the princess. 'Here is mine: let Sister Annina perform her ministry. Tonight, if she will.'

Then she was alone with the Eschalan and a sharp sense of disquiet. She wished she felt more prepared to deal with him, more sure of her vantage – more sure of herself. She offered him some refreshment.

During the bishop's benediction he had turned away. Now he approached her. The intensity of his gaze was fervent; or lethal; or mad.

'Yes,' he said, in a strange, swallowed sort of voice. 'Oh, yes.'

'Something warming, perhaps,' she said, lifting a finger to the footman.

'Decidedly . . .'

'Warm milk and nutmeg,' she suggested spitefully, it being one of the least pleasant beverages she could imagine; and then in fright: 'With a dash of brandy.'

Charan du assented. She did not think he had been listening to her.

The footman left.

The moonshee wore a tangerine frock-coat and lemon gloves. His plait was coiled and pinned on top of his head. He folded his arms behind him.

'There are times,' he announced, 'when the web becomes clearer.'

'Indeed?'

'Almost palpable. You too must know this sensation.'

'Oh, yes,' she said. 'The web.'

He smirked. 'Between superiors, knowledge is possible.'

'Let us always be grateful for that,' said the princess, beginning to be irritated again. The worst of it was, she didn't know whether she was supposed to know what he was talking about, or whether this theoretical pussyfooting was part of it, part of what he had come to do to her.

'Feel how the lines converge!' he told her. 'At this point, in this room.'

She said nothing.

'We must keep our balance,' he continued. 'Balanced, I am strong. Like the blind man, I know everything that is in my reach.'

'You're talking about the murder,' said Princess Nette. 'You know who killed Tumak coh.'

The interpreter brushed this aside. 'Their deed proclaims them,' he said.

Something told her he knew no more about the affair than ever; that this was his impatience speaking. But she had to be sure.

'Do you know who you're looking for?'

The question delighted him. 'Yes! I do!'

Still he would not say.

The princess began to wonder again. Perhaps he *did* know, and was holding it back from her. Why? Because it was a name she would recognise? Because the consequences would be devastating? He looked like an illustration from Mancini on Cartophily: *ASSURANCE: He who manifestly believes all the tricks must fall to him. Meanwhile, his Opponents try to estimate whether or not the Cards have him fool'd.*

'Well,' said Princesse Nette pleasantly. 'Are you going to tell me what it begins with?'

Thoughtfully he smiled, and nodded.

'It begins with a glance, and a word,' he said. 'It begins with a wish, and with an echo to that wish. It begins with a desire, and a decision.'

Princesse Nette wrinkled her nose.

'Charan du,' she said, 'what are you talking about?'

Now for the first time he looked perplexed, yet still avid with it, whatever it was. 'You have no word for it,' he complained.

'If you'd care to tell me one, I would have.'

'No, I mean your language: there is a word in Eschalan, but none in Luscan.'

'Do you not mean murder?' asked Princess Nette. She was sure now he did not.

'I mean love,' answered Charan du. '"Love" would be closest, I think.'

So. This was the moment she had dreaded: come, and found

her quite unready, dreading something else altogether. Startled, she said, 'Then don't think.'

The Eschalan clearly took this as encouragement to proceed impulsively. He seized the lapels of his hideous coat and drew them back, as if offering up his breast.

There was a knock at the door.

It was his hot milk.

Charin du relinquished his dramatic posture and gave the servant a frenzied glare.

'Drink your milk,' advised the princess. 'It will calm you.'

'In my language,' he said between rapid, delicate sips at his posset, 'there is a word *beweo*. It means to sense a shared destiny with someone.'

'We speak of meeting one's match,' said the princess helpfully. She was determined to stay aloof from this as long as possible. With a tiny thrill, she wondered whether he might be stirred to some gesture of ardour which would justify her shouting for help and having him removed; permanently removed, if she made enough fuss to Lan olang. 'But I don't see what all this has to do with me,' she said; and growing bold, 'or why you had to interrupt my privacy to make these declarations,'

'Give me your hand,' he urged, 'and I shall give you my arm. Give me your mountaineers, and I shall give you back your realm.'

'But this is half a dozen different propositions!' she protested, bewildered.

'No, Nette zan Herlach,' he intoned, setting down his cup. 'Your principality needs my strength. I need your compliance. The voice that calls upon you is one.'

He stared at her with his tawny eyes, eyes of a predatory cat. He reached for her hand.

'If you touch me I shall cry out for assistance,' said Princess Nette in a low and breathless voice; and wondered why she did not let him, and do so. His eyes seemed to fix her to her couch, as if he had some awful, unspoken power, something, as he said, he had only to name to damn her utterly.

Yet he closed his fingers and withdrew his hand, slowly, smiling placidly as if her reaction pleased him, as if she had passed some kind of test, fulfilled some favoured prediction.

'Charan du, you are the Eschalan prefect's interpreter, not the prefect himself. You are talking wildly. The gruesome fate of your colleague has upset you.'

He picked up his cup again, nestling it as if to warm his hands.

'The prefect would rejoice at our union,' he told her. 'The emperor himself would welcome it. The marriage of Luscan tradition and Eschalan aptitude. The marriage of an interpreter and a princess: intelligence and power together in one bed!'

He was still smiling, drinking and smiling at her weirdly over the rim of the cup.

'Let us stand together at his side, governing the dispensation of his wisdom,' he exhorted.

'Does His Estimability know you are making these suggestions?' she asked, baffled.

'The prefect is otherwise occupied. The prefect has been distracted from the matter of mortality by the spectre of immortality,' announced Charan du. 'He is convinced the Emperor's Tongue was cut down by one who can never be executed for the act!'

Princess Nette closed her eyes. 'Charan du, you pile confusion upon confusion.'

'Then let me interpret myself. I have just assisted His Estimability in examining a witness who saw the montanos strike Tumak coh, and was himself knocked insensible thereafter. His Estimability takes it into his head that the wound should have killed the wretch; yet he lives. He moves. Indeed, he has run away, after killing a man-at-arms in some barbaric fashion yet unexplained. This, believes Lan olang, proves that *he* was the killer of the imperial herald, and of the missing girl too, no doubt: no rampant mountain brute, but a supernatural marauder!'

Charan du shook his head. 'I can help him no further, not while this fancy leads him astray; but I can help my emperor – and my princess.'

Nette was trying to think. Charan du's idea of a proposal made her want to run laughing and screaming from the room. Yet if the prefect were losing his grip, as his interpreter seemed to be suggesting, the chance Charan du manifestly longed for, the chance to seize power, might well be taking shape before him. Whatever was to happen later, she had to try to head him off; and she had to know more.

'Is this man the gypsy you took? Can you be sure he is not the assassin?'

'No, this was no gypsy, merely a mooncalf with a gypsy's sword. Lan olang hunts the mooncalf, but it is the sword that will lead us to the swordsman.'

'How did this halfwit escape the prefecture?'

'He was improperly guarded,' declared Charan du. His eyes glittered. 'The grasp of the Emperor's Hand has been insecure today. The web eludes him.'

'And the gypsy?' persisted Princess Nette. 'What of him?'

Charan du made an odd, unfolding gesture. 'He too cannot be found. It is most vexing.' He smiled. His teeth were worse than ever.

Nette felt a considerable relief. Then new apprehension filled her. He was lying. Somehow, he was lying.

'You learned nothing from him, then,' she said guardedly.

'Nothing,' he agreed briskly. 'As we expected.'

'Did you?'

'It proves their guilt!'

'Does it?'

He looked at her fondly. 'They throw us a dead fish to distract us from the live one,' he explained. 'These barbarians must be ruled with subtlety as well as force. We are expert at this. We did not win an empire by swallowing dead fish.'

'No, I don't imagine you did,' admitted the princess.

'Yet all fish leave a smell,' he continued remorselessly, 'dead ones especially so! We are on this fish's scent. He will lead us where we want to go. We wait only for your word.'

'It would be wise to wait a little longer,' she advised, desperate to avoid the other thread of this bizarre conversation. 'To let them think all is well. By thaw – '

'By thaw their hands will be drenched with blood!' shouted Charan du. She stared at him reprovingly, but he seemed oblivious. 'By thaw they will have butchered the prefect himself.' He gazed into her eyes. 'I think you fear these creatures. You must not fear them. You must be strong, and quick. They will obey you. If you delay, they will know that you are weak. Let me direct you, Nette zan Herlach!'

'The montanos are not creatures, Charan du. They are men and women, with their own ways. They have ancient rights in the mountains where they live. My father and his father respected those rights. Do you advise me to violate them?'

'Do these rights include murder with impunity?'

'There is law in Luscany, Charan du. It will be brought to bear. My constables will present a crown suit to Chief Entenmann. There are other ways, other channels of influence.'

'We are not unaware of them,' said the interpreter, silkily.

'You can't use them because they are not open to you,' she went on. 'They exist as understandings between people. We know the montanos of old, and they know us. We will find their refuge in a few days. There is a method: courtesies to be observed, considerations to be made. His Estimability appreciates this, as you know. You have conducted many discussions between us. You will conduct many more.

'I understand that you and the other messengers must feel the injury of this death especially keenly. You feel vulnerable, and vengeful. It is only natural. I should like very much to discuss this with you and your colleagues. Please speak to Stevon and arrange a meeting. The Head Proctor will attend.'

He was not looking at her; he did not reply. His shoulders were hunched. She conceived his frustration. He had come rushing in to gain a kingdom; he was dismissed to organise a committee. It was up to her to signal forgiveness of his excesses and the restoration of proper relations between them.

'Rage is never our best counsellor,' she said, sympathetically. 'You come from warmer climes, and I suppose you must think us disgracefully cold-blooded and slothful. But in the north we know our winter, and no human heat can subdue it. We know how to skate: where the ice is firm and will bear passage, and where it is fragile, and will only give us a ducking.'

She dared to smile, and hoped her smile was steady.

'Have patience, Charan du, and we shall all skate more smoothly.'

The prefect's interpreter folded his arms behind his back. He smacked his lips and gave an odd little jerk of the head.

'You may find yourself skating round and round in a circle, madam,' he said. His voice had gone peculiar and gargled again.

'Whatever do you mean?'

'I mean, madam,' he replied, and there was the steel machine once more, 'that you may find your movements a trifle restricted now.'

'Are you threatening me, Charan du?'

'It would be for your own safety, as before,' he said. 'Apprentices with guns, and gypsies with swords: clearly Calcionne is

insecure and troubled once more. The prefect's policy of benefi-
cial influence is not enough. The protection of the princess's
person becomes a matter of some concern. Perhaps this period
does not require you to retire to your apartment. But an armed
guard at your side at all hours – our supervision upon every
occasion – advice on the suitability of certain walks, certain talks:
it would be prudent of us to provide such services.'

He began to stroll about the room as he spoke.

'Consideration should be given to the composition of the royal
household: any doubtful or inadequate officers replaced – which
reminds me, you will be needing a new head gardener. I myself
can suggest one or two excellent candidates for the post.'

'What have you done with Brant?' she cried.

'A precaution merely,' he said. 'All montanos within the
confines of the city have been rounded up and detained pending
interrogation. It may have escaped your notice, Highness, that
your gardener is one such. His Estimability regrets any inconvenience.'

Briskly, neatly, he straightened his coat, brushing two or three
white hairs from his shoulder. Casually he said, 'How much
simpler all these arrangements would be if only you had a man in
the palace, to stand and sit and lie beside you, supporting you
and guiding you in your dealings with your own people on the
one hand, and ours on the other . . . Well, Highness, I know you
will think about these things. Think with your customary admir-
able discretion and care.'

Showing neither of these qualities, Princess Nette went storm-
ing from the room, and nearly collided with a hurrying page.

'Your pardon, ma'am, but there's a man at the gate with a pack
of hounds. He says the prefect sent him after an escaped
prisoner, and asks may he let his dogs loose in the grounds.'

The princess glared at him. 'No he may *not!*' she snapped, and
swept past the gaping boy in a swirl of silks.

Her secretary was not in his office. She sent in all directions to
look for him, but eventually found him herself, in the card-room,
at two-handed palima with her mother. He rose and bowed, and
went scrabbling at once for pen and paper.

'A letter, Stevon, to His Estimability Lan olang Prefect of the
Eschalan Administration. Her Royal Highness Nette Princess of
Luscany commends the zeal of the Prefectorial Moonshee
Charan du, but recommends the prefect to look more closely to

the scope and liberty of the said Charan du, and further requires that the said Charan du hereafter visit the royal palace only upon such occasions as have beforehand been appointed between Her Royal Highness and His Estimability *et cetera*, and then only in the company and presence of His Estimability *et cetera*. The nerve of the man! No, don't put that. But add that I earnestly wish to speak with His Estimability tomorrow morning, in private, about the montano question. All that in his own vile language, Stevon, please, as quickly as you can, and no paraphrases. And I shall want you with me at that meeting tomorrow, to make sure Charan du doesn't paraphrase anything either.'

The secretary hastened away.

'Sit down, Nette, do, and stop puffing and blowing,' said her mother. 'What have you been getting yourself all worked up about now? What's Charan du done?'

'Only proposed to me, mamma.'

'Proposed? To do what?'

'To encumber and disable me; to climb up to power on my back – and on my body; to subject me . . .'

The archduchess looked at her, and then at her hand. 'Well, I suppose he made more sense than you're making, for I don't understand a word.'

'Mamma, he asked – demanded – insisted on marrying me!'

'Oh, is *that* it.'

'Mamma!'

Princess Nette stood up again, staring speechlessly at her mother across the card table.

'Sit *down*, Nette, and stop getting so excited. You're acting like a girl.'

'Oh!' Exasperated, Nette dropped back into the chair again.

'And be careful of the furniture. Now, I take it you're not satisfied with this man's proposal.'

'Mamma, I should like to order his head cut off, and watch from the balcony. I should like to wield the axe myself.'

'Dear me, you are in a temper.'

'How can you take it so calmly?'

'Well,' said the archduchess, perusing her cards and selecting one with care, 'Charan du wouldn't be my first choice – '

'Mamma!'

The archduchess played the card. '– not my *first* choice – '

'Mamma – '

'He is orange, after all.' She reached for Stevon's abandoned hand and turned it over. She raised her eyebrows. 'But we can't always have our first choice,' she remarked, picking up the card she had just played and replacing it with another from her hand. 'Since you have shown no interest in any of the families of Bathista or Ducros; and since circumstances are not ideal – '

'Mamma!'

'– not altogether ideal, you might do worse than Charan du, the prefect's right hand or whatever they call him after that grotesquely anatomical whimsy of theirs.'

'Mamma, it's you who's grotesque. You're speaking exactly like him,' said Princess Nette, aghast.

'He must be a sensible young man, then,' replied her mother, playing a card from Stevon's hand and immediately covering it with one of her own. 'Ambitious – but that's no fault – and intelligent, presentable, conscientious . . .'

'And tyrannous? Do you know they've arrested Brant and all the montanos in the city?'

'A splendid idea,' said the archduchess shortly. 'Send them back to the hills and let them stay there. I told you he was a sensible young man. Crespi speaks very highly of him.'

'Mother, Crespian Vittore is Charan du's spy.'

'Nonsense, Nette. You're becoming irrational.'

'He is, mamma! Charan du pays him to hang around the palace.'

'What does he hear? Me moaning about my ailments,' said the archduchess, and drew another card from the pack.

'He hears more than that,' began her daughter.

'Nette, you're always carping about poor Crespi. I shan't hear another word against him. Not another word.'

'Mamma, I'm talking about Charan du.'

The archduchess closed up her hand, tapped the edge of the cards sharply on the table, and threw them down. 'What about him?'

'Mamma, he threatened me.'

'Nette, he's a man,' said her mother crossly. 'Men like to order us about, whatever their rank. They get excitable when we obstruct them. There's a great deal you don't know about men that a woman of your age and your standing certainly ought to know. As it happens, you did the right thing. Charan du will be a sight more considerate after that letter. Then you can begin to "subject" him, as you put it.'

'I'll wring his neck first.'

'Any woman with two ha'p'orth of sense knows how to rule a man,' continued the archduchess, ignoring her. 'Oh, Charan du may be a bit of a cold fish, I grant you, but at least he speaks decent Luscan, and he has a hand in everything the Eschalans do.'

She reached suddenly across the table and seized Nette's wrist in a bony grasp. 'Use your head, girl! With Charan du in your bed you'd have the prefect in your pocket.'

Princess Nette did not reply.

'That's how it works for us,' the archduchess said. 'Commoners can pick and choose. We have to take the expedient ones. But there are compensations.'

Her eyes gleamed, but there was bitterness in her voice. She shook her daughter's arm.

'You don't think I was in *love* with your father, do you?'

A triangle chimed softly. Abruptly the archduchess let go of Nette's wrist, picked up her glass and knocked back the last of her drink.

'Bedtime,' she said flatly. 'Ring for a man to take me up. Come and see me in an hour. We shall discuss this further.'

The princess shook her head. 'Excuse me, mamma, I am very tired,' she said, and left before she had to say anything else.

She sat for a time in her parlour with only the dwindling fire for light, gazing out at the purple mountains, the black sky, and the spattered stars like flecks of ice. The bishop looked in upon her, and they spoke awhile. Then Princess Nette rose, and went to her bedchamber.

Thisbe helped her to undress, and wash, and put on her nightgown. She took the warming pan from the bed, and tucked the covers around her mistress.

'You look pale tonight, madam,' she ventured. 'Does your head ache? Shall I fetch you a draught?'

'No, Thisbe, thank you,' said the princess, with a smile that was a little drawn. 'I shall not sleep yet. Sit and read to me, if you will.'

Thisbe took a small brown book from the shelf and sat down at the bedside. 'Shall I read "The Shepherd's Elegy", madam?' she asked, turning to a favourite page where the corner was folded down.

'No,' said her mistress. 'Read me the one about the kitchen maid who cuts her hair and goes for a soldier in guise as a boy.'

'Oh, madam, that's a foolish fancy!'

'Even so.'

Thisbe turned up the lamp and found the place. She began to read, but at once the princess stopped her.

'You're a good girl, Thisbe.'

'Thank you, ma'am.'

'Where are your parents? Remind me.'

'Not in Calcionne, madam. My mother is a baker in Tourmalix, north of Cory Waste.'

'That's good,' the princess said, as if to herself. She looked to see the time. 'Is that clock right? Surely it must be later. No? Oh, well . . .' Then she seemed to recollect herself. 'Go to the bureau, Thisbe. Look in the little drawer on the right. Is there a purse in there?'

'This one, madam?'

'Is there money in it?'

Thisbe hefted it. 'Plenty, by the feel of it.'

'Open it up.'

Gingerly the maid opened the strings and peeped inside. 'Plenty,' she said again, and started to bring it to the bed.

'No,' said Princess Nette, 'put it back for now.' And as the girl obeyed, she said, 'If anything should happen to me, Thisbe, and the palace is no longer – safe, I want you to take that purse and go quickly back home to Tourmalix.'

'What are you saying? Nothing's going to happen to you.'

'Promise me, Thisbe.'

'Madam, I can't, it's too much – '

'Promise.'

Thisbe came and sat down again. Worriedly her eyes searched Nette's face. 'I promise, madam.'

'Good. Don't forget,' said the princess, and settled back on her pillows. 'Now you may read.'

But Thisbe had got no further than a half-dozen stanzas into the improbable ballad when there came a knock on the door. She lay down the book and went to see.

'It's Underscrivener Vittore, madam.'

'Vittore? What is it? You may approach.'

He held out a paper sealed with the prefect's insignia. 'A message, Your Royal Highness.'

—9—
What Fortune Love May Bring

'The orange have arrested all the hillfolk in the city.'

There was a murmur, then a clamour, and the minister raised her hand to call for silence. Sister Annina spoke like a woman accustomed to addressing congregations in times of trouble, loudly and plainly so that the very old, the very young, the sleepy and the ones at the back of the cave could all hear and understand.

'Don't be frightened,' she said. Her voice rolled and echoed around the lightless galleries of stone. 'That's what the orange want. They want us to be frightened.'

Serin wondered about her mother.

'The Primary will protect our loved ones,' promised Sister Annina.

There was more muttering at this, some audible denials. 'She's not done so well yet,' vociferated Friano Lydam, known to be no lover of the Primacy. He was hushed, but persisted: 'How are *you* here, anyway?'

'They overlooked me among my sisters. I thank the Primary for that, Friano Lydam,' said Sister Annina.

'I'd overlook you meself,' he retorted, then succumbed to impatient shouts and some rough handling.

'Let the minister speak.'

'Did no one else escape?' demanded another man.

'A party of thirty got away to Berchel's Gap,' she announced, and named names. 'There may have been others; I don't know.'

Here and there in the crowd were flurries of reaction, tears of relief; but some objected, 'They should be here.'

'Berchel's Gap was nearer,' said the minister. 'They'll send someone tomorrow, if there are no Eschalans between.'

Friano Lydam began to make more noise. He was shouted down, but she called: 'Let him speak,' and then he could be heard asking, ' – do we know they haven't followed her?'

'I haven't forgotten the ways,' she assured him loudly.

'Let her speak,' the Entenmann commanded. 'She is the daughter of Braun and Mabel Carver,' he reminded them officially. 'She is ours. She eats with our kin, and with the Lady. Sister Annina.'

'The orange have our people in prison,' she said. 'They will find out anything they want to know. They have not said so, but we think they have taken them hostage for the boys who killed their visitor at the fair. Perhaps if they are handed over, the others may be released.'

But the montanos had been over this issue, and the consensus was, the Esch could have Lukas, Ned, Gwendyn and the others, if they came and got them. It was a decision they held to now, though some demurred; and everyone looked to the Entenmann.

The chief conferred with some of his circle. Then he sat back, scratching his side, saying nothing. An old man begged leave to speak; Entenmann waved him to silence. The minister stood by with her arms folded, watching him brood.

At last he sat forward with his hands on his knees.

'Let me know your minds,' he said.

A young voice – Serin thought it might be Ned or Lukas – called, 'Raid the prison!' and a number of others agreed.

The chief turned to Sister Annina. 'Where are they held?'

'Some at the prefecture,' she told them. 'When they become too many, they brought some to us. Others too, probably, elsewhere.'

Banner Marchan spoke up. 'The posthouse. It's all prisons now.'

'It will be darker later.'

'No! Strike now!'

'We can't sit here!' cried one, agitated, and another in the same tone, 'It's not safe here!' There was a good deal of agreement.

'Wait till we hear from Berchel's Gap,' advised a woman whose daughter the minister had named.

'The High Fastness,' called one faction. 'Across the border,' called another. Everyone began to talk at once. One of the chief's men got up and angrily thudded a staff on the rock until the hubbub subsided, and only the echoes were still quarrelling.

'Are we coneys in a burrow?' he wanted to know. 'The puny oranges won't come up here. Entenmann, don't listen to them.'

Ned Gurny raised his hand, jumped up on a barrel. 'He's right! We don't want to run nowhere. Raid the prisons – raid the prisons – raid the prisons,' and he started a little ragged chanting, which the chief promptly quelled.

'Send the women and children to the High Fastness at any rate,' proposed someone. Many people shouted disagreement, most of them women.

'To Ducros! Across the border!'

'The peregrinage!'

Uproar threatened once more. Sister Annina quietened them. 'Be calm,' she told them. 'Have faith. Set aside your fear.'

'Calm's well for you, Annina,' shouted Ned rudely.

'I know your feelings,' she said. 'My brother is not with us. He is in Calcionne, in prison.'

'What about the princess?' someone called, and a chorus strenuously endorsed the question, as though they thought it should have been asked earlier, as though it had been in their minds all along. 'The princess!'

'The bishop has spoken with the princess,' answered Sister Annina. 'She says the princess asks that we do our duty.'

There was a lull while they all considered this. Then, before the shouting could begin again, Chief Entenmann spoke.

'For all talk of Ducros or the High Fastness, tomorrow will do, when we learn more from Berchel's Gap. Everyone be ready,' he said, raising his voice and looking sternly all around, as if he could see every face in the cave. 'Be ready to fight or go.'

The chief paused and closed his eyes, as if digesting the first part of his utterance. Then he opened them and looked directly at Banner.

'Banner Marchan, you know something of these prisons.'

'Yes, Entenmann, I do.'

'How are your aching limbs now?'

'They will be better for a night's sleep, or what's left of a night,' Banner answered.

'I say no,' rejoined the chief. 'I say they will be stiff and sore in the morning, will they not?'

'Well, they may,' said Banner judiciously.

'How if I told you to ride tonight, to ride to Calcionne?'

'Then I must muffle my groans in my beard,' said Banner. There was some laughter, some cheers and whistling. 'My wife's groans you must muffle yourself,' he added, and the laughter was louder.

'What could you do tonight in Calcionne?' asked the Entenmann.

'Not much at the prefect's, I'd say. And the posthouse will be tighter than a drum now. But a band could have a crack at the primacy, if the minister's willing; and a couple of us could go for Her Highness, if we can get in at the palace.'

'Who will you take with you?'

Banner strode through the press to the chieftain's fire, Streaky Bela beside him. 'All who'd ride stand forth,' he bellowed; and on all sides people thrust themselves forward out of the crowd. Banner began to call names.

Ned Gurny was standing out, and his father in support of him. 'Banner, I'm no use to you at night with my eyes,' he began earnestly, 'but will you not take Ned? He's burning for it, d'you see? Just give him the chance, Banner, ha?'

Banner stared at the fidgeting boy. 'He obeys my every word, and Streaky's, if he rides,' he growled. Ned was nodding vigorously; but Banner went on: 'And he rides unarmed if he rides at all.'

Then Ned began to protest, and Banner to turn away; so Ned had to agree. He stumbled forth, glowering. Streaky Bela slapped him on the back, perhaps rather harder than was altogether hearty.

'We know what a fine sword you are, Neddy,' he said loudly. 'Let's see what else you're good for, eh?'

Banner Marchan stumped on, pointing at men and women and calling their names. Looking around him one last time, he stopped in surprise, noticing a face he'd not remarked at first. He scratched his jaw, and nodded.

'Serin Guille,' he called.

There were shouts of puzzlement and derision.

'Will you ride, child?' asked the chief of the montanos, disbelievingly.

'They've got my ma,' she said.

Her detractors fell quiet. They looked at Banner. Banner looked at the floor.

'Will you take her, Banner?'

'On my own sled, Entenmann,' he promised. Then he put an arm around her, presenting her to the tribe. 'She's an apt little thief, our Serin.'

The night was banked with cloud. In the dim huddle of the city below, one or two lights could be seen for a moment, flickering through the trees: the lights of the Aspenpleyn; the naphtha flares along the Brink; lamps in upper rooms where administrators, or nurses, or gamblers, kept vigil about their business. It did not look like a city in pain, or in peril. Winter night and low cloud muffled all equally.

It was sharply, astringently cold. The novice felt it in her nose and throat; she tucked her chin deeper inside her cowl. She stood in the snow among the pines and looked down the trodden way to Rowe. There was a light there too, the combined glow of a brazier and a lantern, half obscured within a roadside shelter. Her own lantern hung unlit at her shoulder, on the nub of a broken branch. She had preferred to come this far in darkness, for this was the part of the forest she knew well. Even deep in snow at dead of night, it was a comfortable way to walk. She had felt her path around unseen rocks that grew familiar at her touch; she had known where to tread to avoid the low spikes of young trees and the hidden roots of fully grown ones, though snow-piled branches overbalanced constantly, shedding their loads around her with a soft hiss. In her shadow-coloured robe she could walk now into the open and down across the meadows, and still not be seen; but that was not what she had to do. She wished she could, for when she lit her lantern, advertising her presence, then it would begin.

She opened the door of the lantern, fumbling a moment with the cold iron, then found the tinderbox in the deep pocket of her robe, and brought it out. Cradling it in her left hand she struck the steel repeatedly against the flint, showering sparks on the shavings of punk. It was not as easy as she had thought. The cold air suffocated the sparks before they could catch. She tented up her sleeve over her hand, covering the box as well as she could, and tried again. At first it seemed no better. She was in despair of having to go back and have the lantern lit for her; or else go down in the dark and risk being shot at.

At that moment a tiny red eye blinked among the shavings.

The novice blew on it infinitely gently, as she had been shown, and soon it popped up into a flame. Not moving her left arm at all, she fished in the pocket again and drew out a taper, which readily caught the flame up.

In her haste, chilled to the bone, she snapped the box shut before she had got the flame to the candle, and for an instant she saw herself with the taper going out, and the whole thing to do again; but she prayed inwardly to the Primary, Mother of warmth and light, and the Primary was with her. She carried the flame safely into the lantern and set it to the wick. Then the cold forest, it seemed, bloomed with light.

She tapped the lantern closed, flicked out the taper, and replaced taper and box securely in her pocket. With a shiver of relief, she took the lantern from its hook. Shadows jiggled on the ground, trees jumping to and fro. The novice took up the staff that she had leant against a tree, and walked out into the open.

Now her lantern showed only snow, piled high to left and right, and trampled down along the way she was going. Her feet crunched firmly as she trod: her boots were stout; she remembered putting them on that morning to visit the fair. That seemed a great while ago now. The world had turned about since then to show them all a different, unsmiling face.

As she came up over a rise she could see down to the guard-post again. Two small dark figures were standing outside. They had spotted her.

'Help!' she shouted.

Their only response was to point a great long gun at her. It took two of them to wield it.

On the crests of the snowbanks either side the path the wind had carved crazy lace, a filigree of frozen fins and curlicues. It wriggled as she raised her lantern.

'Help!'

She came at a cautious, mincing run down to the road.

The nearer of the soldiers hurriedly stood a forked support under the barrel of the cumbersome gun and ran forward, brandishing their own lantern.

'Come here!'

The novice approached and stood in the light. The soldier came close to look inside her cowl. He was scarcely taller than she. She stared impassively at his crooked teeth, his dripping nose. His breath smelt of beer. 'Who are you?' he demanded. 'Montano?'

'No,' she said.

He gestured. 'Take off hat.'

She pulled back her hood. Now it was his turn to inspect her, to see that she did not have the tan skin and coarse black hair of a gypsy.

'Who?' he said again.

'Sister Jenise of the Primacy,' she told him, speaking slowly and as clearly as she could with her mouth so numb. 'Not montano.' She shook her head in a pantomime of denial, and added, somewhat belatedly, 'Don't shoot,' for his companion was steadfastly training the musket on her, and scowling fiercely.

'Not montano?'

'No. Sister.' She indicated her robe.

He stepped back a little to cast his light on it. 'Sister,' he said, nodding.

'Yes.'

'Late,' he said.

The other took one hand off his gun to point to an ornate clock they had prominently set up inside their shelter. 'Late,' he echoed sharply.

'You must come,' said the novice. 'Someone's hurt.'

The Eschalans conferred briefly. The first one blew his nose with his fingers and spat into the snow, then glared at her, though she had not moved.

'Young woman,' he said. It was a statement, not an address. 'Young to be late. Young to be sister.'

'I'm a novice,' she explained. 'New sister. Please. Someone's been hurt. In the forest. They need help.'

'Hurt. Who is hurt?'

'I don't know who he is. He's a montano,' she said.

'Montano?'

'I think so.'

This, clearly, would not move them. They spoke together, casting suspicious looks at her. Tired of holding up her lantern, she hung it on her staff again, and held that in her left hand, flexing the frozen fingers of her right.

She could see the second soldier was reminding the first that they were supposed to arrest montanos, but the first was not persuaded. He said something, probably that this one should be left to die. The novice could see he did not want to go up into the forest, in the dark, in the snow. He was going to challenge her.

He came forward again. 'Sister,' he said. 'Where from sister?'

'I told you,' she said. 'From the forest. From the hermitage.'

They did not know the word. They looked at each other.

'You must come,' said the novice. 'Come on.' She turned to lead the way. The first soldier grabbed her by the arm, pulling her towards the shelter, but the second shouted at him, No, no, in the Eschalan tongue. He seemed nervous.

The first went back to him. They spoke animatedly, bickering, looking darkly all the while at their prisoner, who did not move except that now and then she shivered. They pulled out a coin and kissed it; one spun it into the air.

The other slapped his thighs. He grinned at his defeated partner, who handed him their lantern and came resignedly up to her again. The novice turned and led him up the frozen path into the meadows, where it was very dark and still. The orange took every step with great caution, looking about him in the desolate night. He drew his sword to menace her.

Softly, the novice began to whistle a childish hymn.

> The Primary made trees and leaves
> And all things good and green
> The snowy-headed mountain
> And the valleys in between.

The soldier pricked her with his sword. He had had an idea. 'Sing!' he commanded her.

'What?' she cried.

'Sing! Sister sing!'

'But I need my breath – for the climb.'

He whacked her with the flat of his blade. 'Sister sing.'

Her voice floated out into the night.

'The Primary made trees and leaves . . .'

'Good!'

Despite her lack of sleep, her exertion and the steepness of the path, singing actually seemed to stir her on, the novice found as she tramped. It also helped her not to scream, or laugh. She sang all the verses, loudly and rather flat, then stopped.

He struck her again. 'Sing.'
'But that's the – ow! All right, you asked for it.'

> The Primary made Eschalans,
> And all things smelly and orange.

She sang fearlessly, then wondered what on earth rhymed with
orange.

> And if he'd put his sword away
> I'd kick him in the sporrange . . .

'Good,' he said. 'Music.'

They entered the forest. The novice looked around warily, but
nothing moved except the shadows of the trees, fleeing her light.
She led her captor faithfully on, up the rocks by the blasted fir,
kilting up her robe to climb. She could hear him behind her,
coping, breathing hard.

When she reached the clearing she paused, looking back. He
came out of the shadows, his eyes like topaz shining in the
lantern-light. He caught up with her and took her by the arm,
pointing up at the old hut.

'Yes. In there.'

They crossed the clearing and stood at the foot of the outcrop
by a frozen spring, a cascade of curdled ice dripping down a
black gash in the snow. She showed him with her lantern the
steps chiselled in the rock, all full of snow, and the shrouded
hulk of the ruin above, its gaping window like a cavity in old
bone.

The soldier reached for the staff, to take the light from her.

'Bring him,' he said.

The novice held on.

'He's hurt,' she said. 'I can't.'

'Yes. Bring him down.'

'He's very heavy. I can't carry him. Please, you must come.'

The soldier reached up and unhooked the lantern.

'No,' she protested.

'Go up,' he said.

'I need the light,' she said, trying to take it back.

He held it away from her, high above his head, splashing the
raw face of the rock with a yellow glow. He gestured with his
chin.

Planting her staff before her, the novice began to climb the steps. The light rushed up around her, swaying as he followed. She looked down, wanting to tell him not to crowd her; but she went on up, and he too, less readily.

The hermitage door was ajar. All was dark within. The soldier held up the lantern to look between the sagging shutters.

'He's lying down,' the novice told him. She made to go in. The soldier lunged at her, pulling her aside. Then, lantern in one hand, sword in the other, he stood on the broken step and pushed at the door with his foot.

The door creaked and gave a little. Dirt, or something, sifted down from the gaping roof.

The Eschalan started slightly, hesitated; went in.

The novice held her breath.

Narrow fingers of light came combing through the decrepit shutters.

'No one,' he said.

She went in.

He turned accusingly, like a demon of annunciation, lighting the ruined hut, revealing nothing, nothing but a bare cot and a rusty dish. The sky above the roof was black.

She looked around, disbelieving, baffled. 'He must be outside. I don't know where he's gone.'

She held the staff with both hands, across herself.

He hit it hard with the flat of his sword.

She dropped it; bent for it; found his sword in the way. She stood up, her arms spread.

'I expect he'll be back any moment,' she said, quickly and quite loudly.

The soldier went to the door and looked outside. The novice went too, as though to follow him out, but he turned and directed her back in.

'Please,' she said. 'I don't know.'

He looked at the cot, then at her, then at the cot. He set the lantern down on the floor and picked up her staff.

He poked her in the belly with the end of it. He gave a little grunting laugh, then threw the stick off-handed, out of her reach. He said something in Eschalan.

He tweaked the hem of her robe with the tip of his sword.

The novice skipped back into the corner, pinning the cloth of her robe between her knees.

'No,' she said.

He sheathed the sword. He came at her, embraced her.

She drew in her head and tried to push him away with her arms.

He kissed her, lavishly. He smelt sour, his mouth was foul. She felt his hand sliding up her leg.

She pulled out the knife and stuck it between his ribs. It was all the way in before she knew.

He hugged her tight.

Seen close to, his face was waxy and pale as cheese. He gazed into her eyes and spasmed, and seemed to be choking on something.

Then it all started to dribble out of his mouth. She broke his clasp and drew back from him. The knife stayed where it was.

He fell down her, bleeding. She put out her hand, but let him fall to the floor, where he lay shuddering. He kicked the old dish and it rolled clattering into a corner.

She picked up the lantern.

She heard noises then in the clearing below, people moving about. Someone shouted her name.

She bent to pick up her staff.

The Eschalan made a sort of squealing noise; then he stopped. She looked at him. There really was quite a lot of blood.

Banner Marchan rushed wildly in, sword drawn. He looked at her, then at the body, swearing hoarsely and at length. Faces peered in at the door and window.

Serin gave a yelp and threw herself into his arms.

'His friend gave us trouble.'

At the guard-post she saw that his gigantic firearm had done no good to the sentry who had stayed on duty. It stood propped over the brazier, its works blackened, its stock burnt away. Of the fusilier himself there was no sign.

They rode down through the slush of Rowe, Serin in her uncle's sled with Friano Lydam. No householders appeared at the windows to see who was passing. What with the market by day and the military by night, there was altogether too much going on in the street for any of it to merit their attention.

At the aqueduct the raiders parted, these to the primacy, those to guard the escape. Bela's party took cover while Banner Marchan delivered his niece to the sisters' gate.

'Are you sure?' he asked her.

She gave him a look of affectionate scorn.

He gave her the knife back, clean.

The primacy was silent and still. Serin knocked and woke the porter, who opened the postern. She was a stumpy old woman with hardly any hair.

'Who are you?' she asked as Serin stepped inside. 'What are you doing in our robe?'

'The bishop and Sister Annina sent me,' Serin told her. Neither of them had, strictly speaking, but it was simpler than the long explanation.

'What do you want?' asked the woman, blinking crossly. 'It's the middle of the night,' she added, rather superfluously.

'Where are the prisoners?'

'In the dorter.'

'How many guards?'

'Six. Two at the door, two at each end of the passage.' She hesitated. 'What are you going to do?'

'Whatever we can,' said Serin. 'You can go back to bed now. There'll be some noise and some upset, but you'll be all right if you stay put. Don't get up until it's all over.'

She turned to raise the bar of the gate.

The porter stood biting her lip. Then she came and lent her weight.

'I want to help,' she said.

Serin thought for a moment. 'Can you keep the orange away from the dorter?'

'I could lock a few doors.'

'Go on. Then hide.'

The porter glanced at the dark figures approaching from the sled, then said: 'Good luck,' and ran in to get her keys.

As the others made for the dorter, Banner drove on past and into the grove. He dropped Serin at the cemetery gate, and turned the sled.

'Give me two fifths,' she told him. Then she put up her hood again, and walked quickly into the Garden of Eternal Regret.

The monuments that leaned towards her were doubly shrouded in snow and in darkness. Serin gave them hardly a glance. Their gestures of wistful admonishment seemed to be addressed to a vanished time, one when death could be contemplated and accepted, when it did not come marching up to your door to drag you away through the midnight streets.

Clumps of snow hung dimly from the branches like fungal excrescences. Serin saw one that resembled a rotted cauliflower, and another for all the world like a monstrous white owl. Then she looked again, and saw it was the head of a man.

Everything went blurred for a moment, and Serin thought she would faint, but she slumped back against a tree with her eyes closed, biting her hand. When her heart had recovered, and the world was steady once more, she made herself look out.

The head had not moved. It was not facing her. In her own head there was shrieking and shouting, but the scene was frozen, without a sound.

If he was not hanged, then he was sitting up in the tree, which was not, Serin thought, something any Esch would do. No one that white could be an Esch anyway. She looked at him, and then she cupped her hands to her mouth and gave a long, low mournful whistle.

His cry came floating to her through the trees.

'Arethusa!'

She ran to stand beneath his perch. His bald head peered down between black branches like a mad moon.

'It *is* you,' she said.

'How did you know I was here?' he asked excitedly.

'I didn't,' she said. 'I thought you were – I thought – ' She turned away from him suddenly, looking at all the headstones and shivering.

'Yes,' he said, unabashed. 'I thought the same of you! Are you safe? Are you all right?'

'Oh, yes,' she said. 'I'm one step ahead of the Esch, I haven't had any sleep, I'm frazzled to a flinder and I think I'm going mad, but I'm all right really. How – are you?' she finished, somewhat uncertainly.

'The strangest things have happened since you left me at the fair,' he told her.

'I didn't – well, I suppose I did, but I couldn't help it. I was kidnapped. I'm in an awful hurry,' she said, apologetically, but still hesitated, gazing up at him.

'Have you seen any dogs?' he asked.

'Dogs? There are dogs on my uncle's sled.'

'They're not after me, are they?'

'No,' she said, perplexed.

'Then I think I'll come down,' he said, and dropped lightly to the ground in front of her. He rubbed snow from his bare hands. 'Are you running away too?'

'No – I'm going to try to get into the palace.'

'That sounds interesting. Everyone will be asleep, won't they, seeing as it's night? May I come?'

She opened her mouth to deny him; but instead said, 'Well, yes! Why not? But we must hurry. And you must be quiet, and do exactly as I say.'

'Always, Arethusa,' he said happily, and took her arm. 'I was intending to go back to the Hyacinth House when it grew dark,' he told her as they hastened through the snow. 'It was the only place I could think of to go – rather like a wolf returning to its lair, you know. The only place I have ever really been happy, as far as I recall. Happiest when you were there, Arethusa! But it's very nice here, isn't it?'

Serin said only: 'Hush.'

She walked him quickly out of the cemetery, and along the avenue to the bottom of the palace garden, where she looked around.

'All right,' she whispered. 'I don't think there's anyone about.'

'Oh, there isn't,' he said confidently. 'I can see exceptionally well in the dark now – much better than I used. Is that the palace?'

'Yes, but we're not going straight there. This way,' she said, and led him around into frozen shrubbery.

'Who kidnapped you, Arethusa? Did you steal this gown? It looks very warm.'

'It's Sister Annina's,' Serin said. 'I didn't really steal it.'

'Who is Sister Annina?'

'She ministers to the montanos.'

'Ah, so you did go with them. But why did they knock me down?'

'They were frightened,' she said.

'So was I,' he replied.

'Look, it's all a bit complicated to explain now,' said Serin, 'but what's happening now is that there are some other montanos, my uncle and his friend, and we're going to try to rescue the princess. I have to go to the palace and open the door.'

'Won't you need a key?'

'We're after one now,' she said. 'Annina's brother has one.'

They stopped outside a small pavilion made all of glass. Inside Serin could just about see piles of tools, and the shapes of plants bundled up in sacking.

'Is he here?' her companion asked doubtfully.

'No, but the key is.'

She tried the door. At first she thought it was locked, but then realised there was ice gumming up the frame. She tugged at the handle without success.

'Shall I try?' he offered.

'It's stuck,' she said.

He pulled on the handle, forced his fingertips into the crack of the door, and prised it free. Serin winced, but it did not seem to have hurt him.

'Do you know where to look?'

'There should be a sort of table with two drawers.'

'There is.'

'Have a look in the right-hand drawer.'

Under a large pair of scissors lay a small iron key.

'That must be it.'

She took it up, and as an afterthought the scissors too. 'I've got a knife,' she said. 'Do you want these?'

'Do we need them?'

'In case we have to fight.'

'Oho, look!' The old man opened his coat and proudly showed the Eschalan sword.

Serin wondered if he would have the first idea how to use it. She hoped they wouldn't find out.

He looked so odd in the darkness of the glass pavilion. His painted face seemed to be glowing slightly. Luminous paint, she thought. But it seemed to be glowing through the paint.

'We should cover our faces.'

She pulled on her cowl, then reached to help him turn up the broad wings of his collar. Her hands brushed over his otter tippet. It was falling apart. But she fluffed up the rotten fur, wondering if it made him look any more respectable, more normal even. The effect was fairly macabre. She paused, her hands against his cold cheeks. He raised his own hands and laid them lightly over hers. His eyes shone in the snowlight.

Serin snatched her hands away.

'We have to go.'

Fresh snow covered the gravel paths. They hurried up between dim lawns. There was a lantern at the door of the palace, and an Eschalan soldier in the porch. He hadn't seen them.

'Don't say anything,' whispered Serin. 'Let me.'

The soldier was hunched half asleep. He did not challenge them until they were two yards off. 'Stop! Who are you?'

'I am Sister Jenise,' said Serin. 'This man is a doctor. The princess sent for us. Let us in.'

The soldier was unconvinced. 'Why in garden?'

'We had to get some herbs.'

He did not understand.

She turned to the flowerbeds. There was nothing but snow.

Along the terrace was something in an urn that looked as if it might still have some leaves on. She made a move towards it.

The sentry became alarmed. He pulled out his whistle.

Serin reached for her knife, but the old man had stepped lightly forward to place his hands on the guard's shoulders, looking intently into his face. The guard groped for his pistol; then his hands fell to his sides. His face looked as if he had had a great shock. He was gagging and gurgling.

Serin's nameless friend then set the finger and thumb of his left hand gently around the man's throat.

'Your sword!' cried Serin.

He did not seem to be listening. With a turn of his wrist he knocked the man's jaw up and aside, and dipped his face under it, as if to kiss him on the neck.

The noise they made between them was disgusting, but she stared and stared. The blood began to run down the old man's neck. It dripped into the black fur at his throat. He stopped a moment to lick his lips. His tongue was very long and muscular. It was black, and glistening wet.

The blood kept welling from the soldier's neck. It ran down among the trodden snow. The wild man fell to feeding again, his eye rolling over Serin like a dog's, not knowing her.

It took him a long, long time to finish. Then he laid the body thoughtfully in the snow, out of the light, out of the way of the door.

'Is it done?' whispered Serin. Her heart was beating faster than she'd ever known. She felt her own blood battering beneath her cold, tight skin.

He said only: 'The key!' His mouth gaped wide in vast soundless laughter. There was blood all over his chin and down his front.

Somehow she got the key into the keyhole and opened the door.

His arm about her, they peered into a dim vestibule. A huge marble staircase wound up into the darkness.

'My uncle will be here any minute. Perhaps we should wait.'

'Do you know where the princess sleeps?'

She nodded.

'Then let us find her without delay!'

He glided past her into the hallway, prowling across and leaping up to cling to the banisters. All his movements had a feral energy and grace she had not seen in him before. She tiptoed to the stairs, hardly noticing her surroundings, watching him.

He vaulted one-handed over the banister and sprang lithely on to the step above her.

'How mavellous!' he said. His voice was strong and vibrant.

'Hush!'

He sniggered, and swept her up in his arms.

'Arethusa, I feel – I feel – Oh, I don't know *what* I feel! Kiss me, Arethusa.'

She struggled to free her gaze from his, found her body limp and unresponsive to her will.

'Are you afraid?' he murmured.

'You'll bite me.'

'Indeed I shan't,' he said. 'Come.'

Still she strained away. 'There's blood on your mouth!'

'Your enemy's blood, Arethusa. Your enemy that is no more.'

'Well – wipe it off, then.'

Gently he set her down, and smeared his sticky mouth with the sleeve of his coat.

Then she was in his arms again, his lips cool upon hers.

—10—

Wax and Wane

Princess Nette sat in bed, turning a folded paper back and forth between her fingers, but not opening it.

'How did you come by this, Vittore?'

He answered her vaguely, as if the thing were a matter of distant and unparticular memory. 'I – ah – happened to be at the gate, Highness, at the time: I mean when it was delivered . . .'

'Just now.'

'Yes, Highness.'

'Indeed,' she said carelessly, still toying with the letter. 'Have you added volunteer night porter to the list of. your many duties?'

'I was merely consuming an idle hour,' he said, apparently with some difficulty, 'watching the road – seeing who might come – and go; as it were.'

'As it were,' said the princess. She held the letter across her face and regarded him keenly over the top of it. 'What is in this? Do you know?'

He stood uncomfortably by the bed. 'I couldn't possibly imagine, Highness.'

At last she cracked the wax with her nail, unfolded the paper and glanced over its contents, then handed it back to her visitor.

'Read it to me, Crespian.'

Warily he took the letter as if afraid it might burn him, then fished a pair of spectacles from his pocket, unfolded them and positioned them on the bridge of his nose.

'*His Estimability Lan olang –*'

'No – sit down and read it. Not there: here.'

Princess Nette patted the bed as if enticing a cat, then drew up her feet and hugged her knees like a young girl.

'Thank you, ma'am . . . personal honour . . .' he mumbled as he sat stiffly on the eiderdown, and began to read:

His Estimability Lan olang to Her Royal Highness Nette Princess of Luscany: Greetings. My thanks for concerning yourself with the work of the Moonshee Charan du, who assures me he will take greater care to avoid inconveniencing you in future. My apologies for my inability to wait upon you in the morning, but I am on the track of the beast that slew the imperial herald: an old man frail in appearance and most mild in manner, but possessed of savage powers quite unknown to nature. I must seek the help of the illustrious Professor Jonal, though I fear there is more here than even his sciences can explain. It is a creature most obdurate to death. Beware it, I beg of you. On my return, I shall indeed wish to discuss the mountaineers, especially in respect of their preferred funeral rites, for some appear to have died in custody.

For the space of a heartbeat, Princess Nette did not speak. Then she said calmly, 'Do *you* know of this improbable monster, Crespian?'

'I fear not, Highness.'

'Then why not stay a little and tell me what you do know?' she said; and looking across at Thisbe, with a smile quite unlike her expression earlier: 'Goodnight, Thisbe. You may leave us now.'

Doing her best to conceal shock and confusion, the princess's maid began to sidle from the room.

'Oh, and Thisbe?'

'Yes, ma'am?'

'Don't forget your promise.'

'Yes, ma'am. I mean, no, ma'am. Goodnight, ma'am.'

'Goodnight, Thisbe. Crespian?'

'Yes, madam?'

'Say goodnight to Thisbe.'

'Oh. Ah. Goodnight, ah – Thisbe.'

'Goodnight, sir.'

Plainly of the opinion that her mistress was in a most unusual humour tonight, Thisbe escaped from the chamber.

'Now. Crespian,' said Princess Nette, pronouncing his name most precisely, as she lay back and stretched out her legs under the covers. 'You were about to tell me what it is you know.'

The underscrivener swallowed.

'About what, Your Highness?'

'About everything,' she answered languidly. 'About the day and the night, the orange and the white, the comings and the goings . . . Whom did you see while you were at the gate? . . .'

'Why, no one but an old seller of roast chestnuts, madam . . . a drunkard who had lost one snowshoe . . . a party of those women who gather at the Dreisepont and accost unwary strollers . . .'

'Harlots, were they?'

'I believe so, madam.'

'How strange, to make one's living so.' The princess reflected. 'What is the attraction, do you suppose? Surely they do not continue to enjoy it?'

'I imagine they know no better, madam; or have no choice,' said the underscrivener thickly. He cleared his throat and looked down at his pale, fine hands.

'Might it not be freedom, of a sort?' she speculated.

He did not immediately understand her.

'To be used by all men, but possessed by none,' she elaborated.

'I think it is more usual for several women to work under a single man – as it were,' he said, colouring.

'As it were,' she echoed.

'A master, who assumes responsibility for them, and protects them.'

'In return for most of their earnings, no doubt. What sort of men are they, though, who have recourse to these women? Do you know that?'

'Soldiers; transients; husbands out of favour with their wives,' hazarded Vittore. 'The young who feel themselves unloved; the elderly who know it is so.'

'Why, Crespian,' smiled the princess, 'you are a perfect compendium of knowledge. Have *you* ever hired the service of a harlot?'

'I may have done,' he said rapidly, not looking her in the face, '– years ago – I don't recall . . .'

'Why, were you too drunk? Or have your amorous escapades been so numerous you've lost track?' She wriggled pleasurably.

'I wish you would not press me, madam.'

'*Do* you, Crespi? I don't think you do,' she said archly. She moved across to cuddle her legs against him beneath the covers. At first he tried to move away; then reluctantly, drawn by the intensity of her dark eyes, he met her gaze. He looked hunted, insecure.

'Madam,' he said reproachfully.

'Do you know what I should like, Crespian?'

'No, madam,' he said nervously.

'I should like to trade places with one of the Dreisepont women,' she said. 'Just for one day – or one night.'

There was a significant measure of relief in his agitation as he said, 'Primary forbid!'

'It's a vain whim,' she went on. 'I don't suppose I should like it really, you know.'

'Indeed not.'

'But it seems to me my life is not so different from theirs, in many essentials.'

He regarded her in baffled dismay.

'My life too,' she explained, 'must seem to many to be one of freedom and power, great power over others. Yet my work consists of an endless series of encounters with men, most of whom want something from me I am quite unable to give. Somehow, they exact satisfaction from me. I am what is required. Yet it is not me they come for at all.'

She looked at Vittore, who had not understood any of this, with a small frown of reflection. 'I am not sure that's quite what I meant to say.'

'Your Highness is a model to us all,' he said placatingly.

'There you are, you see?' she said. 'That's it exactly.'

But he didn't. 'Madam,' he announced, 'I must beg to take my leave of you.'

'Why?'

'My presence is required elsewhere.'

'Where?'

'At the gate.'

'You have an appointment?'

'Yes.'

'With a woman from the Dreisepont.'

'No!'

'With another.'

'Yes. That is, no.'

'You said you were there in all idleness.'

'So I was,' he said helplessly. 'But there are things there I left unfinished, when His Estimability's letter arrived.'

'What sort of things?'

'Things,' he temporised, 'which are altogether unworthy of Your Royal Highness's attention.'

'You seem,' said the princess cautiously, 'to be almost ashamed of these things, whatever they are.'

'Trifles,' he said wildly. 'Nothing, nothing at all.'

'Then they cannot be so urgent as to rob me of your company,' she said decisively.

'Oh, but madam,' he said; then lapsed into a fretful silence. He stared unhappily at her clavicles.

When she reached over to adjust the lamp, his eyes avoided the bodice of her nightgown. 'Let me do that for you, madam,' he said quickly.

'No thank you, Vittore,' she said steadily. 'I can manage it. There is a certain small pleasure in doing things for myself, you know, now and again.'

Vittore fiddled with one of his rings as though it had suddenly begun to irritate his finger.

'I should not be here with you like this,' he said weakly.

'How, then?'

'I mean it is improper. What will people say?'

'They will say the princess is very properly paying some attention at last to her most devoted servant, Crespian Vittore,' she replied. She settled back in her bed, in a nest of shadows. The gentle light at her side softened her features and seemed to bring a little warmth into the chilly room. 'Are you not my most devoted servant?'

'Of course, Your Highness.'

'Then do as I say.'

But she said nothing then for some minutes. She lay looking upwards into the gloom as though listening for something; and Vittore for his part sat attentive to her breathing, like a prisoner waiting for his warder to fall asleep.

'How still the night is,' she said at last. 'One could fancy the whole city carried off by wolves – or sudden plague – or all frozen where they lie . . .'

'Highness,' he chided her gently. 'It is not healthy to entertain such thoughts before sleep. You will give yourself a nightmare. Would you like me to read to you?' he went on, briskly. 'Did I not hear the maid reading to you when I arrived? What was that?'

'A military memoir,' she said. 'It is all violence and bloodshed now, all!'

In a panic he cried, 'They mean you no harm, Highness, I swear!'

Calmly she asked, 'Whom do you speak of, Crespian?'

'Why, of – of – these phantoms, these fancies that frighten you . . .'

'Will you protect me from them?'

'Trust me, madam.'

'Then lie here beside me.'

He acquiesced.

She raised herself on one elbow to look down at him.

'Would you not prefer to take off your boots?'

He sat up to do so. And when he lay down again he found her arms about him.

In an upper room at the posthouse Charan du saw the fourth member of his conclave admitted, then ordered the door to be shut and no one to disturb them. His mood was black as he took his seat, surveying the faces around the fire.

Ap riuli's broad, blank brow and deep-set eyes were as stolid as ever. But Ap riuli would laugh and talk, and it was then that his character and his consent would be revealed, in the snapping of his even, tiny teeth. Charan du was sure of Ap riuli.

Tega kesel might be more of a problem. She was young, the only one younger than Charan du himself, and presumably ambitious, being postmistress of a capital city so early in her third decade. She wore her hair fashionably short on top and long about the ears. Yet her signifying features were her narrow, pinched-looking nostrils and her long chin. She was a being without passion, a woman of intellect, not action, propriety, not daring. Her support was crucial. He would have it, he thought, if he could convince her that the gain would be the guild's, not glory for him alone.

His only real opponent would be Aten lo, the imperial nuncio. With his high cheekbones and his judicial little beard, he was the very soul of calculation and discretion. He would be the man who would have to account to the emperor for whatever happened tonight and tomorrow. Unless he could be sure he was not betraying His Supremacy's directions to the province, Aten lo would prefer that nothing happened. He was openly scathing of the featherbrain Lan olang, yet he would never countenance anything that resembled rebellion. He sipped gilliflower wine and looked, as did they all, to Charan du, their firebrand colleague, to begin.

Charan du stroked his rat, curled on his lap, drowsy from the heat.

'I have spoken to the princess,' he told them.

'And?' said Aten lo, setting down his glass.

'She resists us still.'

'I knew it.' Aten lo sat back, his fists on his knees. 'You alarm her with your wild advances. These northerners have a delicate pride. You are too bold.'

'It is time to be bold,' said Charan du, immediately angered. 'We must be bolder yet.'

The imperial nuncio gave a sharp sigh of exasperation and spat into the flames. 'Women require subtlety,' he said, not loudly. He had said all this before.

Ap riuli laughed and caught Tega kesel's eye. The postmistress's expression did not change.

'How does Her Royal Highness enact this resistance?' asked Ap riuli. 'Will she alert her gypsy friends?'

'I think she will find that difficult now,' said Tega kesel. 'You moved swiftly enough there, Ap riuli. It was well done.'

'And conclusive,' added Charan du, keen to invoke their friendship as soon as possible.

Ap riuli waved a fleshy hand. 'A scrawny handful of miners eluded us. This marvellous weather will do the job for us!'

'But if they reach the main camp,' objected Tega kesel.

'So much the better,' said the signaller. 'They know nothing. They will spread fear and dismay.'

She looked doubtful.

'I understand the whereabouts of the main camp is confirmed,' said Aten lo.

Ap riuli stirred his wine with his finger. 'Our man's body was found at dusk on the road below Scarpine.'

Tega kesel lifted one hand in a gesture of despair. 'They might be anywhere up there.'

'But they are cornered,' said Ap riuli. 'The lower slopes are impassable now.'

'Then you may starve them out,' she concluded. 'Are they not dependent on support from Peirruich?'

'Consider, Tega kesel,' said Charan du, 'these gypsies are little more than animals. They grub subsistence from the frozen soil. Where crows and wild dogs can survive,' he pronounced with distaste, 'the montanos also can.' He seemed to have forgotten the formidable scavenger he was at that moment fondling.

'More to the point,' Aten lo broke in, 'they delight in this weather. I think you are wrong to be so confident of your fugitive miners, Ap riuli. I think you should crush them at once.' He pinched finger and thumb together, as if snuffing out a candle. The signaller blinked slowly and insouciantly. The nuncio did not pursue the point, but reached for the tampoy. 'More wine?' And Ap riuli held out his glass.

Charan du fumed with impatience at these civilities. 'I disagree,' he said, addressing Ap riuli. 'Waste no shot on the stragglers. It is on Scarpine that we must concentrate our efforts. The princess – '

'You have failed with the princess,' interrupted Aten lo.

'Not at all, respected colleague. I gave her a warning, and an opportunity, which she chose to reject. She does not appreciate which way the wind is blowing. She is mistaken.' Charan du smiled, to show he had everything under control.

'Letters passed between her and the prefect this evening,' said Tega kesel.

'What was the matter of them?' asked Aten lo.

'A complaint from Her Royal Highness against our colleague Charan du, as I heard it,' she said. 'In reply, an assurance of good behaviour in future.'

Ap riuli laughed hugely at this; and Charan du smiled wryly, seeking to turn the jest to advantage. 'His Estimability confides in me his concern that I may have treated Her Highness with insufficient diplomacy. Then, knowing my scorn for this mad goose, he rides off to visit the even madder professor and leaves me behind! What wondrous conference the two sages must be enjoying.'

He was gratified to see Aten lo smile slightly at this.

'Chaos!' guffawed Ap riuli.

'Which the guild will have back in order by the time he returns,' said the interpreter simply, and replenished all their glasses.

'Tonight?' queried the postmistress. 'My agenda for tonight had contained nothing more enterprising than sleep.'

Charan du detected an undertone of deference to him, perhaps to appease a touch of guilt for having mentioned the letters. And Aten lo would be happier to talk in these terms than any the bluffly seditious Ap riuli might introduce. This was his moment.

'The messengers are alert at all hours,' he said to Tega kesel, charmingly. 'Alert to travesties of correct administration – ' (That for Aten lo.) '– to enemies without and within.' (And that for Ap riuli.) 'We have offered Princess Nette the gloved hand and she has refused it. Now is the time to remove the glove, to use the naked hand.'

'It's the middle of the night,' demurred the imperial nuncio, who was indeed visibly flagging.

'A good time,' said Charan du vigorously, 'an excellent time, to arrest the princess.'

He scratched the rat behind its ears. Lazily it flexed a pink claw.

Aten lo grunted with surprise, but raised no objection.

'To arrest Princess Nette? On what charge?' asked Tega kesel.

'On suspicion of instigating the murder of Tumak coh,' said Charan du.

'Is that probable?' she asked.

'I should think a case could be constructed,' he replied, 'from the testimony of your interrogated witnesses, could it not, Ap riuli?'

'We could get some of that lot to say anything,' answered the signaller cheerily.

This was not quite the tone of response the interpreter would have preferred. 'In any event,' he said smoothly, 'the actual charge is not so important as bringing the power of the crown securely under the power of the Empire.' He glanced quickly at Aten lo to see how he was taking this.

The fine patrician face showed no discernible reaction in the firelight, but Aten lo spoke then. 'Well,' he said. 'Well, well, well.' And, after a pause and a sip of wine: 'Other than appeasing your own sense of grievance, ambitious colleague, what would this imposition actually accomplish?'

'It will instruct Her Highness that her realm is a possession of Eschaly, and that she herself is answerable to our administration. It will enable us to set out to parley with the montanos at first light, before they realise we even suspect their hiding place.

They will not dare ignore or attack a party that includes their monarch. Their loyalty is unquestioning. The princess will speak for us, and they will obey. We may, through her, require of them what concessions and hostages we choose. Thereafter, when they are fallen into despondency and disarray, we may crush them at our leisure.'

There was no reply to this, not even from the imperial nuncio, who sat contemplatively turning his glass in his fingers.

'For too long,' continued the interpreter quietly, 'we have striven to weaken and dilute the power of the Luscan throne. We have been encouraged in this policy by having the throne occupied by a young woman unused to the wielding either of statecraft or of the sword. The vicious destruction of the imperial herald, Tumak coh, and the sorrily wayward response of the prefect show us that we have become lax; that this policy, among others, has been a policy of weakness, not strength. Now it is time to reverse this decay, to acknowledge the power still vested in the principality by the loyalty of its subjects; to seize that power and master it, before what has happened in Nairi happens here.'

He paused for a heartbeat, sure he held them all in the palm of his hand; then he said, '*Now* is the time: this very hour.' He drained his glass and rose, the dozing rat under his arm. 'Who rides with me to the palace?'

'I'll fetch a squad,' said Ap riuli.

Charan du forestalled him. 'The less disturbance, the less difficulty. Three or four of us will do better than a host under arms.'

'Then let it be three,' said Aten lo, getting up slowly, 'for I'm away to my bed.'

He did not wish them good luck, or offer any other pronouncement; and Charan du had the greatest of pleasure in bidding him courteously goodnight.

As the nuncio was escorted from the room by his curate, Charan du addressed the others. 'I trust you are both still with me. I will not have it said tomorrow that the headstrong Charan du assaulted the palace on some impetuous folly all of his own!'

'I'm coming,' said Ap riuli, snapping his fingers for his coat.

'Tega kesel?'

'Fatigue almost persuades me to emulate the nuncio,' she replied, 'but let us see this thing properly done. How shall we get into the palace without great alarm and outcry?'

He smiled, and handing the rat to a servant, ushered them out to the stairs.

'My associate Crespian Vittore has instructions to meet us at the gate.'

Crespian Vittore, the underscrivener and spy, lay rigid in the arms of the princess. She stroked his fair, flossy hair. In the darkness her fingers found the end of his plait and began to undo it.

'My mother . . .' she said.

'Her Royal Grace the Archduchess,' he responded.

'Yes. Do you and she ever talk about me?'

'Sometimes.'

'What do you say?'

'It is her way, you know, madam. To be – critical.'

'Yes. She tells me I know too little of men.'

He did not reply.

She combed out his hair between her fingers. She stroked the nape of his neck.

'Tonight you will teach me something, won't you, Crespi?' she murmured fondly.

'If – I can, madam.'

'You are so modest!' Princesse Nette hugged him, pressing his face between her breasts. Then suddenly she released him. 'Sit up. Let me look at you.'

She moved the lamp so that its light fell full on him. His hair hung down over his cheeks in soft disorder.

'For the Eschalans,' she remarked, 'it is a gross offence to appear before a superior with one's mane unbraided. But I imagine you knew that, didn't you?'

'I – believe – I had heard – something of the sort,' he said, trying to tidy his hair and tuck it behind his ears. His voice was jerky, as if there were some constraint upon it.

'You're so knowledgeable, Crespian, so thoroughly primed on all points. I am sure you know a great deal,' she said, setting down the lamp and taking his hands, 'about women.'

'All too little, I fear,' he replied, with an attempt at brightness; and he shivered.

'Are you cold, Crespian?' she asked, sympathetically. 'So am I. We shall be warm enough in a while, shan't we? But first I fear we must make you colder yet.'

She unfastened his yellow stock and began to unbutton his waistcoat.

'Slip off your jacket,' she said. 'That's better. Now hold me.'

The princess knelt up out of the covers and pressed herself against him, her cheek on his shoulder. He put his arms about her.

'No one has held me since I was a little girl.'

'Your Highness, I – '

'Don't speak, Crespian. Don't speak a word; for I can hear by your voice you are about to protest again, to say that this is wrong. What is it?' she asked, wriggling suddenly free. 'Don't you like me? Is there something wrong with me? Am I not as other women are?'

She was in earnest for an answer. His arms bore the warm memory of the form beneath her gown.

'You are the loveliest in all Luscany,' he said awkwardly. 'It is only that, that – Highness, I fear – '

But she would not let him speak. She put her hand upon his mouth; then took it away, and replaced it with her own mouth. Her lips were moist and firm. She kissed him. He roused himself, endeavoured to respond, but she had drawn away again, and he would not, could not reach for her to draw her back. She was once more busy at her unbuttoning.

She removed his waistcoat, stroking her hands down his shoulder-blades; she took his left arm and then his right, removing his cuffs and planting a small kiss in the centre of each palm as she did so; she unfastened his shirt and reached inside to feel his woollen undershirt.

'This is warm,' she said. 'But it must come off, for tonight we must uncover the inner Crespian, the real man!'

She tugged at his shirt where it was tucked in; then, with a look at him half mischievous, half sly, reached to unbuckle his belt and loosen the waistband of his breeches; and she let her hands linger a little on the buckle, and a trifle below the buckle. Then she had the shirt off, and the undershirt, and had wrapped her arms around his smooth chest, hearing the racing, skipping of his heart and smelling the smell of him, which she thought reminded her of clean straw.

'How many women have you held like this, Crespian? A childhood sweetheart, a scullery maid, the buxom daughter of some country duke? But I must not ask, must I? It is not proper, and you are a proper man and will never, ever tell.'

'Not to a soul, madam.'

'I admire you for your secrecy. Oh, I know you may not think so, but it's true. I know I can always trust you.'

'Madam, I only wish – ' he began, and gasped as she grazed his nipple with her teeth. 'I wish – I were w-worthy . . .'

'That we shall see,' she said, rubbing her hand in circles on his belly, letting the tips of her fingers stray into the top of his open breeches. He gave a small moan and convulsively tangled his fingers in her long black hair as she nuzzled his throat. 'We shall see,' she said, in a muffled voice, 'how worthy you can be. Let me take these off,' she said, pulling at his breeches.

Crespian Vittore slumped back on the bed and raised his hips, pushing his breeches down while Princess Nette pulled them. It took a while. At last she stood with them in her hand, and tossed them carelessly on to the pile of his other things. He lay sprawled in his woollen trews and silk stockings, propping himself up on his elbows now and smiling foolishly at her.

The princess knelt to unfasten his garters.

He struggled to sit up. 'Madam, you must not kneel!'

She raised her head and looked up between his knees. 'I must do what pleases me,' she said mildly. 'Is that not so? Pleasure? Do you not speak,' she went on as she drew off his right stocking, 'of a man pleasuring a maid?' She drew off his left stocking. 'Is that not what we are about, do you think?' The stockings joined the rest.

'Now,' she said. 'Stand up. Stand there, by the foot of the bed.'

He rose, a little hesitantly. She smoothed the bedclothes where he had lain and hopped up to sit cross-legged there, her night-dress drawn taut between her knees. She gave him a beautiful smile.

'Take off your trews,' she said.

Shivering violently now, he did so, and stood naked on the crimson rug, holding them before him in both hands.

'Put them down. Let me see you.'

She looked him over coolly, almost dispassionately.

'My. So that is a man.'

He held out his arms to her.

She raised a monitory forefinger. 'Not yet, Crespian. There is something we must do first. Kneel.'

'H-Highness?'

'Kneel down. Your boots are there somewhere, aren't they?'

He nodded, fumbling under the bed, looking up at her all the while.

'Take the laces out,' she told him. 'Give them to me.' From her voice it might have been the most commonplace instruction in the world.

With shaking fingers he picked the thongs free. He stood up and handed them dumbly to her.

'Now go to the foot of the bed and stand with your back against the bedpost. Clasp your hands behind you.'

Swiftly she tied his wrists together, then tied them to the bedpost.

'What is it, Highness? A game? A – joke?' For all his terror, he strove to be pleasant.

'Now I have you where I want you, Vittore. Where I've wanted you for a long time.'

The princess ran her hands lightly down his arms, down his flanks, kneeling before him to caress him all the way down to the ground. Then she ran her hands up behind him, caressing his buttocks either side of the bedpost; and began again at his feet, stroking up the inside of his legs.

Suddenly he blurted out, 'Your Highness, I cannot let you do this. I am not loyal to you. For years I have been receiving money from the prefect's interpreter, Charan du.'

The princess stood up. 'I know,' she said.

Tears were running down his face, glistening in the lamplight.

'He is coming to carry you off,' he said hoarsely. 'This very night! I was to be at the gate to let him in.'

Princess Nette went to the dressing stand. She took up a hairbrush.

'I thought it must be something of the kind,' she said. She began to brush her hair with long deliberate strokes.

'He will force his way in,' whimpered Vittore. 'You must flee!' He gave a small cry. 'I hear him in the corridor!'

There were indeed footsteps outside, approaching at a run, but they did not sound like the Eschalan interpreter's.

Whoever it was knocked at the door, and, before the princess could answer, opened it.

A pale, thin young girl stood there, dressed in a charcoal-coloured robe. Behind her came an old man in a long, shabby black coat, its hem wet with snow. He had dark stains of something smeared about his mouth.

'Your Highness,' began the girl, but said no more, gaping at Vittore.

The princess was bewildered. 'What is it, sister? Who is this man?'

More hurrying footsteps. A pair of gypsies burst into the bedchamber, swords drawn.

Crespian Vittore gave a shriek. At once Princess Nette snatched something, his trews, from the bed and stuffed them forcefully into his mouth.

The younger of the gypsies smartly shut the door. The elder, a large, bearded fellow, crossed at a stride to the girl in grey, and put an arm about her with brusque affection. Then he saluted Princess Nette.

'Your Royal Highness,' he said fervently; and he and his comrade went down on one knee.

'I thought you would never come,' said the princess.

'We have a sled,' said the man. 'We must hurry. The orange – '

He stopped, disconcerted, at the sound of more footsteps. There was a knocking at the door.

'Madam? Madam?'

'It's all right, Thisbe,' said the princess loudly. 'Go back to bed. All's well.'

Throwing down the brush, she went quickly and dressed, and came back with a pair of boots and a cloak of wolf's fur. She sat on the bed. The sister ran to help her on with the boots, the stoutest she owned and richly lined. Then the princess stood, swept the cloak about her, and strode towards the door.

'Ma'am,' said the elder gypsy, 'what about – him?' He nodded at the naked courtier.

She looked briefly over her shoulder.

'Kill him,' she said.

Vittore gave a muffled cry. The montano drew a knife.

But the old man was there already, prancing on tiptoe out of the shadows. He flicked back his coat, and there was a sword in his hand.

Reaching the captive, he plucked the ridiculous gag out of his mouth. Yet Crespian Vittore made no sound, but stared into his face with wide and hopeless eyes, and did not cry out even when the ancient thrust with his sword and, in his first and only clumsy movement, twisted it up into the traitor's vitals.

Vittore sagged. The executioner withdrew his blade and, stepping back, wiped both sides on his sleeve.

Vittore's knees buckled. He slipped and, still pinned at the wrists, sat down heavily, all askew.

The royal party left him alone in the room, bleeding on the crimson carpet.

Charan du was impressed with the way Tega kesel rose to the challenge. Showing no sign of lethargy now, she clattered downstairs, rousing half her household and calling for the sleigh. Ap riuli, meanwhile, was thumping and banging around in the little pantry that did the posthouse for an armoury, cursing the page who stood nervously among the explosives holding a lamp. At the half-landing Charan du stopped, beckoned to the servant who was following him down with the tray and poured himself a last glass of tampoy, which he tossed back in a silent toast to victory: victory accomplished and victory ahead.

'Keep still, damn you!' roared Ap riuli in the armoury.

As Charan du came down the last flight, he saw an old man cross the hall and present the postmistress with something on a tray. 'Perfect,' she said, and smiled at Charan du, holding up a hefty pair of black iron handcuffs.

The interpreter passed on into the stableyard where they were lighting the carriage lamps and harnessing up a pair as white as the snow on the flagstones. The night was cloudy, the air stark with cold. Charan du jumped up into the driver's seat, rubbed his hands together and briskly pulled on a pair of stiff leather gauntlets. The ostler handed him up the reins, with copious instructions and admonishments. When at last Ap riuli and Tega kesel came bustling out, he waved the importunate woman aside. 'Yes, yes.'

She turned to motion a couple of staring stable-lads to open the gates. Charan du tugged the reins, flicked the lash, and off they jolted.

'Where do we take her?' called Tega kesel. 'Not to the prefecture!'

'We'll hold her here until morning,' Charan du called back. 'I shall teach her what's required of her. At first light we'll ride for

Peirruich and the mountains. The keenest escort you can muster, Ap riuli.'

'And a company behind to deal with any trouble,' replied the signaller. 'Confusion, but it's cold.' He slapped his arms.

The postmistress played with her handcuffs.

Soon they swung into Brinkway, the horses toiling valiantly up the hill, then past the Bunch of Chives and across the Aspen-pleyn, which looked yellow and grimy in the lamplight. A few desultory flakes of snow floated around the bunting, which no one had ordered to be taken down.

The ponderous silhouette of the Hall of Accomplishment loomed. Tega kesel drew their attention to it.

'What do we tell the prefecture?'

'Nothing!' exclaimed Ap riuli, and farted loudly.

She gave him a cross look. 'We must tell them something. We should tell them everything.'

'We shall,' Charan du assured them over his shoulder. 'But we shall send all the messages to His Estimability at the house of Diaz Jonal!'

The signaller began to chuckle appreciatively.

'If some of them go astray in the woods,' the interpreter continued, 'what a pity it will be!'

At the great gate of the royal palace of Luscany, however, they found nothing but icicles and silence. The postmistress shivered, and tucked her fur up over her chin. 'Where is your man?'

'Crespian Vittore has ever been both cautious and conscientious in my service,' Charan du reassured her. 'He will come shortly. Depend on it.'

They sat and waited in the cold and dark. A sharp little breeze blew flurries of loose snow about their heads. The horses started to grow restless.

'He's fallen asleep,' averred Ap riuli.

'No!'

'Perhaps he has mistaken the place or the time,' supposed Tega kesel. 'Perhaps he has been delayed by some unexpected duty.'

'There can be none at this hour,' said Charan du. 'At night the palace is like a citadel of the dead. The household take to their beds and sleep.'

'So might we,' yawned Ap riuli.

'Perhaps he has been here already, and the gate is secretly open,' Tega kesel suggested.

'That must be it,' agreed Charan du. He left the sleigh and leaned confidently on the gate, which remained nonetheless shut, as did the postern when he rattled its handle. As he returned to his companions, however, there came a light at the small window, and the postern opened, disclosing an elderly porter with a lantern.

Charan du hurried up to him. 'We are from the prefecture on urgent business. Please admit us at once.'

The porter shook his grey head. 'I've no orders.'

'Our business is with Underscrivener Crespian Vittore. Is he not here?'

'Mr Vittore? No, not these two hours past,' said the porter. 'And who may you be, sir?'

'I am Charan du, the prefectorial moonshee!' declared the Eschalan, affronted. 'Do you not recognise me?'

'Well now, sir,' said the man slowly, 'my eyes aren't as certain as they used to be, you know: not in the dark, and what with your hood, and all of you gentlemen being, beg your pardon, sir, much the same to look at . . .'

Charan du interrupted him. 'Please send for Crespian Vittore and tell him we are here.'

The porter regarded him, thoughtfully chewing his lip. 'That's not our procedure, sir, not in these cases. But if you like to wait a moment or two, I'll send the boy to wake the steward, sir, and he'll decide what's to be done. And he'll need to know the names of your companions too, sir, if you'd be so kind.'

'Why don't you ask them yourself?' Charan du replied haughtily. He turned aside, pulling off his gloves and tucking them under his belt.

The porter's face barely registered the rebuff; but he made no haste as he stepped out across the threshold, holding his lantern high.

Charan du held his knife higher, and brought it down. The old man pitched face forward into the snow, without a sound. The lantern went out. Charan du had already ducked in at the postern and was drawing the bar of the gate.

'That was not your man, I take it,' said Ap riuli, and drove the sleigh in.

Charan du, wedging one door, didn't bother to reply. Tega kesel jumped down and wedged the other.

Three Eschalan guards came running from the main building, but stopped, startled at the sudden appearance of three ministers in the courtyard. At a gesture from Charan du one of them hurried to unlock a door. Charan du pushed inside. The soldiers made to follow.

'Stay here,' Ap riuli ordered. 'Keep the gate open. If there's any trouble as we leave, deal with it.'

Led by Charan du, the three Eschalans went swiftly and noiselessly upstairs. In the corridor of the royal bedchamber a maid in mob-cap and nightdress peeked cautiously from her door, gasped, and immediately disappeared from view.

'Oho,' said Ap riuli, and stopped to try the doorknob. When he grasped it he heard a key turn. He bent down to look through the keyhole, but the key was in the way.

There was a cry. It was Tega kesel.

She and Charan du had gone on ahead. From the sound of it, all was not well in the princess's room. Had they been ambushed? Ap riuli cocked his pistol and crept up to the door.

There was no light in the chamber. The interpreter and the postmistress stood over a huddled shape: someone lying on the floor.

The signaller could see a lamp on a nightstand by the vacant bed. He lifted the glass, found lucifers and set a flame to it. 'Who is it?' he asked as the light flared. 'Is it the princess?' But the figure by the bed was a man, a Luscan, clad only in his own blood. His arms were canted oddly up behind his back.

Charan du rose, looked purposefully about the room, and seized on a jug of water. He dashed the contents full in the unfortunate's face.

'Where is she?'

The man gasped. Ap riuli had heard that gasp before, always from those who would shortly have no breath to gasp any more. As if in confirmation, the man's abdomen next heaved mightily and his mouth spewed black blood. Tega kesel's hand flew to her own mouth and she spun away from him. Ap riuli silently took her place, leaning over with his hands on his knees.

'Where is she?' Charan du demanded again.

The dying man foamed and frothed and shuddered. His head

reared up and fell, his face crumpled against the toe of the interpreter's boot.

'G-gypsies,' spluttered the bloody mouth; and then the face was still, like the face of a landed fish. The eyes stared fixedly at a view beyond this world.

Charan du withdrew his foot. He picked up something, some discarded garment, from the floor and wiped the blood and bile from his toe. After that he wiped spatters from his leg and from his hand, then let the rag fall.

'That, I take it, was your man,' said Ap riuli.

Once more Charan du did not deign to answer. He looked over at Tega kesel, who was vomiting in the corner. He did not speak to her either.

'Ap riuli,' he said at last, 'fetch a troop. Fifty of the best men. Join me on Scarpine. Tega kesel.' She stood up, composing herself. 'As soon as you are recovered, you may return to the posthouse and send a message to the prefect. The ice gypsies have kidnapped Princess Nette zan Herlach, and we have gone after.'

'Shall I send to the professor's house,' she asked, her voice low, 'or straight to the prefecture?'

'To confusion, for all I care,' he replied, calmly. He felt tired, tired in every fibre of his being. He left the bedchamber.

Ap riuli was standing at the end of the passage, looking out of the window. Through the black trees of the grove came a flickering orange glow.

'It looks as if they're at the primacy too,' the signaller observed.

Charan du turned sharply and walked away along the dark corridor.

──11──

A Restless Sound,
So Many Dead

Down an avenue of yews they sped. Serin's Uncle Banner sat poised over the haunches of his dogs, plying a black whip, looking from the back like some grey bear. Behind him sat Princess Nette in the fur of a wolf. She had had a naked man tied to the foot of her bed. 'Kill him,' she had said.

Serin had become tired and disconsolate. She looked at her companion, but there was no comfort there. He was still turned sideways in his seat, staring at her with that silly smile. The chill light of the snowbanks and the pallor of his own cheeks showed his make-up was flaking badly. Bits were falling off him. He had lip-wax and blood smeared all over his face.

Seeing him kill the man in the bedroom had not been like with the guard outside, not at all. Nor like the soldier up at the hermit's hut. The princess's man had been naked. He had been tied up. Serin wondered who he had been, what he had done, how he had threatened his mistress.

Seeing the old creature stab the naked man had been more like seeing what Lukas did to him at the fair, down beside the frozen river.

'*Arethusa*,' he whispered, grinning like a human skull.

As the primacy came into view, Serin knelt up on her seat. She saw a crowd of people milling out of a door. Most of them were women: some in grey robes, like her; some in the scarves and motley of the ice gypsies. There were violent cries, three shots, the breaking of wood.

'Mother!' yelled Serin. 'Mother!'

At the same time, Banner Marchan began to call for Streaky Bela.

Serin jumped off into the snow, to run to the building. The old man grabbed her. 'Arethusa!' Struggling, she unseated him. His grip was inflexible, but he weighed next to nothing.

The princess looked round, while Banner drove on.

'Bela!' he called.

People shouted to him, pointing.

Serin stood up, the old man clinging to her like a parcel of roots.

'Stay,' he begged her.

Wildly she tore herself free, ploughed a few steps further, then stood and gazed. None of the women was her mother.

A figure fell from an upper window. Before it landed she saw it was a man, an Eschalan.

Smoke began to billow through the broken glass.

People were fighting in the doorway. The gypsies were mounting up, two to a horse. Skiers raced for the grove.

Friano Lydam arrived on a palace horse. He shouted something Serin did not catch, gave her an exultant grin, and rode on to join the crowd around Banner and the princess.

Serin's supplicant hovered at her back, not touching her. 'Arethusa, the building is on fire!'

'If you want to help, go and find my mother,' said Serin.

He stared at her with his head on one side. From his open mouth came a melancholy hissing sound.

'Go on,' she commanded. '*You'*ll be all right.'

He drew his sword and waved it dangerously around his head. Leaping and bounding, off he went across the snow.

'Amber Guille!' Serin called. 'Ask for Amber Guille!' Then she took the knife out of her pocket and ran after him.

'Serin!'

Friano Lydam rode down upon her, snatched her under the arms and flung her across his horse. The knife went flying from her hand into the snow.

'Your uncle says you've done enough.'

She swore loudly at him, then subsided. 'At least – let me – sit up,' she panted, jolted at every pace.

'Soon as I can.'

They joined the exodus from the primacy, via the unguarded gate. Running people disappeared into the streets.

Under the viaduct, Friano reined in and took cover. 'Quick now.'

Serin grabbed the horse's neck and twisted round, throwing one leg across the withers. 'Go! Go!' she said, pushing herself upright.

They followed the rest of the band up out of the city. At the edge of the forest they stopped again and turned. No pursuit was evident.

'Did you see my mother?'

'No,' said Friano. 'Who was the old man? Your father's father?'

'No,' said Serin, then paused, wondering if he might be.

'Some old retainer of the palace, then. But he seemed to know you.'

'I don't know who he is.'

The horse snorted warm clouds in the darkness. Friano stared down the hill. 'Ha,' he said. 'Here's Banner.'

Torches could be seen coming smoothly across the meadow. Friano stood his horse away from the path, letting others pass while he and his passenger watched. When Banner and the princess arrived, escorted by four people on two horses, Friano rode out to greet them.

'Good raiding!' bellowed Banner Marchan. His face was red and perspiring as if he'd roasted it at the fire. 'Did you see them, Friano? Did you see them, Serin? No more idea than a burrow of coneys!' His team panted and ate great quantities of snow.

Streaky Bela rode off a way, to look down Rowe. He signalled. 'They're coming.'

Banner waved Friano on ahead. Serin stopped him.

'Where is she?' she asked her uncle.

Banner shook his head, saying nothing.

'Did they all get out?'

All he would say was: 'She wasn't there.'

Princess Nette sat behind him, saying nothing. She looked pleased, and exhausted, and sometimes apprehensive. The torches were extinguished. Everyone rode on: Friano and Serin, Banner's escorts, Ilse and Helgen, each with an exhausted fugitive clinging on behind, then Banner with Princess Nette. Further along Streaky Bela came up through the trees to join them.

The band rode in single file up a black tunnel of trees. Serin's eyelids began to droop. Between whiles, for an instant, Serin was elsewhere: treading the icy cobbles of Threadpole Street, or lost in the dimly lit corridors of a big old mansion, with something dogging her heels. '*Bit of snap in a fifth!*' it wheezed. '*Snap up!*' She felt its pointed fingers dig at her shoulder, and sat upright with a start.

'Were ye sleeping?' Friano murmured.

'Mm.'

They were going down now, and along a gully. The lurid porticos of dream enveloped her again, only to burst in flakes of unreasonable light and vanish like the echoes of a shout. Her chin was on her chest; Friano's left arm supported her. In the woods up on their left a nightbird chittered in alarm.

Slowly they wound their way up to the ridge. Soon they would be out of the forest awhile, passing above the silent cottages and bleak pastures of the hill-farmers. Perhaps they would catch up with the rest of the rescue party here, riding easier now they were nearing their own land, wild land, away from the vicious city. She wondered if the mad old man had got away, out of the blazing building. She would not have been at all surprised to see him scuttle out from the boulders ahead. Beyond and beyond, the mountains rose, black against blue-black cloud.

On the ridge it was very cold. The huffing of the dogs, every creak and click of harness, sounded sharp and distinct in the frosty air. Like Serin, the two escapees from the primacy were drowsing and jerking awake as the horses swayed. Only Princess Nette slept entirely, buried in the furs of Banner's sled.

Of the band that had gone ahead there was still no sign. They must be already climbing on to the shoulder above Peirruich, or even up the perilous path to Scarpine. It was hard to imagine there was another living soul abroad in the frozen stillness of the night.

Now the ground rose up on either side until they were threading a defile, a crooked gap between huge tilted slabs of rock. Streaky Bela was in front.

'Stop,' he said.

Serin came suddenly awake as they all stopped.

'What's happening?'

Streaky was dismounting, walking back down the line.

'What is it, Streaky?' asked Friano.

'Orange,' said Streaky.

There were muffled exclamations.

'A couple of dozen. Maybe more. Soldiers.'

'Did they see you, Streaky?' asked Banner from the rear.

'Not a chance.'

'Can we take them?'

Ilse was out of her saddle, climbing silently up the rocks. She signalled them forward.

The party rode out of the defile and gathered on the shelf of a great bay in the side of the mountain. They looked down across an apron of snow and saw, not two hundred yards off, dark figures moving steadily along. How Streaky knew they were Esch Serin could not tell; but she did not doubt it for a moment.

Banner, who had left his sled in the defile, stood peering into the gloom, muttering execrations. Ilse came slithering across the rock, jumped down next to him. He clapped her on the arm. She and Helgen strapped on short skis and went whirring softly off down the mountainside with their bows.

'Uncle Banner?'

'Hush.'

Straining to see where the two montanos had gone, Serin caught sight of a blocky shape standing up among the trees. It was hard to see when she looked for it, but definite enough out of the corner of her eye. She was sure it could only be one of the ventilator shafts of the Peirruich mines. She thought of Ned and Lukas, and wondered if Ned's party knew the Esch were following so close behind. Of Helgen and Ilse she could see no sign.

For what seemed a long time, nothing happened. The Eschalan riders were moving away up the track.

Suddenly there was a soft thump, and a cry. Then a horse began squealing below: a horrible noise. It would not stop. There was shouting and cursing.

Now there were more horses coming up the track; stopping; milling about. Serin saw someone move in the snow; heard whinnying, a human scream, excited babble, a whistle blown.

The figure in the snow went skimming by; stopped; crouched; came straight up towards them at a run.

It was Ilse, her skis over her shoulder. Banner reached for her arm and pulled her up on the ledge. They both stared down at the fracas.

A voice called. 'Banner Marchan!'

Banner raised his hand to bid them all keep silent; but the horses were whickering, alarmed by the noise of the wounded horse below; and because of the horses one of the dogs began to whine.

'Banner Marchan!'

The voice was nearer now. The Eschalan was moving back along the track.

'I know you're there, Banner Marchan.'

How could they know? Serin looked round at her uncle, who shook his head.

'We have your man, Banner Marchan.'

There came a yell of pain and anger. It sounded like Helgen. Ilse muttered something brief and savage and kicked snow.

Banner cupped his hands at his mouth.

'I hear you, Charan du. You shouldn't shout so loud.'

'Come down, then. Talk to me.'

'You come up.'

'Come down, Banner Marchan. Come alone, or the man dies.'

Their words echoed forlornly down the mountainside.

'Don't trust him.'

Serin turned at the voice. Princess Nette was standing right at her elbow, shivering in her furs.

'You'll kill him anyway, Charan du,' called Banner. 'You'll kill us all.' He sounded remarkably jovial.

Streaky Bela was stealing off along the path with a bow. Ilse had slid back down off the ledge.

'Come down, Banner Marchan.'

There was a pause.

'The man is dead,' shouted the Eschalan.

Either this was untrue, Serin suspected, or Helgen had died more silently than the orange had intended.

Banner began to shepherd Serin, the princess and the two escapees from the primacy back into the defile. Someone had given the man a sword. He shook it determinedly: he would not retreat. The dogs blocked the path, clambering over each other and the sled.

Meanwhile, Friano had gone galloping off around the bay. There was a shot from below; then more uproar as Streaky and Ilse let fly. The resolute swordsman from Calcionne went wading off after Ilse.

Friano came galloping back again.

'Go!' he cried hoarsely. 'We'll hold them off!'

A dart whizzed past him and buried itself in the snow. A second time he turned and traversed the arc of path, drawing Eschalan fire.

In the gloom of the defile, Streaky's horse and Helgen's shuffled their feet and tossed their heads unhappily. The woman from the city was urging Ilse's horse past the sled, which the dogs had contrived to turn sideways and tip up on its end. One dog was trapped underneath and yelping shrilly. Serin and the princess stood trying to calm the horses while Banner pushed through to disentangle the dogs. Behind and below the skirmish yawed raggedly this way and that.

'What now?' asked the princess.

Between grunts and curses, tugging and slapping at his encumbered team, Banner Marchan said, 'We'll make for Berchel's Gap. There's a camp there.'

Serin remembered Sister Annina's news. She stroked the horse's neck, murmuring reassurances she did not feel.

The sled came free suddenly, scraping down the rock wall, turning right over. One of its runners caught, nearly knocking Banner off his feet. Everything was scattered across the path.

The woman from Calcionne looked back, then dismounted hesitantly, as if unsure whether she would be any help or whether she would be better off staying in the saddle. She came back down the path towards them. 'I wonder if we shouldn't,' she said, but was interrupted by a sound like the snapping of a branch.

They never knew the rest of her speculation, or its relevance. Serin saw her stop and sway suddenly forward, as though some invisible hand had slapped her unexpectedly on the back; then, half turning from the waist, sway back a little on her heels. Her hands flew up and grasped the air, and her head rocked back on her neck. She opened her mouth again and something black splashed out. She toppled in a heap on the pathway.

Her horse snorted, pawing at the snow.

'Banner Marchan,' said the voice, from the far end of the defile. 'What have you done with the princess? Is that her I see behind you? Bring her to me, Banner Marchan.'

Banner did not obey. Instead he turned to the two women, his sovereign and his niece.

'Ride!'

There was a sharp metallic sound, the mechanism of a gun being readied. Serin scrambled up into the saddle.

'No!' cried Banner hoarsely; but he did not seem to be begging for his life. He stood square in the midst of the defile, not facing his assailant across the brawling dogs and the upturned sled, but pointing up the mountainside.

Princess Nette was still on her feet. Streaky Bela's horse was whinnying and shying from her.

'Princess!'

Serin, clinging tightly to her reins, leant down to her, holding out her arm. The princess seized it, set her foot on Serin's foot, and Serin hauled her up.

Turning the horse's head, Serin took a last glance back along the dark cleft of the defile. She saw the Eschalan fire: a yellow flash that sprang from his hand and lit him, the dead woman, Serin's gesturing uncle, horses, dogs and sled in huddled confrontation. She heard the echoes of the shot fired in that narrow space, like flung pebbles cracking on unseen rocks; and then a vast and ponderous creaking, far above.

She did not see whether or not the Eschalan's shot struck and killed her uncle. Princess Nette's arms were tight about her waist. There was a sudden flurry of snow and grit in her face. The creaking sound became a deep thick rumble, a shudder of rock. Serin kicked her heels in the flanks of the horse that had been Helgen's, and shouted in its ear. She could not hear her own shout for the tumult of other voices: the voices of soldiers and horses and dogs, screaming; the voice of the mountain.

They tore into the open and wheeled left, racing around the bay through a torrent of dirty snow. It was in their mouths and in their eyes, harsh and cold. They were deaf with the roar of the great grey wall of it, bulging swiftly down the mountainside to swallow them all. But the horse ran headlong, squealing in terror, and the women clung choking and gasping on its back. It ran on unguided through the storm of earth, off the path, past the bend where there had once been a track winding up to Scarpine, across the rocky slope and into the trees. And still it ran, trying to swerve from the long low growl that was battering through the forest, snapping and shattering trunks and branches.

Serin hauled on the reins, battling the horse's frenzy. It was no use. The horse tore the reins from her hands and fled downhill from the face of destruction, from danger into darkness.

Serin fell forward, hugging its heaving neck. At their back she heard the thunder, growing louder, gaining on them. She tried to murmur soothingly in the horse's ear, but all she could manage was a thin and breathless whine. She looked up. They were heading straight for a tree.

She shouted and kicked. At the last second the horse swerved, bucking, unseating the princess, who screamed and fell, pulling Serin on top of her. Helgen's horse was gone at once, away into the night.

Gasping, Serin staggered to her feet, plucking at the princess's coat and shouting something about a tree.

'*Behind a tree!*'

Then the wave struck. They were engulfed. And the wave rushed on.

For a space there was no sound but a mighty whisper sliding away below.

Then the snow heaved. A shoulder broke the surface, then a head, coughing, gagging. Arms scrabbled, uncovered heavy cloth: beneath it, a small elbow. Princess Nette locked her own arms around it and pulled, pulled, shovelled away black snow and pulled again. Serin Guille came up, her head lolling.

Princess Nette shook her, slapped her cheek, pounded her back. If Serin had been badly injured, the treatment might have finished her. But they had outrun the worst of the terrible tide, which had spent its force blundering down through the thick forest. The horse had brought them to the edge of the disaster, to lie floundering in the shallows of it, ragged and bruised, but aching, alive.

Serin came to freezing and wet, held in a freezing wet embrace, retching and spluttering over someone's shoulder, her legs still buried in snow. Around her in the wood she could hear the cries of other anguished animals.

A great quiet fell then. The night seemed suspended, as if numbed by death. The snow shifted and settled; there were creaking pattering sounds. Trees sighed and dropped branch-loads. Yet these things seemed only to accentuate a greater stillness, the shadow of the shock.

Wearily the women crawled from the pit they had made and collapsed in the snow together a few feet away. After a minute, Princess Nette raised herself on one elbow and looked closely at Serin.

'My hand hurts,' said Serin. 'And my arm. And my ankle.'

The princess took a handful of snow and rubbed Serin's

forehead with it. Serin saw that it came away pink, but she could not feel any pain there.

'Does that hurt?'

'No,' she said.

'It's not deep,' the princess told her. 'And it's as clean as it's going to be for now.' She sounded exhausted.

Then Serin noticed that the shoulder of Princess Nette's cape had blood on it where she had been leaning. At that moment that was the most important thing in the world.

'I bled on your coat.'

'Doesn't matter.'

'But – '

'It's all right. Are you all right?'

'I'll be all right.'

Serin stared at the blood on the fur: a black stain glinting. She felt she could see it very clearly despite the dark. She thought of the soldier's blood on the old man's lips; of the blood of the thin man in the princess's bedroom; of the blood of the orange soldier pooling on the floor of the hut. She remembered wiping blood out of her uncle's beard. She thought of the first time she had put her hand between her legs and brought it out sticky with blood. Then she realised two things: that she was drifting into a dream again; and that it was horribly cold.

She got up, favouring her sore ankle. Her head was very clear suddenly. She held out her hand to the princess.

It was only then that they found the princess's left leg was almost useless. The problem seemed to be at her hip. Serin pulled aside the sodden cape and looked doubtfully at the joint through her dress. She remembered the diagram in the *Anatomy*, but felt diffident to examine the injury more closely.

She was sure it would not be wise to move her, but even less so to let her lie out in winter, in the black hours before dawn. She took the princess's arm around her shoulders and helped her up.

'It's not so bad now I'm upright,' commented the princess, white-faced. She looked all around. 'Where are we? Do you know?'

'Not really, but I think we should go this way.'

Slowly they limped from tree to tree, uphill.

'Your name is Serin,' said the princess soon.

'Yes.'

'Serin what?'

'Guille, madam.'

'And you're not a sister, are you?'

'No. The robe was part of the plan. It's Sister Annina's.'

'The montanos' minister.'

'Yes.'

'Her brother works at the palace.'

'Yes.'

'But you're not a montano.'

'No, madam. My mother is. Was.'

The princess stopped, leaning on a spruce, partly to take her breath, partly to look at Serin again.

'You're the girl who went missing,' she said. 'At the fair.'

'Yes, madam.'

They moved arduously on.

'Did you kill him?' asked Princess Nette. 'The orange?'

Serin shook her head.

'Pity,' said the princess. 'Well, no. I can't suppose you'd tell me if you had.'

Serin thought about this.

'I might,' she said.

There was a pause.

'So . . .' said the princess, expectantly.

'I saw them kill him. They knocked me out. Took me away.'

It was Princess Nette's turn to ponder.

'I can't truly say I understand,' she admitted.

'It doesn't matter,' said Serin.

Hopefully she scanned the tops of the trees, but there was still no sign they were anything but lost. They continued to climb, as best they could.

'I saw you once,' said Serin. 'At the party for Mr Jessup's hot water.'

'Did you?' replied the princess. 'I meet so many people,' she said, excusing herself.

'I didn't really meet you,' Serin said. 'You wouldn't remember. I'm no one important.'

'Indeed you are. You saved my life.'

'Not yet I haven't.'

'Is it much farther? I don't think I can walk much farther.'

'I'm not leaving you.'

'I'm very grateful, Serin . . .'

'You saved my life too,' Serin objected. 'In the snow. Just now.'

'I suppose so. I didn't think about it. So we're equal,' Princess Nette concluded. There was an odd note of hopefulness in her voice.

As they plodded to the next tree, she said, 'Do you suppose anyone else escaped? Your uncle . . . the others . . .'

'I shouldn't think so,' said Serin. She thought of Uncle Banner, buried as they had been, but forever. And she had escaped. It seemed unjust, but no more so than everything always was. She thought she wouldn't think about it any more, not just yet.

'Charan du, too,' said Princess Nette. 'It's hard to believe.'

'The one with the gun? *There* it is,' said Serin suddenly. 'At last.'

They swung round to the right, moving with new energy and purpose.

'What is it?' asked the princess. 'However did you find it?'

'It's a ventilator. A sort of chimney,' she said. 'Not for fire, for the mine. For air. It's shelter, anyway.'

The door was blocked, like the first one, by snow. Luckily this one was on something of a knoll, so the snow was not all the way up to the top of the door. More work. Serin was past caring. She knelt, and let the princess lie. They both scraped at the snow, the princess with both hands, Serin with her good one, until they could squeeze through the door.

Inside it was pitch black. Serin made sure of the fence around the pit, and sat the princess up against it, covering her as much as possible with the filthy wet wolf cape before sitting down beside her.

'Come closer. Don't be silly. We must keep each other warm.' The princess put her arm around her. 'Serin? Are you comfortable?'

'I'm all right, madam.'

'I wish you might stop calling me madam.'

'All right.'

'Call me Nette.'

'All right, Nette,' answered Serin obediently.

'I mean it,' said the princess. 'I need it. I need to be reminded I'm still a person. Still alive: Primary,' she said in weary wonder.

'Hush. Safe now.'

Minutes passed.

'So many dead . . .'

'I'm going to sleep,' said Serin.

'I couldn't,' said Nette. 'Oh Serin, please don't. I'm – I'm absolutely terrified.'

She laughed agitatedly.

'What a marvel. I was not frightened, all this time; and now I am. I had not thought of it, all this while; now I have, now I – am. Please stay awake, Serin. Watch with me; talk to me. Please, Serin.'

'I don't think I can.'

'Then I shall talk to you. When my father died, I was about your age, I think. I am sorry for your uncle. He was a good man. Or perhaps he is alive!'

She hugged Serin.

'Serin, listen: When my father died, I was at school, in Bal Mouline. Do you know it? It sits in the lap of Perimont like Earth in the lap of the Primary. Your robe reminds me of that school. Our superior was called Sister Ysanne. She had enormous teeth and bad eyes. She brought the letter to me in the prayer garden. I was appalled – no, outraged. That's what I was: outraged. It seemed so absurd, so inappropriate. He was no soldier.

'We had it given out that he died in battle.' She sniffed, shivering. 'There was no battle. Not within a dozen miles. He was killed by a prisoner, an orange soldier who had been cut off from his troop in Orvalle and was supposed to have walked for something phenomenal, I don't know, two months, before he was caught. He claimed, so far as anyone could understand, to have been all unaware he was in enemy territory. It was some sort of victualler outfit that picked him up, stealing ducks, as I recall. They kept him as a kind of trophy at first, chained to a post. Then they set him to work, peeling the parsnips and suchlike.

'My father was making a Royal Visit. The orange saw his chance of glory, I suppose. Everyone was looking at papa, no one at him. It wasn't a dart that killed Prince Dolo, it was a vegetable peeler.

'I was incensed. For some reason, I blamed Sister Ysanne, or at least suspected she had read my letter. At any rate, I turned on her and kicked her on the shins. Then I took a boat and rowed out on the lake, alone, which I was supposed never to do. The other girls were permitted; not I. But now I was Princess of Luscany.

'I drifted all the afternoon. There was a particularly wild and spectacular sunset, or else I thought it was, because of the state I was in. I rarely bothered with sunsets normally. When I did come back, finally, it was because I was so hungry. The carriage was already there, waiting to bring me home to Calcionne.

'Do you know what I did, Serin, all afternoon in that boat? I sang all the songs I could remember my nurse had sung to me. What a despicable, childish thing! Yet there was no other way I could find to comfort myself.

'My mother was thunderstruck. I think it broke her: the indignity as much as anything. Before that I remember her being gentle and rather vague. When papa died, she refused to listen to anyone. It was she who made up the official story, the one you were taught, Serin. After that, she rapidly became bitter. She could be devastatingly sarcastic. We quarrelled, how we quarrelled. I told her sarcasm made her vulgar! Can you imagine it? Well, you don't know my mother.

'But this is not the way to talk, not with your own mother missing. I understand there was no raid on the prefecture. There are some prisoners there, you know. The ones the orange think are important. I'm sure that's where your mother would be. Where they were going to take your – uncle.'

She shuddered.

'Oh, hark at this, this is worse and worse. Forgive me, Serin; Primary forgive me. I should be better employed telling you the story of the Butter Troll, or Jack and the Stickleback, or the time when once all cats were grey. Or I could sing you the songs I sang that afternoon on the lake. There was one: *If the sun should wed the moon –* '

Serin had lain through all this like a log, oblivious, unresponsive; but something in Nette's nervous rendering of the old tune roused her, and she found herself, without thinking, singing too:

> And if the moon should bear a maid
> Wouldn't the stars be amazed?
>
> And if that maiden had a horse
> And if that horse could cross the sky
> Wouldn't the stars be surprised?

Together they sang all of that one, then *Peacock*, *Pennylock*, *Ship's A-Homing*, and *Pumpkin Fair*.

Somewhere about then, Serin fell asleep. When she woke, the

darkness had lifted a little. She looked at the princess, fast asleep beside her, head on Serin's shoulder, mouth half open. The princess's fur was in Serin's face; but that was not what had woken her.

Her arm ached when she tried to move. Her hand felt twice its normal size. Around the edges of the pain she could sense grief, accumulating, waiting to prostrate her.

But that was not what had woken her either. All that was what she came back to upon waking. That, and the cold.

Outside, the scraping sounded again.

She wondered if she were about to die. To have survived all this only to finish here, cornered, and get no further. She wished she could think of anything or anybody that might protect her, but there was death, now, everywhere. She had helped to bring that about; now it was her turn.

She looked at Princess Nette, a picture of helplessness. Should she wake her, warn her? They could set a trap. But they had nothing, nothing but themselves: both injured, exhausted, shocked.

Serin didn't see why they should both be discovered.

Perhaps it would be only Ned and Lukas again, she thought; and she opened the door quickly and stepped outside.

Standing a little way off was a man with short skis and a long gun. He was dressed roughly, chiefly in sheepskins, which he wore with the wool side in. On his head was a hat that came out in a point above his eyes, and had flaps to cover his ears. Everything about him was smudged and grimy. Though she could not see his face for a peculiar pair of wooden, slatted goggles, Serin thought he was not very old. He had a slight, blond moustache. His gun was pointed just over her head.

She had never seen anyone who looked like that.

'Serin?' he said. He sounded uncertain. 'Serin Guille?'

'Otto Meringer!'

—12—

Wild in the Woods

The gypsies would not take me with them. Indeed, they shunned me like creatures afraid. I think they disliked my tactics. Not that they availed me anything: Arethusa's mother was nowhere to be found.

At last, the excitement proved too much for one of my retiring habits; and perhaps I overtaxed my powers. I remember a room of blazing furniture; then flame, simple; then nothing.

I woke on a table with grey sisters looking down at me. The room was full of sisters and the injured of both races.

I tried to get up. They told me I was wounded badly, and must not move.

By this time I had many wounds, none of them at all significant. I asked which might be giving them concern.

They told me I was wounded inside. I had been bleeding from the mouth.

I assured them I was perfectly fit, and begged them tell me, where was Amber Guille? They could not. I told them I must be up and about my search. They raised objections, but I leapt at one bound from the table to the door, after which they made no effort to detain me.

The fire had been extinguished, and the corridors were full of frenetic Eschalans. If there were any prisoners who had not escaped, they had already been secured, out of sight and out of reach. I hurried outside to tell this to Arethusa, but she too had gone, vanished like snow among snow.

I felt the night wind, and knew that it was cold. I understood then that she did not return my love. Now I think it was foolish of me ever to hope. She was young, and I am old, who knows how old. One day perhaps she will be old.

I believe it was a fool's errand she sent me on, about her mother, to be rid of me. Yet she had been kind to me, and I did think she admired me a

*little. And she had allowed me to kiss her. I think often of that kiss —
snatched madly in the first giddy flush after imbibing: a rake's kiss, a
lecher's kiss, but a kiss all the same. With that I shall have to be content.*

*I stood in the snow, abandoned, sick at heart. I was unworthy of
Arethusa's love, unwelcome in human society. The mountaineers, the
outcast race, had outcast me. I had become no better than the dogs that
hounded me; worse. I would fly the city and live like the wild beasts in the
wood.*

*From the roof, an Eschalan saw me and cried out. They fired small shot
at me. I turned and shook my fist and screeched a miserable screech. Then
I took to my heels.*

*In the Garden of Eternal Regret a corner of the royal mausoleum
sheltered me for two fifths of an hour, but I did not feel safe. That was no
place for me. Even the tomb refused me a home. To the woods, then, and
Primary grant me a cave, the merest crevice in the rocks, to pile my bones
together. Or would even Her face be turned from me?*

*How sorry for myself I felt! I was distracted from my wits by
melancholy. Now, perhaps, I reflect that Arethusa, her uncle and all may
have expected me to follow after. Or they left me for dead, and why not?
Perhaps I shall not last forever. They were in danger, and quite properly
preserved themselves, and returned to their own.*

*If I disappointed them, I do not regret it. My impulse to solitude,
confused and nervous as it was, was right. It was a voice of nature, the
bidding of the Lady. She did not lead me to a cave, but to something
better, a good place to sit and contemplate Her changing moods. Yet still,
even in the calmest hours, I could wish I had never left the mud by the
river and the company of the dead, where I was filthy and ignorant as a
crow.*

*I get ahead of myself. I did not find this eyrie at once, but ran among
the trees. The snow did not impede me. I ran until I was lost, then
wandered until the sky began to grow pale.*

*It was my plan to hide all day and go about only at night. This, I
decided, would lessen the chance of my discovery, and also suit my poor
eyes. That first morning, however, while I traversed a stretch of bare
rock, the early light showed me that I could not afford to stop. On my left,
in the valley a little way below, stood a tower of stone. I groaned aloud at
the sight of men gathered on the parapet. Was I to be nowhere free of
them?*

*One pointed at me. They ran to an apparatus they had, a tube mounted
on legs, and turned it in my direction. One put his face close to the end of
the tube. I suppose it was one of their guns.*

I made haste to lose myself once more in the forest, but my exertions of the night and the arrival of day weakened me. I did not hear that they fired their gun, nor the barking of any dogs, but they tracked me easily. I heard the birds making a complaint, and then horses coming behind me. I continued to climb out of the valley, but two riders caught up with me. They drew apart and swiftly trapped me between them.

They were the orange: the old prefect with his eyes starting from his head, and a burly man-at-arms, who drew a gun.

There came a shout. 'Don't damage it, man!' A third assailant was approaching, a fat man, bald as myself, mounted on a labouring mule. He seemed excited.

The servitor looked at his master, who said a word. Then the man put up his gun and uncoiled a great whip that he had hanging by his saddle. He lashed out at me, but missed.

'Leave it alone!' cried the fat man. 'Go and fetch Dr Guille!'

Now Arethusa's name was Guille, as I recalled. I wondered whether the doctor might be her father, whose boots I had ruined. I had no desire to be troubled with him. In any case, the orange were taking no notice of the fat man. The servitor struck at me again.

This time the lash curled tight around my forearm. It maddened me. I was afire, whether with anger or pain I know not. I grabbed the whip and flung myself backwards into the snow, jerking the man from his seat. The whip fell from his hand. I seized it and pounced upon him. With the handle I beat him about the head, once, twice. Then I flung a loop of the lash about his neck and pulled hard. I felt a snap. I tore away his headcloth and bit him under the ear.

The two old men were shouting. Other men-at-arms might arrive at any moment. I took little from the one I had, a couple of swallows merely, but it was sufficient. I turned to the fat man, growling; but his mule had bolted, throwing him to the ground.

The prefect was backing his horse away. I sprang to his side. He gave a high, wild scream. I snarled, and grabbed him by the leg. He kicked. I clung. I still had my sword, my little Eschalan sword. I drew it, and stuck it up through his belly until it met bone. I left it there and fled.

I have not seen a single orange since, or none but him in whose notebook I write. For weeks I roamed in the depths of the forest, and only lately came back to look down on Calcionne. I needed that one sight to fix my resolve nevermore to trouble its streets. Then it was that I chanced upon this place, this little broken house high on its rocky pedestal. I knew it was my place as soon as I saw it, its empty window staring blindly down at me. When I found its broken-necked occupant, lying on the floor all blackened and frostbitten, I felt quite at home. Though he wore an Eschalan uniform, it was as if he had been waiting to welcome me. He lies there yet like a faithful hound, stinking.

I had a dream the other night, of the fat man, the bald one who came at me on his mule, and a thin man all in black. I called for help to Arethusa, whom I could see between them a little way off, sitting on the ground in her grey robe, whistling. I called her 'sister'. She could not come to me.

Dreams arise like wraiths from the pit of my oblivion, and make a mockery of truth.

Soon it will be spring. I watch and pray, and set these few recollections down so as never to forget, and in time perhaps to understand. I rise once more with the owls. I cry to them. They cry to me. I am content.

From the clutches of sleep, Princess Nette awoke to a shaft of daylight in a dark place. Above her head snow and dust clouded an ellipse of pale sky. Her breath steamed in the cold air. She came awake to pain, which her dream had been busily translating into other things. Her nose and lips were numb.

She was sprawled against iron railings, covered in a sodden fur. Her legs did not seem to belong to her. In front of her was a wall of planks painted with tar. She recalled where she was; that she had left her home; that she would never go back again. Then she remembered the girl, Serin Guille. She was no longer beside her. Nette looked as far as she could over her left shoulder and her right, and wondered if she should not call out her name. Perhaps Serin had been taken; but why Serin and not herself?

In a while she thought: perhaps Serin had abandoned her. It made her sad to imagine it, but she could not blame the girl. What had she done herself but betray her crown, her country, her mother, everybody?

Well, it was not so; or it would not be so. The country was the people, she reasoned. With the hillfolk, the montanos, she could fight the orange. The war was not lost, not yet. Alone they could not win, but they could die fighting.

Or they could die of broken hips in airshafts miles from anywhere, surrounded by snow. Should she shout, should she not? The pain sawed ceaselessly at the delicate supports of Nette's lucidity.

She wondered what was happening at the palace. She thought of Crespian Vittore's corpse tied to the end of her empty bed.

She imagined her mother's grief and rage. The prefect's staff would get little sense out of her.

Nette hoped Thisbe had taken her chance and gone. She trusted her to find somewhere to hide until she could get out of Calcionne. Once she reached Tourmalix the tale would be all around within the day, eventually across in Ducros. That might do some good, perhaps.

She shouted.

Nothing happened.

She shouted again. In a spasm her eyes filled with tears. She felt them run down her face. Crying made her leg throb. She stopped crying then, but whimpered for a long time, drifting on the pain. She wished Serin would come back. Serin had leaned against her, whistling in the darkness.

> Seven shirts of silk and satin . . .
> Six stacks of silver sequins . . .
> Five fans of flaming feathers . . .

When she heard a noise of people out in the snow Nette bit her lip and lay shivering, curled up on her right side now, listening hard. The door opened and a man came in. His beard was black, his furs were white. He touched her leg. Nette screamed and fainted.

When she came to they had strapped her to a stretcher and propped her against the wall. People were working at the railings, fixing a heavy beam across the hole. There was a contraption of chains and a wheel.

The master enginer came and squatted beside her, opening a small brass flask.

'You're safe now, ma'am. You're in good hands.'

'Mr Jessup? What are you doing here?'

'We'll take care of you, ma'am.'

'But I thought – '

'Hush.'

He tipped the flask to her lips. It was brandy and it was wonderful, like being warm again.

'All right?'

'More.'

His team hammered and clanked.

'What are they doing?'

'It's to take you to safety, ma'am, where we can see to your leg. They'll be ready soon.'

'There was a girl with me, the lost girl, Serin Guille . . .'

'She's safe too. You'll see her in a couple of minutes.'

They lifted her stretcher and set it gently on the rail.

Nette looked down. She was perched on the lip of a shaft of cold air. There were blacker patches down in the darkness where galleries ran off to left and right. One of the openings glowed with a faint light. Beneath that, it was simply dark.

She stared at Jessup in horror. They were bolting chains to the poles of her stretcher.

'What are you doing to me?'

'Hush now, ma'am, and save your strength. It's but a little drop, then you'll be among friends and you won't need to fear any more.'

'You're going to drop me down there?'

'We sha'n't let ye fall,' he said. His voice was patient and calm, as if he were talking to a child. Nette closed her eyes and took a deep breath.

'More brandy,' she said.

He put the flask in her hands, and pressed her hands briefly between his own. 'Take the flask,' he said. 'You can carry it down for me.'

Nette unscrewed the cap and took another swallow. It was awkward to drink lying down.

They had fixed the chains to a loop at the end of a cable that ran over the wheel. The wheel was fixed to the beam across the hole. Ropes hung from the stretcher, draped across the rail. The people on the ropes shouted down the hole and other voices, metallic and echoing, answered from below. Then they were counting, and heaving, and Nette felt herself sway up and out, suspended in a cone of pale clouded white above a dark well. Convulsively she prayed and gripped the edge of the stretcher, though what good that would be she couldn't imagine.

They held the ropes to stop her spinning or banging into the sides of the shaft. As the ring of faces passed jerkily upwards she caught sight of Enginer Jessup. His smile was meant to be reassuring, she supposed. Next moment she was hanging in the darkness, surrounded by slick black rock. The air smelled of earth. Nette wondered how far she had to go.

Panic and pain clamoured fiercely for her attention, but she

was too exhausted, too numb to care. It was hard to believe this
was as smoothly as they could go with her, but a residue of pride
prevented her from yelling. Every shudder jolted her leg as if she
had hit a rock. She concentrated on prising one hand free from
the stretcher to take the flask from her cloak. She held it to her
chest, gazing up at the silhouette of the beam and the wheel, and
the little faces peering intently down at her. It was even more of
an effort to let go with her other hand so that she could open the
flask again.

Curiously, not holding on made her feel better and braver. She
lay in a daze, descending, trying to relax and trying not to
wonder why they wanted to send her, with a broken hip, down a
mine.

She passed one dark gallery, and then another. People came
down here like this to work, she thought: to spend every day of
their lives crawling in muck and water, in narrow spaces far
underground, hacking things out of rock. And they did it for a
wage that barely kept them warm in winter. They did it for her,
and she never gave them a thought. She waved to them from her
carriage.

Then there was light behind her head, and cheering. Arms
reached out to pull her in, to lower her on to a trolley and release
the chains that had supported her.

'There she is, then!'

'Well done, Your Highness!'

Well done? But she'd done nothing. And what was this now?
They were trundling her along on rails, crowding round to have
a hand in pushing the trolley down a tunnel where they couldn't
even walk upright. Grimy faces looked down on her with bright,
white smiles of joy and pride. That one, the woman with the
lantern, surely she knew her?

'Aulioline? Countess, is that you?'

'We'll soon have you there, madam.'

Unsatisfied, Nette stopped craning round over her shoulder. It
was hard to conduct a conversation with someone preceding you
as you went bumping headfirst through a crack in the earth,
black rock dripping a foot or two above your face.

The tunnel went on and on.

'This really is very kind of you all,' said Nette doubtfully. She
remembered the flask she was clutching, and offered it to one of
the men.

'Would you like a drink? There's not much left, I'm afraid. It's Mr Jessup's. Would you give it back to him for me? You do know Mr Jessup, don't you?'

This amused them all.

'Oh yes, ma'am. We know Mr Jessup.'

At last the ceiling rose, and there were more lights, and more people jostling and cheering, children, men and women welcoming her into a large, low chamber, and Serin Guille among them with her arm in a sling and a bandage on her head.

'Hello,' said Serin, reaching for the princess's buckles with her good hand.

'Serin, praise God, you're all right. Where are we? What is this place?'

'This is where they live.'

'Who *are* they?' asked Nette, looking confusedly all around, blinking in the torchlight.

'The outlaws.'

So it was the countess, that woman with her lantern, Countess Aulioline, who hadn't been seen for years. And the young man at Serin's shoulder, she knew his face too, but she couldn't remember from where. He looked a trifle embarrassed at her stare.

A man offered her a hot tin mug. 'For the pain,' he said, and watched her anxiously while she drank. He too was obviously in awe of her presence. Well, that she was used to, if nothing else.

The tea was green and tasted strongly of sage. She wished she had not let the brandy go. But yes, she did begin to feel better, or at least more detached. The pain was the pain, but there was a space now between her and it.

They wanted to take her aside and see to her leg, but she wanted to talk to Serin first. She had begun to recognise more faces: people who had been sent away; people who had run away; faces that she knew were the faces of farmers and miners, though they were all miners now, seemingly.

'What do they do down here?'

'Argue,' said Serin.

'We practise, ma'am,' the young man put in hastily, 'with our weapons.'

'I know you now,' said Nette.

'Otto Meringer, ma'am. Your – ' He hesitated, but decided to say it. 'Your servant.'

'But you're the boy who shot at Mr Jessup. What are you doing here?'

'It was the prefect I was after,' he told her. 'I'd hit him now.' He looked at her gladly. 'Maybe now I'll get the chance.'

Nette could not leave it alone. 'Why did you pretend you wanted to kill Mr Jessup?'

'I didn't want them to suspect. See, it was one of Karel's guns.'

'Now you live here.'

'Yes, ma'am.'

'Does he live here too?'

'No, ma'am. He lives in the city. But he keeps us going, Karel does. I wouldn't be alive if it weren't for Karel, no more than you, ma'am.'

'It was Otto who found us, Nette,' said Serin; while Otto glanced at her, surprised by this familiarity. 'He heard us singing.'

'Very cheerful it was too,' said Otto.

The man who had brought the green drink interrupted. 'Madam, we must deal with your injury.'

'Not if you're going to cut it off,' said Nette. 'Will I have to have a wooden leg?'

'A simple fracture I'm sure,' he answered nervously. 'But you must pardon and permit me to examine it.'

'Don't ask me then,' she told him. 'Do it.'

He shooed everyone away, even Serin and Otto. They peeled off Nette's cloak and carried her behind hanging rugs to a little recess with a low plank bed. A woman brought a pan of coals and a bucket of wet cloths.

The man fussed with a pair of lanterns, then reached out hesitantly.

'Madam, I must – '

'Oh get on with it, please!'

'Here, let me,' said the woman, and undressed her quickly but carefully. Nette did not care that she was half naked; on the contrary, she felt as if she were wrapped up in a little cloud.

'Have you any more of that tea?'

The man poured her a second cup, even gummier than the first, while the woman fanned the coals and sponged the princess down with fragrant hot water.

They splinted her, bandaged her, covered her over and let her lie. 'It would be a good idea not to move very much,' said the man.

'What a treat,' said Nette drowsily. 'I hope everyone else agrees.'

They bowed and left her alone with a candle and the shadows of somnolence; but not for long. There was a cough, and Otto Meringer put his head cautiously around her curtain.

'Come in,' she said, and he did, and squatted beside her bed.

'How many are you?' she asked him.

'Two hundred and twenty-three,' he said promptly. 'All over the system.' Then, seeing she did not understand: 'Scattered in the mines. Wherever there's a safe chamber.'

'You have guns.'

'Yes, ma'am.'

'You'll need them.'

His face brightened. 'We'll show them! Even Karel can't say no.'

'Why should he?'

'He always does.'

Nette tried to think about this. Nothing came to mind.

'I want to talk to him,' she said.

Otto hurried out. As he passed through the hangings, she glimpsed her attendants sitting at a respectful distance, knitting voluminous shapes out of stringy brown wool. Back in the main cavern, she could hear the noise of machinery being dragged about. The noises were dead, contained. Nette began to feel the fear of the place, the weight of rock suspended above her, the possibility that –

Mr Jessup arrived and hunkered down.

'How do you feel, ma'am?'

'Enclosed.'

He nodded sympathetically. 'It's a problem, at first, for them that's not used to it. But it's safe.' He thumped a balk of timber. 'Duke oak, this, twenty years old. It doesn't crack and splinter down here the way it does in the open.'

'Mr Jessup.'

'Ma'am.'

'Why didn't you *tell* me?'

'With spies at your table?'

'But in private . . .'

'Safer for you not to know, ma'am.'

'How many other people know?'

'In town? Not many. They're only safe here as long as the orange don't find out. They've been close just recently.' He shook his head, grim.

'So you think they won't find out where I am?'

'They'll think you're dead, ma'am, in the avalanche. If everyone keeps their heads down for a few days – '

Nette closed her eyes. 'Mr Jessup, you have two hundred and twenty-three people here.'

'They can do it, ma'am. They're a good bunch.'

'Mr Jessup, they're an *army*. They've no business to be hiding in holes.'

'They're not two hundred and twenty-three able-bodied, not all of them,' he said. 'And with respect, ma'am, they've not all cause to love the crown.'

'They've less cause to love the orange, I trust. And you have guns. What are you waiting for? Listen. The prefect was out of the city last night, at Jonal's. You can ambush him. You must attack now, while they are disorganised. You know these people. There will be fighting between guild and guild.'

She raised herself up on her right elbow.

'You have surprise on your side. And the Primary. Who knows how many the avalanche killed?'

'It's not like that,' Karel said patiently. 'They're a good bunch, like I say. They're surviving. They work together, mostly. Yes, I've given them guns. They can protect themselves. They'll protect you, ma'am. But an army they're not.'

'That's not what Otto Meringer says.'

'He's a boy,' growled Karel dismissively. 'Oh, I know what you're thinking, ma'am. I've thought it myself. But it's foolish, they're not ready.'

'They'll *never* be ready,' she advised him.

'One day – '

'Today.'

'You'd send them to their deaths.'

'I'd send them home.'

She looked up at him, eyes like dark smudges in her white face.

'I don't say it as your sovereign. I tell you as a witness, as someone who's come out of the city and, thanks to you, I'm still alive to tell you what it's like. Why won't you *listen* to me?'

She glared at him.

He sat back, looking glum.

'I want to talk to them,' she said. 'Call them together. As many as you can get in one place.'

Unexpectedly, he smiled. 'No need for that. You can talk to them all at once. And they can talk back to you.'

She looked at him uncomprehendingly.

'It's a device of mine . . .'

'A device? Show me. Take me to it.'

The man who had bandaged her came hurrying in. 'Madam, you really shouldn't be moved – '

'Show me!'

They carried her back into the main cavern and set her down beside a strange pair of brass horns dipping from the wall like snakes. The lanterns showed her complicated tubes running off in all directions.

While Otto found trestles for the stretcher, Karel explained it to her.

'You speak in here and they can all hear you. At North Face, all up the Doyne Line: everywhere. Through this one they talk back.' He smiled wryly. 'They like to talk back.'

'Nearer. Let me see.'

Nette reached out to touch the dusty brass.

'Can they talk to each other?'

'No. This was the best I could do, in the time.'

'The best,' repeated Nette, and laughed.

'I'm a busy man, as you know,' he said, offended.

'Forgive me, Mr Jessup. I'm not insulting you. This – this is perfect.' She patted it. 'This is a weapon, Mr Jessup.'

He stared at her bleakly.

'It always is,' he said. It did not occur to her until later that he had spoken in Bryle. But he looked like a man who recognises his own defeat. Mancini, thought the princess: *The player who believed the Ace was down already.*

'We must use it at once,' Nette concluded. 'What does it need?'

'Pull the ring, ma'am. That blows a whistle and they all listen. Then you shout in here.'

So Nette pulled the ring, and heard many little whistles squeak back from the horn. She knew already what she must say. 'This is Princess Nette,' she cried. 'Go. Go now. The city is yours for the taking.' Then she lay down.

There was nothing to hear at first but the hollowness of brass, and air stirring in it. From the tunnels people came to stare at her. Then there was consternation, cheering, running. Serin appeared from somewhere, reminding her of something else.

'The montanos,' said Nette. 'Have you spoken with the people at Berchel's Gap?'

Nobody seemed to know what she was talking about.

'There's a cave. Serin, can you show them?'

The girl was not sure.

'Fetch a montano, someone. They will know where.'

Otto looked stern. Karel looked at the floor.

'There aren't any,' said Serin. 'Not down here.'

'No montanos? Why not?'

'You can't trust them, ma'am,' said Otto gravely.

Nette's expression did not change. She glanced at Serin. 'Yes I can,' she said.

'They don't want to know about us,' Otto persisted.

'They want to know about me,' said Nette. 'They want to know about their sons and daughters who died in prison, or in the snow. They want to avenge them. There are things in Calcionne too, that they may want, I imagine. Serin, go with him to Berchel's Gap. You'll find the cave. Tell them, send a fast horse to Scarpine, to tell the Entenmann, and all get down there immediately, with whatever weapons you can. Karel, don't argue.' She was sagging. 'I must sleep.' Her face was bloodless. 'If I can. I'd be grateful for some more tea,' she said quietly.

She was asleep before they brought it.

Nette zan Herlach dreamed she visited the dormitory of the retired soldiers, and discovered that, though they spoke of nothing but past glories, many of them were still in their prime. Many were able to fly, or perform other superhuman acts; but they were bound by some obscure historical pledge to refrain. They invited her to inspect certain articles of furniture they had made.

She woke, cold but sweaty beneath the blanket. Her leg ached, and her whole side. Voices in the tunnel had disturbed her.

It was Serin, and a montano woman.

'Nette? This is Blair.'

Blair, Nette noticed, had brought a crossbow down the mine with her. She seemed very excited.

'Why did they leave you here, Highness? They shouldn't have left you.'

'Have you come from Berchel's Gap?' Nette asked them.

Blair nodded.

'They didn't want to believe us,' said Serin, looking askance at Blair. 'But they sent someone up Scarpine, and Otto's taken the rest to the palace.'

'You must follow at once, princess!' insisted Blair.

Nette thought of the doctor. '*It would be a good idea not to move very much.*'

'No,' she said.

Blair obviously thought she was afraid. 'They'll take the palace, they say,' she assured her.

'Good,' said Nette. 'But not for me. Not any more.'

Blair looked perplexed.

Serin contemplated the supine princess. She scratched her ear. 'You don't have to *stay* there,' she pointed out.

Nette relented. There was mother to consider, and the rest of the household. You couldn't simply walk away from that, even with a broken leg.

'Very well,' she said. 'Take me home.'

Not everyone had left the mine by any means. Elderly colliers helped the three women manoeuvre the stretcher in and out of the lift cage, and found them, in lieu of anything better, an old cart, which they padded with rags.

They rode laden with blessings and advice in the wake of the outlaws, under a milky sky.

Even before they came within sight of Calcionne there was smoke on the breeze.

Primary, thought Nette zan Herlach. What have I done? But she said nothing.

Beside her, Serin shivered.

So they sat there awhile, on the snowy slopes above Melkonnen and the Apron, gazing. Then Blair clucked her tongue and tugged the rein, and they rode down into the burning city.